RETURN TO
SULPHUR RIVER

art anthony

RETURN TO SULPHUR RIVER

Return to Sulphur River

For information about this title or to order other books and/or electronic media, contact the publisher via email at aanthony@pldi.net.

ISBN (softcover): 978-0-9988078-2-9
ISBN (hardcover): 978-0-9988078-3-6

Printed in the United States of America

DEDICATION

To our forefathers and foremothers and the difficulties they endured, the sacrifices they made, and their endless fight for rights and freedom, which has built this great nation we live in today. May we follow their example and not lose all they built.

ACKNOWLEDGMENTS

Thank you to my wife who has supported me throughout the writing of this book. She has been my typist and advisor, and most of all she has been patient with all my ups and downs.

LIST OF CHARACTERS

Art Logging	The main character, a seventeen-year-old boy and thirteen-month Civil War veteran who continues with his friend Darrell Stroud to try to build farms and protect their families. He now has a 5,600-acre farm and cattle ranch. These events take place during the reconstruction period after the Civil War.
Darrell Stroud	A twenty-one-year-old Civil War veteran, continues to be Art's best friend in every way. Darrell runs a 1,200-acre horse farm next to the Logging's homestead.
The Boys	Art and Darrell as friends built together a tough reputation. They became skilled gunmen in the army, and do not hesitate to use their skills to settle disputes and protect their families. They do not start anything but will retaliate better than most gunmen.
Velma Stroud	Darrell's wife and mother of his stepson, Erik, and his own daughter.

Mr. Stroud	Darrell's father who runs a horse ranch in Jefferson, Texas.
Sharon Logging	Art's wife and mother of his son, Art Jr., and daughter, Patricia.
Maggie Mae (Logging)	Art's mother that remarried after her first husband, died. She and Art's sister live in Red Oak, Louisiana with her new husband, Abe Martin, and his daughter.
Patricia Logging	Art's sister living with her mother in Red Oak, Louisiana.
Colonel Abe Martin	Married to Maggie Logging after Art's father died, owns a plantation twenty miles north of Shreveport in Red Oak, Louisiana.
Cynthia Martin	Abe's daughter. Her mother died five year ago, and she raises and trains cow dogs.
Ted Wilson	Abe Martin's helpful neighbor.
Lewis and Mary Rogers	Sharon's parents who live in Marietta, Texas, also part-owners of Naples, Texas Bank.

Buddy Rogers	Sharon Logging's thirteen-year-old brother.
Charles Rogers	Sharon Logging's twenty-three-year-old brother, helps the boys many times.
Ace Sutton	Friend of Charles Rogers, also helps many times.
Robert and Mae	Ex-slave friends who help the boys. The boys had befriended them during the war. They have their own farm north of Naples.
Sherman and Trixie	Ex-slave friends who help the boys. The boys had befriended them as well in the war. Like Robert and Mae, they too have their own farm north of Naples.
Mr. Smith	Owner of the general store in Marietta.
Jesse Lassiter	Local vindictive lawyer previously convicted, escaped, and fled the state, returns trying to make examples of the boys.

Gene McCoy and family	Long-time friends of the Loggings family and run Bryans Mill general store and mill.
Dr. Lilly	Family doctor for the area and a good friend.
Mr. Shaw	Closest neighbor to the Loggings family. His family moved away when he was drafted, and Art buys his farm.
Ion Shaw	Mr. Shaw's sixteen-year-old daughter and Art's first girlfriend. She ran away from home at - thirteen and returns after the war.
Onnie Shaw	Mr. Shaw's thirteen-year-old son. He is very helpful to the boys and is self-reliant.
Mr. and Mrs. Barnes and son, Bobby	Friends of the Loggings family from New Boston, Tx.
Mark and Lola Anthony	Friends who run a large horse farm three miles north of Bryans Mill.
Chandler and Kelly	Mark and Lola Anthony's older son and wife who help run the ranch.

Hunter and Maggie	Mark and Lola Anthony's younger son and wife who also help run the ranch.
Hawk	A twenty-five-year-old Choctaw Indian from Oklahoma territory. Art's friend.
Running Bear	Hawk's eighteen-year-old brother.
Straight Arrow	A Choctaw Indian who is a friend of the boys.
Earnest Albright	Farmer and friend of Confederate General Taylor, who stored captured Yankee supplies at his farm.
Clint Lawrence	A cotton buyer living in New Orleans. The boys sold cotton to him when they were in the Confederate army.
Sheriff Bass	Sheriff in Naples.
Sheriff Brown	Sheriff in Naples.
Mr. and Mrs. Hill	Owners of the Naples General Store, farmers and part-owners of the Naples Bank. Helpful friends as well.

Tommy Brundet	A rebellious boy who turns his life around to be a helpful friend.
Mr. Brundet	Tommy's father who faithfully tries to protect his son's bad choices.
Ed Wright	Farmer friend of Art's, helpful when buying cattle and in other ways.
Eagle Feather	Chief of the Choctaw in southeastern Oklahoma, friend of Art and Darrell.
Pete	A tough guy hired by Lassiter to cause trouble for the boys.
Todd Berry	Is helpful Texas Ranger who joins the state police. He is sometimes helpful to the boys.
Dr. and Mrs. Ellis	Shorthorn breeders in Linden, Texas.
Bob and Ralph Simmons	Art and Darrell helped them, protect thier 2,000-acre ranch from Lassiter. They are also good friends.
Captain Nance	A Yankee officer assigned to the Naples area, promoted to colonel due to successfully starting a black community. The boys were a major help. He was reassigned to Austin.

General Young	A Yankee officer in charge of the occupation of north Texas.
Colonel White	A Yankee officer in charge of Fort Smith, Arkansas after the war.
Paul Parkinson	The former owner of the farm west of Art's. He sold this farm to Art and now has large ranch south of Shreveport.
Louis	The manager of one of Art's farms, has wife and three children.
Ed	The manager of one of Art's farms, a bachelor.
Judge Boyd	The presiding judge in Naples.
Andrew	A blacksmith who helps set up the boys' sawmill between Bryans Mill and Naples.
Larry Steveron	A traveling preacher between Marietta and Bryans Mill with wife, Susan, children Colin, Kyle, Lana, Clay, Lauren, Lane, and Lyndi.

Joe and Jed	Brothers who try to rustle Art's stock. After Art caught them, they began working for Art and became good, successful friends.
Lieutenant Thomas	The Union commander of a squad stationed at Naples.
Sergeant Jones	A Union soldier stationed in Naples with a squad of soldiers.
Colonel North	Union officer helpful to the boys.
Master Sergeant Best	He assisted in training civilians to shoot as ordered by Colonel North.
Steve Hand	Fort Smith carpenter.
Bob Schmitt	Fort Smith blacksmith.
Mr. Ryan	A businessman that buys the first steamboat Art salvages on the Arkansas River.
Phil and Mrs. Jenson, and children Paul, Betty, and Luke	A homeless family Art helped, and they became good friends.

Roger Russell	A builder who shows the boys how to build their stone houses.
Bill Stalworth	A cabinet-maker from Marietta.
Tom	Captured unbranded cattle and sold these to the boys.
Melinda Yeiser	A school teacher at Bryans Mill; she is widowed with two daughters, Katelyn and Haylee.
Bob Horton and family	Run the ferry across Sulphur River close to Bryans Mill.
Mr. Goodman	A shorthorn breeder in Marshall, Texas.
Lawyer Hastings	Naples's lawyer representing Lassiter in legal matters.
Mrs. Lucas	A widow with a large farm five miles north of Art. She has two daughters, Ashley and Sara.
Mr. Ardmore	Runs a machine shop in Shreveport.
Jack	Works for Mr. Ardmore.

General Bond	A Union general in Shreveport, Louisiana.
Tom Downing	Once known as Mt. Pleasant's Lawyer who later became a judge in Naples.
Governor Pense	Governor of Texas during the reconstruction era.
General Mays	A Yankee general in charge of army procurements in Austin, Texas.
Gene Bates	A Yankee commander at Fort Worth.
Mr. Case and Son	Live north of Sulphur and sold horses to Darrell.
Arch	Top hand for Lassiter who turns helpful on cattle drive.
Jelly	Lassiter's foreman.
Neely	An ex-Union soldier from Kansas who helps on a cattle drive.
Tom and gang	Burn Onnie's barn and rustle cattle from Onnie Shaw.

David Townsend and cousin Alex	Two men who worked for Art while in Jail and after being released eventually worked for him and live on the Old Parkinson's farm.
Phyllis Williams	A widowed school teacher. She and Art get married after the death of his first wife. Mother of Art's new son, Kenneth.
Hank Wilson	A horse trader and Phyllis's ex-boyfriend.
Bohanan	Made furniture for folks in the area.
Ted	Bohanan's neighbor that bullied and terrified all his neighbors for the past two years.
Tony Young and Katie	Neighbors to Bohanan who had been terrorized by Ted for two years.

Art and Darrell drive cattle and horses to Ft. Smith, Arkansas from Bryans Mill, Texas up thru Eastern Oklahoma to sell to the Union army.

They drive another herd from Bryans Mill to Ft. Gibson, Oklahoma.

SUMMARY OF ART'S FIRST BOOK SULPHUR RIVER, WINNER OF FIRST PLACE IN TEXAS AUTHOR ASSN 2013 BOOK CONTEST FOR WESTERN FICTION

Set during the last sixteen months of the Civil War, a poor fifteen-year-old northeastern Texas boy, Art Logging, has been farming for his family for three years because his pa has consumption. His thoughts are that they are not making any progress.

The Confederate Army forces the boy into the war, taking his father's place in a mandatory call to serve. Art tries to get the farm in order for his family to live for a few months without his help.

In the Confederate Army, Art meets a nineteen-year-old boy named Darrell Stroud, who befriends him. Together they receive the training readying them to fight in the historical Red River Campaign. The boys discover some of the Southerners are really going to profit after the war, as there is a huge amount of livestock and Confederate equipment stored on a farm in Hope, Arkansas.

The boys feel they should have some livestock and equipment of their own to sell when they get out of the army to help start their own farms.

Prior to that, they survive training. Since the boys are young, fast, and already good shots, they actually turn into well-trained soldiers who are deadly with pistols and rifles.

They see action in the Red River Campaign of 1864 with the Yankees trying to capture Shreveport and Texarkana to cut off supplies for the South coming through Texas and Mexico. They also became involved in helping the South sell cotton to the North during the war. Clever and always looking toward making money, the boys end up selling some cotton to the North on their own.

While Art was away from home, his father dies, his mother remarries, and together with his sister, moves to the home of his stepfather, Colonel Martin, located twenty miles north of Shreveport.

When discharged in December of 1864, they find four runaway slaves hiding in Art's abandoned childhood farmhouse. The South has severe laws against harboring or helping slaves. The boys make a decision to get the slaves to safety under Northern protection. In the meantime, the runaway slaves help the boys gather a herd of wild cattle to drive north, because this is where they can get the best price for beef. This also makes sure the boys get their crops planted with the help of their newly made friends.

The South is devastated. There are so few ways to make money even after the end of the war. When the boys try to pay the taxes on the Logging's farm, they find a corrupt lawyer trying to stop them, beginning with questioning their honorable discharge. This lawyer is a nemesis for the whole year. The boys persevere against several attacks against them and their farms.

Plans for the cattle drive change when they find out Fort Smith will pay more for the cattle and horses than the buyers will further north. The boys' Choctaw Indian friends guide the cattle drive from the Red River through hostile Oklahoma Territory to Fort Smith, where the slaves find freedom.

A later trail drive to Fort Gibson, Oklahoma, gives them the opportunity to sell both horses and cattle to the Yankees. The boys chanced being tried as traitors, hoping the Confederates would not discover them supplying the Union Army.

Art meets and becomes involved with his future wife while buying oats from a farmer in the neighboring town.

Gunfights, showdowns, Confederate and Union Army battles, trail drives, girlfriends, and making money any way they can are the adventures of Art Logging and his friend, Darrell Stroud.

CHAPTER 1

Art Logging had now grown into a man. He was six foot two, slender, well-muscled from hard work, and had expressive eyes, as blue as the sky, which let you know his intent at all times. He strongly believed in fair play and justice and was quick to defend his rights and beliefs. He and Darrell Stroud, a slight contrast to Art, medium built with dark hair and eyes, also well muscled with the same beliefs and determination to defend them, whatever it took, had become friends when they were drafted in the Confederate Army and served thirteen months. They were discharged approximately four months before Lee surrendered to General Grant. The boys had grown up a lot while in the army, well trained in marksmanship and were a pair not to be reckoned with. After being discharged over twelve months ago, they had accumulated a lot of land and stock, realizing their dreams of owning their own farms. Art and Darrell had successfully defended their farms against a corrupt lawyer and sheriff. They had successfully driven cattle and horses to Fort Smith and Fort Gibson with the help of Choctaw friends and black slaves. The previous summer, they both met local girls and married them. They each had a son. Art was only seventeen and Darrell was twenty-one.

Art now owned five different farms that totaled over five thousand acres. He had approximately six hundred head of cattle and a sawmill, which was not yet setup and running. Darrell had a horse farm of approximately twelve hundred acres with about one hundred blooded horses and a herd of about twelve head of longhorn cattle. Art had a bachelor named Ed running one farm and a man named Louis, who was a married man with a family, running another farm.

He had been selling a lot of corn to McCoy's store and mill in Bryans Mill, located eight miles from his farm. He usually planted corn and cotton, but had decided to plant only corn this year because he thought the price of cotton would be very low. Darrell had already planted one hundred acres of oats, and the boys were going to swap crops.

Darrell and Art were discussing Darrell's plans. Darrell said, "My dad's pretty sick, and I want him to move up here with us so I can better see after him. I hope I can talk him into selling his horse ranch and moving. I know he'll not like leaving his many old friends. My dad's lived there over forty years." Darrell continued, "I'm going to sell my twelve hundred acres north of Naples to the new sheriff in town and buy two thousand acres south of your farm. We plan to build a new four-bedroom home with running water and an inside bathroom, about six hundred yards south of your farm. I want to build it out of brick with a large front porch. We will need a bigger house because dad will be living with us, and Velma is pregnant. Also, I figure this will better protect both of our families. Don't you agree Art?"

Art asked, "Where will you get the brick mud?"

Darrell said, "From the Sulphur River."

Art was excited that his good friend would be close by, and the wives and children would also have friends close. The women were already good friends, the boys were close in age and would have someone close to play with. Sharon, Art's wife, was medium heights with dark curly hair and brown eyes that lite up whenever he was around. She had a nice figure and was the perfect picture of the girl next door. Velma, Darrell's wife, was petite with blonde hair and hazel eyes. Also, nice to look at and had a perky personality. The girls were raised in the same area and had a lot in common. Being raised in this area, both girls knew this was a hard life and were prepared for the life they had chosen. Art said, "You know if you're building a new house, I'll never hear the end of it from Sharon until I also build a new house, so I guess we better get the sawmill running and build a kiln close to the mill so we can start making the bricks." He also said, "I'm going to build my house out of special stone found thirty miles from here and Darrell, you might want to consider that. It appears we're going to have to continue to protect ourselves and our property since no one else wants to help. Who will you buy the land from?"

"Lassiter," said Darrell. "He now lives in Kansas and is happy to sell the two thousand acres for seventeen hundred dollars. Part of the deal with selling my farm to the new sheriff is that I can still harvest the hundred acres of oats planted on my old farm."

During one of the boys many talks, Art said, "Darrell, what do you think about us entering some of the shooting and horse racing contests they have around here?"

Darrell answered, "I hadn't thought about that, but it might be a pretty good idea because at least our names will become known. Just what do you have in mind?"

Art replied, "I thought it might be a way these rustlers, thieves, and so forth might think twice about attacking us if they knew we were good enough with guns to take care of ourselves and think it just wouldn't be healthy to try to steal from us." Besides, it only costs a dollar to enter, and we just might win some money, which never hurts."

"Sounds good to me," said Darrell. "I think one is coming up at Mount Pleasant soon if the weather's good."

On Saturday, all the folks, Darrell and his family, Art and his family, Louis and his family, Phil and his family, Mr. Shaw, Onnie, Joe, Jed, and Lewis Rodgers and his family all loaded up in three buggies and four wagons and went to Mount Pleasant's horse racing and shooting contests. Since it was about a three-hour trip, they left at six o'clock in the morning. The women packed boiled eggs, sliced ham, biscuits, jelly, and tea for lunch.

Velma asked, "Darrell will you pick up some ice at Mount Pleasant to keep the tea cold so we'll have cold drinks all day?"

"Sure," he said. "That shouldn't be a problem."

They arrived at nine o'clock, and all the men competing in the shooting contest signed up and paid their one dollar entry fee. The winner was to receive four hundred dollars. Over three hundred men were signed up, and Art said, "Darrell did you notice it looked like a lot of these men paid their last dollar to enter."

"I did," said Darrell. And I'm sure you noticed that at least ten of Lassiter's crew are here." We better give them a good show and shoot our very best." The rifle contest took all morning, shooting at three different places. The boys both shot at the 100-yard place, and both put five shots in the bull's-eye along with twenty-four others. The twenty-six went to the 125-yard range where each one would have fifteen seconds to shoot all five rounds. Art and Darrell both put four shots in the bull's-eye and one very close outside. Not one of Lassiter's crew was in this group, and that put a smile on the boys' faces. Two men put all five shots in the bull's-eye and decided to split the four hundred dollar winnings rather than have a shoot-off. The boys did not know the winners.

At the same time, the pistol contest was going on, and there were over four hundred men entered in that contest. Four stations were needed for the 25-yard targets. Art and Darrell both put six shots in the bull's-eye, and so did forty-nine other people. In the shoot-off, the target was fifty yards. Darrell shot first and put all six shots in the bull's-eye. Art put four in the bull's-eye and two close outside. Only one other guy had six shots in the bull's-eye, but he didn't want to split the winnings. Therefore, the target was moved to seventy-five yards. This time, they both missed the bull's-eye twice, but they were very close. At that time, the judges said, "We are declaring this a tie and will split the winnings between you two." So each man received two hundred dollars.

It was now one o'clock and time for the horse races. This took another hour as they narrowed it down to four horses that had each won a race. The last race was with those four to determine the winner. A man from Mount Pleasant was the winner of that race. There was a lot of money bet on these races. During the day, there were also horseshoe tournaments, foot races for the children, and a number of other activities. All the boys' group participated in several of the events and everyone had a good time.

Art said, "Well, I think that was a worthwhile trip. And besides, it was fun for all." Everyone agreed. They got home at 6:30 p.m., put the horses up, and as soon as they unloaded and cleaned everything, everyone was ready to go to bed.

For the last seven months, Art and the people that worked for him had been logging hardwood and pine from his farms. Art had accumulated two hundred cut hardwood and two hundred pine trees. All of these trees were at least twenty-five feet long and twelve inches in diameter. Art had already installed a debarker and a sizer with his sawmill. The boys spent several days hauling the special mud from the Sulphur. Everyone was out collecting large rocks, and they collected two wagon loads. The next day Louis and Ed began to build the small kiln to cook the bricks. In two days, they had built the rock kiln, filling the cracks with the mud from the Sulphur River. This was really just a big stove with one open front door and a small opening in the rear where the fire was set to heat the kiln. The boys thought they could cook from five hundred to a thousand bricks at a time, if they could build some metal racks inside the kiln. They then began to cure the kiln by slowly heating the inside and outside of the big oven. This took a week.

Darrell said, "I'll need a thousand bricks just for the chimney of my new house."

The boys set about learning to cook brick. They cooked during the day and let it cool at night, then took the bricks out to see if further cooking was necessary, which would then be done the next day. It took three days to cook bricks to where Darrell thought they were ready. They continued to cook more bricks using this procedure.

Darrell's wife, Velma, came to the sawmill and said, "Darrell, you need to go to Naples to sign the papers selling your farm and see Lassiter's lawyer to pay him for the new farm."

Art said, "Darrell, we also need to get started on your nice horse barn where your family will have to live until your new home is completed." Darrell had made a deal with Louis, his wife, and Ed, who worked for Art, to help him complete the barn. It was understood they would also have to be available to help Art plant the hundred acres of corn.

The next day Art's old neighbors, Mr. Shaw and his son Onnie came to see him. They had a wagon loaded with all their possessions. They both looked gaunt, unkempt, tired, and a bit defeated. Their clothes were tattered and torn. Mr. Shaw said, "We would like to move back to our old farm and sharecrop if no one else is living there." He also asked, "Do you need any other help?"

Art said, "No one is living in your old farm. However, I can't pay anything until the saw mill is started. Would you and Onnie like to help at the saw mill? You would make a dollar fifty a day, and Onnie would make one dollar a day?"

They were really interested in making money, since they had zero. Art also told them about all the rattlesnakes that were found at their place. Art said, "Go to McCoy's and buy whatever food you need to sustain you and Onnie for a couple of months and put it on my bill."

After about an hour of talking about the events of the past year, the problems with the rustlers, and the necessity of guarding his farm nightly, Mr. Shaw said, "Onnie and I would be glad to take a turn guarding every five days."

Art gave them two repeater rifles, and they all went out and each one shot about ten practice shots. Art told Mr. Shaw, "Come see me in about a week after you get settled."

Mr. Shaw said, "I sure would like to get some corn planted this year."

"I will have enough extra seed for sixty acres of corn and thirty acres of cotton and you could borrow my plow and disc for about a week."

"Thanks, Art, I know I'll owe you one half of my crop."

Art laughingly responded, "Let's get a crop first."

After the Shaws got settled, they came over and brought a deer. They all proceeded to butcher it and hang the meat in the smoke house. Mr. Shaw also wanted to pick up the seed and planting equipment.

Monday morning at six o'clock, Andrew, the blacksmith who had assembled the sawmill, Art, Darrell, Mr. Shaw, Onnie, Ed, and Louis started the sawmill. Art had located the sawmill on Bare Creek at the old Parkinson farm on Naples Road nine miles from Bryans Mill and eleven miles to Naples. This was one mile from Art's home and about three miles from Louis and Ed, who ran the other farms for Art.

They only had three minor problems the first day. Art also was told by Andrew, "I need at least three thousand board feet for a project of my own."

Tuesday the sawmill had six breakdowns, and Art was glad to see Mr. Shaw had helped fix them.

That meant Mr. Shaw was taking personal interest, and maybe he could run it without Art being there. Darrell was also training Onnie, who was now thirteen, how to make bricks. The rest of the week there were only nine more breakdowns, and Mr. Shaw fixed all of them. Saturday afternoon, at five o'clock the saw mill crew finally stopped. Art paid Mr. Shaw nine dollars and Onnie six. They had processed seventy hardwood logs and ten pine logs. For the next week, Art and Darrell ran the sawmill for twelve hours a day for six days, and had taken care of the wood for Darrell's, Lewis Roger's, McCoy's and Simmons's barns. Darrell and Onnie were busy all week making covered lumber racks, and they would have to do the same thing next week. Darrell said, "We should build an office large enough to have two rooms, in case someone needs to stay over."

While working, they found they couldn't keep their six-shooters on because they would be in danger of the guns accidentally firing. They had been working without their six-shooters a lot and that would have to change. There was always a threat of being attacked. Art and Darrell realized they should sell some of the guns they had collected over the last eighteen months. They had eighteen repeater rifles, carbines, and about that many six-shooters.

Darrell told Art, "Velma, her son, and I will take your buckboard to Texarkana and try to sell the guns. We could buy new holsters made to carry our guns on our back, and also some other things we need."

Art said, "Darrell, let's have the new leather shop in Bryans Mill make the special holster so we won't have to make another trip to Texarkana to pick them up, and we can put off the trip to Texarkana until absolutely necessary."

Darrell agreed, "Okay, have you talked to him about this?"

Art replied, "No, but I will Sunday."

Sunday was church at Bryans Mill. Everyone attended and relaxed for a day. The preacher, Larry Steverson, lived in Marietta and came to preach every other Sunday in Bryans Mill. Pastor Steverson was a large man, six foot seven and weighting at least two hundred seventy pounds. Art had been concerned about the preacher and his family traveling without any protection. He had decided to offer him a Henry rifle, a Sharp carbine, and a Colt six-shooter plus ammunition in hopes those would stop anyone from trying to attack the preacher or his family. In Northeast Texas, there were a lot of murderers, robbers, and thieves who were hungry, desperate men.

Art pulled the preacher aside and told him, "I would feel better if you and your family would take these guns to protect yourselves from the outlaws operating in this area."

Brother Larry and his wife, Suzy, had seven children, Josh, Jacob, Lana, Clay Lauren, Alayna, and Lyndi. Suzy was a perfect Preacher's wife. Not quite back to her girlish figure, outgoing, loving and had all the attributes to support her husband's profession. The preacher called all his family together to discuss what Art had said and offered them. The preacher told his family, "I really don't like the idea, but I'm afraid if we don't have some protection, something bad could happen to our family someday." They decided to accept Art's generous offer. Art immediately went to the edge of the woods to set up a safe place for practice shooting.

At four o'clock, when most of the church goers had finished picnicking and socializing, all of the preacher's family went with Art to the edge of the woods where he taught each family member how to load each weapon and then fire three practice shots. By the time Art had finished his instructions and firing practice, it was five thirty, and everyone was ready to go home. The preacher said, "Thanks Art for the guns and help." Everyone got home late.

The next day, Art's crew went to Darrell's old farm and moved all his livestock and equipment over to his new farm. The women also moved wagonloads of the furniture from Darrell's to the old Parkinson farm house, which Art now owned. The following day, Darrell was taking his family down to his dad's horse farm in Jefferson. They would return in two months, when Darrell's barn was completed. Art and Darrell needed two hundred fifty metal brick molds to make more bricks.

Darrell said, "If they're available in Marshall, Texas, twenty miles from Jefferson, I'll be back in a couple of weeks." Ed and Louis and his wife worked on the new barn for two weeks. Darrell returned with the metal brick molds. Art and Darrell spent a day getting special mud from the Sulphur, filling and setting the molds on the racks in the brick oven. That week they experimented with the amount of time it took to cook the bricks. They cooked five hundred bricks that week.

Everyone was working on Darrell's barn. The barn could have been finished in the next week, but Art, Ed, and Louis worked eight days planting ninety acres of corn. They then worked three days straight on Darrell's barn, and then three days finishing planting corn. Darrell and Art talked about security of all their animals and property.

Darrell told Art, "Everyone has been missing stock, and I personally lost twelve horses before I sold my farm north of Naples." Darrell had the ex slave friends, Sherman and Robert, check to see if any blacks were leaving their community at night. They checked for two weeks and found none of their black friends had left their homes after eight o'clock in the evening. Darrell thought the blacks were being blamed to cover up the real rustler's identities. Art and Darrell had befriended the ex-slaves and were helpful in getting them started in their new lives. The boys had a lot of trust in Sherman and Robert and their wives, Mae and Trixie. A lot of people did not like the boys because they had befriended the ex-slaves.

Darrell said, "We need to be guarding your farm at night because that's where I think they'll try to hurt you since many of these rustlers have attacked your farm seven times in the past two years. I have seen a lot of unidentified horse tracks around your farm recently."

It was decided Art would begin the watch that night from ten until three. Louis and Ed took their turn the next two nights, Darrell the fourth night, and the Shaws the fifth night. The first night Art had guard duty there were no problems. Art slept late the next day. Next week Ed, Louis, and Art were going to be busy harrowing weeds out of the corn.

About a week later, Art was just beginning his guard duty when he heard horses on the road. He rode six hundred yards to warn Darrell and ask him to get Louis and Ed. Art immediately and quietly returned to his farm and could see the four rustlers beginning to drive off fifty cows and ten horses. Art circled north and west to stop the rustlers. He dismounted, steadied his rifle on a tree, and when they came within sixty yards, he opened fire. With seven shots, he hit one rustler and two more of their horses when they tried to ride off. Then Art wounded one of the younger boys. The other rustlers decided to dismount and fight, but when Darrell, Louis, and Ed showed up, the rustlers surrendered. Art was really surprised that one of the rustlers was a loudmouth named Tommy Brundet, whom Art knew and could not stand. Tommy was a typical young boy, nothing usual about him other that his loud mouth and attempts at being a bully which had not worked for him so far. Both wounded rustlers were shot in the upper leg, but the bullet did not hit the bone. The older rustler's flesh was torn up badly. Art sent Ed to get Dr. Lilly in Naples to treat the wounded rustlers. Two eighteen-year-olds readily confessed to Art that Tommy had recruited them to help steal the cattle and horses. Darrell put the two eighteen-year-olds on the porch of Art's house, and Tommy and the older rustler in the barn. The older rustler would not admit to anything.

Art sent Louis to get Mr. McCoy, the general store owner, and ask him to get Tommy Brundet's dad to also come because it was urgent. Mr. McCoy also sent his son to get Sharon's dad, Lewis Rogers, and her brother Charles. When they all arrived, they got the same story. Sharon's dad was really upset and wondered why Art had not sent for the Union troops. He started in on Tommy's dad and told him, "He should have just killed Tommy."

Art went into the barn and took the ropes off Tommy, gave him his gun, showing him it was loaded. He told him, "Come out because I've had enough of your lying, bullying, threatening, and trying to steal from me. When you come out of the barn, I'm going to shoot you."

Tommy ran out of the barn, shot at Art, and missed. Art shot Tommy in the hand. Everyone knew it would take a year for his shooting hand to heal.

Art then told the rustlers, "Here's the deal. You're each to furnish twenty hardwood trees and twenty pine trees at least twenty-five feet long and twelve inches in diameter, delivered to my sawmill within thirty days." Art was going to take all their guns, horses, gear, and money. Art continued saying, "You're not to come within five miles of my place. If you violated any part of this agreement, you will be turned over to the army, admitting you had tried to rustle my cattle and horses."

All signed the agreement except Tommy, who refused. Art said, "Darrell will be taking him to the army in Naples." So Tommy's dad made him sign the agreement. Dr. Lilly and Sharon arrived at eight o'clock, and it took him two hour to treat the prisoners. Dr. Lilly told Tommy, "I'll have to see you in four days to take another look at that injured hand."

Mr. Brundet said, "He'll be there."

Art said, "He better not come down the Bryans Mill-Naples road, or I'll shoot him."

Mr. Brundet started complaining, and Mr. Rogers said, "Art, just send for the Union Army at Naples."

Art said, "Okay."

The rustlers all said no, and then the Brundets said they would stick to the agreement. Dr. Lilly, Tommy's dad, and Mr. McCoy all signed the agreement as witnesses. Art told Darrell about the agreement and Darrell went into a rage. He said, "Art you should have killed him! He's going to end up ambushing or hurting someone in our family." When Darrell read the agreement, he got even madder. Tommy's dad took Mr. McCoy's wagon and transported his son and the other older rustler home. Then everyone except the Rogers left. Louis and Ed also went home and said they were not going to guard the farm that night. Charles, Sharon's brother said, "I'll help guard the farm for two days, and then I'll go back to my farm."

Mr. Rogers said, "I want Sharon and the baby to come home with me until next Sunday." Sharon had started a deer roast and told Art and Charles how to finish cooking it.

Art told the two young rustlers, Jed and Joe Smith, they could have breakfast because they looked like they could use a good meal. Sharon cooked a great meal of eggs, ham, grits, biscuits, and gravy. The brothers told Art that was the only meal they had eaten in three days, and they really ate like it. Jed and Joe were eighteen and nineteen, respectively, medium height and weighed somewhere around one hundred fifty pounds. They looked like they could work hard if needed. After the meal, Sharon, the baby, and Mr. Rogers left.

Art told Jed and Joe, "You can take your horses and pistols. Take two axes and a crosscut saw." He showed them where and how they could cut oak trees. Art told them, "You can bunk at Ed's place and come by after finishing the day's work, and I'll send groceries home with you." Ed did not like having the Jed and Joe bunk where he lived, but Art said, "It'll only be for a month or so." Art went to bed, and Charles went out and chopped wood for two hours, then checked on the roast. Art woke up at five o'clock well rested and feeling good. Charles had eaten at three o'clock and fallen asleep. Charles pulled guard the next two days without having any trouble. Then he left, and Art and his hands decided to suspend their regular guarding routine for the next three weeks.

In ten days, Jed and Joe had cut and trimmed thirty oak trees and borrowed Art's big timber-hauling wagon and mules to haul the logs to the sawmill. Art told them, "You can make a dollar a day, plus room and board to help guard all the farms. Also, I'll pay you two fifty for each tree that's cut and transported to the sawmill. You can continue to bunk at Ed's."

Ed was not complaining about them anymore, as they were good workers and tried to keep things organized. Jed and Joe had also shot a deer and certainly knew how to cook it, making a tasty meal.

CHAPTER 2

A rt and Darrell had many discussions about the politics in northeast Texas. The US military was doing the same job they had been doing in Texas since the end of the Civil War. There were a lot of outlaws north of the Sulphur River and up into Oklahoma. The Yankees only had three thousand soldiers in Texarkana to the Dallas area to protect over one hundred fifty thousand square miles. They had fifty, five-man squads at small towns in that area. The Yankees also had three thousand soldiers on the Texas western frontier, mainly to fight the Comanches. It took two months to deploy these troops. Most of the time they were busy going after murderers, rustlers, and thieves, which left them little time to protect those settlers. The Comanches had a force of ten thousand, including their friends, the Kiowas. The Yankees also started hiring people to run the new Friedman organization, which was to protect and help the blacks. Art and Darrell knew two of those agents who were so anti-black that the boys didn't see them being much help to the blacks.

The West Texas settlers hadn't had anyone protecting them since the Yankee soldiers left when the Civil War started. The Confederate soldiers who were supposed to protect the western frontier ended up chasing draft dodgers and outlaws. In northeast Texas, there were lots of murderers, rustlers, and thieves who were hungry, desperate men. They seldom protected the settlers. Many of the West Texas settlers had moved at least one hundred miles away from the frontier. Only the real tough had stayed in that area.

When the Civil War ended in April of 1865, the Texas governor, Marrah, and other Confederate officials fled to Mexico before the Yankees arrived. The lieutenant governor, Stockdale, assumed the governorship until President Andrew Johnson appointed Andrew Hamilton as provisional civilian governor on June 16, 1865. Hamilton had been appointed governor-in-exile of Texas in 1864 by Abraham Lincoln. This took place when the Yankees tried to capture Texas but were turned back.

Hamilton did not agree with President Johnson about the treatment of the Texas-defeated Confederates. During his term, he had tough times with Indians, outlaws, and money. One of his main responsibilities was to have a constitutional convention in 1866. This convention was to nullify the act of secession, slavery, and the Confederate States' debt. The delegates were to be elected and had to take the oath of amnesty as prescribed by the president. Only white or black males twenty-one years or older that had also taken the oath could vote on these delegates. No one had checked to see if the delegates had really taken the oath or were even eligible to take the oath. The convention did nullify the act of secession, slavery, and renounced the States Confederate debt. The delegates also set an election for all state and local offices for June 25, 1866. There were enough ex-Confederates elected that they really didn't get anything else accomplished, and Hamilton resigned after fourteen months. He had not been able to get along with the Unionists or ex-Confederates.

In September of 1865, the Union had formed the Freedmen's Bureau. Their main goal was to help the blacks go from being slaves to being free. Most of the blacks had no place to go, and therefore, would be stuck with having to work for farmers, many who had been their slave masters. The bureau tried to help them make sure the farmers paid them a fair wage and also encouraged them to work in the rural areas because there weren't many jobs in the towns for them. At that time, the largest towns in Texas were Galveston and San Antonio, with populations of two thousand each.

In the election of June 1866, voters elected James Throckmorton as the new governor of Texas by a four-to-one margin. James had served in the Confederate Army for two years. Previously he had voted not to secede from the Union. Most blacks were intimidated, by various means, to not vote. In August, the Texas legislation met. During his governorship, Throckmorton was pro-Confederate and many blacks and Unionist were actually murdered. Not many whites were brought to trial during his tenure. Governor Throckmorton was also accusing the military of not doing their job protecting the settlers on the western frontier. The Unionist accused him of using the rangers to enforce his pro-Confederate views. The Yankee Texas commander General Griffin complained bitterly about Governor Throckmorton. The Texas legislatures also sent two pro-Confederate Senators to Washington, but the US Congress would not seat them.

In March of 1867, the US Congress passed the first Reconstruction Act, dividing the old Confederacy into districts.

Texas was in the fifth military district, and General Philip Sheridan was in control. In July, Sheridan removed Governor Throckmorton and over four hundred elected officials, at least one official in each of the fifty-seven counties of Texas. Sheridan's reason was refusal to cooperate and a punishment of those who had committed outrageous acts against men both white and black. Sheridan also removed all the officials in San Antonio and Austin. The new military commander of Texas, General Canby, made sure everyone appointed to replace these officials were capable of taking the oath test passed by the US Congress in 1862.

This eliminated all Confederate soldiers and elected officials during the Civil War as they weren't even eligible to take the oath.

Art and Darrell knew at this time they had to be very careful because the Yankees were more in full control of not only the taxes and political government but also the federal government. Some carpetbaggers controlled the local government. In order to vote or participate in any politics, you had to be twenty-one years of age and could not have been a Confederate soldier or official.

Darrell was more upset than Art and said to him, "Why aren't you upset about this as much as I am?"

Art answered, "I'm not twenty-one years old, so I couldn't vote anyway."

CHAPTER 3

Art and Darrell had previously been successful trapping wild longhorns that had no brand. They had found it hard to trap these cattle when there was plenty of feed and grass for them, but in the winter when they were hungry, it was easy to trap them. Art had trapped about sixty longhorn cows the previous winter and put them all on his family homestead farm. Even Darrell had trapped some cows on his north Naples farm. This had been the third winter the boys had trapped these cattle. The first winter the boys had trapped over four hundred head of wild longhorn cattle. They knew the wild cows would be even scarcer next year. It was said there were over twelve million wild longhorn cattle mainly in central, south, and west Texas, and the ranchers in those areas were going to drive most of the wild longhorn cattle to the northern markets because there was no other way to make money in Texas at this time. Of course, Art and Darrell had already successfully taken two herds north to Yankee forts.

With Darrell's barn completed, he was returning to Jefferson to move his family back to Bryans Mill. He was to also pick up more brick molds from Marshall. He had talked his dad into a trial of living with his family. He drove a wagon to Jefferson to pick up his family and all of their belongings. His dad would drive his own wagon with his belongings. Art and the others moved all of Darrell's furniture from the Parkinson farmhouse over to his new barn and unloaded it. Ed, Louis and his wife would receive forty dollars each for helping build Darrell's barn. Darrell was to pick up more plans for building barns just like his. Art knew a lot of farmers who wanted to build new barns, and he thought if they had plans, more of the farmers would buy the lumber from them.

Art and Darrell decided to both build their new homes out of stone from a quarry twenty miles away. It would take eighty wagonloads to complete the houses. Art immediately contracted Jed and Joe to haul all the special rock for the homes for five hundred dollars. They could use Art and Darrell's wagons and mules. The wagons were special heavy-duty wagons, and the boys were able to deliver six loads a week. Art gave them each a Henry rifle and figured with their six-shooters and the sixteen shot Henry, they should be able to fight off anyone. Besides, nobody really thought anyone would want a wagonload of stone.

It was the twentieth of March, and Art told Darrell, "We're going back on regular night guard duty. We have spotted several different cowboy groups trying to secretly look over the herd."

Velma, Darrell, and his dad had returned and made small changes in their new horse barn to make it more livable. Art, Sharon, and the baby went over to help the Stroud's get set up at their temporary new home. Art cut wood for four hours and was completely worn out. When everyone sat down to eat, he talked to Mr. Stroud, Darrell's dad, about the problem of guarding all their stock and families.

Mr. Stroud suggested, "We could set up a telegraph system between all the farms. This would mean the guard could warn all the farms with one signal. I know a man who can do that, but I would have to talk to him to see how much it would cost. It would take six miles of wiring and five terminals. Most of the wiring

CHAPTER 4

Art and all the people that worked for him had been doing nightly guard duty on a rotating basis for the last three weeks. Everyone was getting tired of it. Art asked, "Louis and Ed, could you hold on for two more weeks?" They agreed. When Art finished with the harrows, he took them to Mr. Shaw who had already plowed.

Art and Darrell had so many barn orders it would take the sawmill running for a month to get caught up. Art planned to start next Monday. They could now produce one thousand bricks at a time, in three days, with the new racks and forms Darrell had gotten in Marshall. The third week, Lewis Rogers, Gene McCoy, and the Anthonys all picked up their lumber. Art collected $3,800.00 and Darrell sold four thousand bricks for $1,000.00.

On Sunday, everyone attended church in Bryans Mill. Onnie had shot a deer Saturday night, and they had setup a spit that morning at church to cook it, and it was ready to eat by one o'clock. The one-hundred-fifty-pound deer was completely eaten, except for two two-pound roasts. Onnie said, "I'll be taking the roast to the sawmill on Monday for lunch."

In the afternoon, the preacher told Art, "I'm sure glad we had the rifles today because there were several men that rode past us as we were coming to church this morning. They stopped, but when my sons picked up the guns from the floor of the wagon, they decided to ride on."

Darrell was going to harvest his oat crop at his old farm, and was going to get Robert and Sherman, his ex-slaves friends and Art to help. They finished harvesting in ten days and got over four thousand bushels. Darrell sent Art, Louis, Mr. Shaw and Ed each five wagonloads of oats. All these farms belonged to Art. It took Darrell, Robert, and Sherman two weeks to bring the rest of the oats to Darrell's new barn.

It was now May the twentieth. Darrell had over five thousand bricks on order and the wood for the inside of Art's and Darrell's houses. Wood for six barns had to be cut. They had enough new orders that it would take at least one month to finish. Ed and Louis needed to weed one hundred acres of corn plus Mr. Shaw's thirty acres. Everyone thought they needed to take off two weeks to take care of all the crops.

Art told Darrell, "We need to get a steam engine to saw and cut wood faster."

Darrell agreed, however, even a small steam engine could cost over ten thousand dollars, and the boys knew they could not afford that. If they could get a used one, it would be much cheaper.

Art said, "I remember a Yankee paddle wheeler that was taking supplies to Fort Gibson, Indian Territory, from Fort Smith that was sunk by General Stan Waite on the Arkansas River. It was partially on land and partially in the river. If it's still there and the steam engine is not damaged, maybe it could be salvaged. I could travel up to the Oklahoma Territory and see if I could salvage the steam engine. I plan to leave in about three weeks."

Darrell said nothing but was thinking, *Well, another one of my buddy's ideas.*

The boat was in Indian Territory, and Art knew he would again need help from his Indian friends. Art told Sharon, "I'm going to look for my Indian friends to see if the paddle wheeler that was sunk is still there and if the engine's good." Art and Darrell knew they had to get more work done at the mill.

They started the sawmill about seven o'clock Monday morning, and in the first three days, they only had six breakdowns. Mr. Shaw quickly fixed those with the help of others. About one thousand bricks could be made in a week. Onnie could do all brick making from getting mud on the Sulphur, to cooking them and still help guard Art's farm.

CHAPTER 5

In two weeks, the whole crew and their families again went to church in Bryans Mill. After church, Mr. Brundet and Tommy came over to Art, Darrell, and the crew's picnic table. Art was dreading another confrontation with that loudmouth Tommy. His father grabbed Art's hand and shook it and said, "I want to thank you for not sending Tommy to jail."

Tommy also told Art, "I'll be delivering forty trees to the sawmill next week, and I would like to order enough lumber for a barn."

Art told Mr. Brundet, "It'll be about three weeks before I'll have the lumber ready."

Tommy said, "Art, I have heard that the rustlers are going to try to steal your cattle the next Sunday that you're in church."

Art was so upset he asked Darrell, "Will you ride back now and make sure the farm is protected?" Darrell grabbed some food to eat while he was riding.

Everyone else ate lunch and left at one thirty in their wagons, trying to get home as quickly as they could. No rustlers showed that day, and they made preparations to surprise them when they came in two weeks.

Tommy delivered the logs that week, and by the time they cut wood for seven barns and Art's and Darrell's houses, they were out of timber. They would have to cut trees for two weeks to take care of any new business that might come along.

On the Saturday before Bryans Mill church, Art asked the two Anthony boys, "Will you hide on my farm? The plan is for me, Darrell, and his men to double back and catch the rustlers between us and you boys." The Anthony boys were both close to six feet tall and very muscular from working with horses and general farm work. They were very good with a gun and also their fists. Not many men were willing to take them on in a fight.

Art, Darrell, Ed, and Louis hid their horses about two miles from Art's farm, and as they traveled in the wagons toward the church, they jumped off and let their wives drive their families on to church. They covered the north and east areas while the Anthony boys were already hidden in the south part of Art's farm.

Everyone was at their predetermined position, and at ten thirty, ten rustlers crossed the Sulphur heading for Art's cattle. They worked about twenty minutes rounding up over a hundred head. Art had two of them in sight about sixty yards away, and he shot them both. Then all the other defenders opened up, and when they were finished, five of the rustlers were killed or wounded and two more of the rustler's horses had been shot. That left three rustlers making a run for it. Before they got off Art's farm, two more were shot. Art and Darrell told their group, "Tie up the six injured rustlers, leave the three dead ones where they are."

Louis was sent to get the Union Army and Dr. Lilly. Art asked, "Ed will you get all their guns, money, and horses because I'm going to keep all that."

Darrell asked the Anthony boys, "Will you stay until the law arrives?" The law didn't get there until three thirty that afternoon.

When Sharon and Velma told their stories at church about the pending attack on Art and Darrell's homes, several men from the church left with the Loggings and the Strouds as they were returning to the boys' farm. Gene McCoy was leading the group. They were hoping to get there in time to help. However, when they arrived the fighting was over. The group did help clean up and realized how really dangerous it was for everyone in this area. They all agreed, "We need to organize and stick together to protect our families and property."

Everyone left except Gene McCoy and his son, who stayed until the Army finished their investigation. Art and Darrell had not yet returned when they left.

The boys had taken off after the rustler who had gotten away, and trailed him until he crossed the Red River going into Oklahoma Territory. They just could not pick up his trail and returned home at about three in the morning. Everyone had returned to their homes and Velma told Art and Darrell, "You both need to go to Naples to tell your stories to the Union Army Lieutenant Thomas."

The next day, Art and Darrell decided to have a long talk about the danger and what they needed to protect themselves, their families, and property. The idea for a telegraph system had been discarded. Darrell suggested, "We can continue to use Jed and Joe Smith for at least six months and have them continue to bunk over at Ed's. No one else lives there, and they have a roof over their heads. We need to pass this information on to all the farmers in the area and try to get them organized to protect all their families. Also, we need to get the metal bullets for the Henrys and check if we have to correct the Henrys before they could shoot metal bullets."

Art and Darrell had fourteen Henry rifles that only shot the old ammunition, and many of their friends had Henrys. Their friends had another twenty-six Henrys for a total of forty. Darrell contacted Sergeant Jones in Naples, and Sergeant Jones said, "The Henrys need a small conversion, which would cost ten dollars per rifle. This could be done in Texarkana by a gunsmith who lives there. The new metal shells are five hundred dollars for a thousand rounds."

Darrell asked, "Is that your price?"

The sergeant said, "You'll even have to get permission from the Lieutenant to buy them. I don't know why, but the detachment at Naples don't even have Henrys, and we only have two thousand rounds for them. All the men in our detachment use the Sharp carbines, which load from the butt of the stock."

Darrell, knowing they also had a total of twelve Sharp carbines asked, "How much is that ammunition?"

The sergeant answered, "Five hundred dollars for one thousand rounds."

"Will you talk to Lieutenant Thomas?" asked Darrell.

Sergeant Jones told Lieutenant Thomas what he and Darrell had discussed, and Lieutenant Thomas said, "I don't know what else I can add to what Sergeant Jones has told you."

Darrell said, "You expect us to pay for our own ammunition and protect the eastern side of the territory? You don't even use the Henry ammunition, and we could sure use that."

Lieutenant Thomas said, "Darrell, you're only getting this kind of good treatment because of what Colonel Nance and Phillips put in their report about how helpful you've been to the Yankees."

Darrell replied, "For God's sake, don't say that in front of any of the locals, we'll have to fight everybody. You should at least give us four thousand rounds, two thousand for our Henrys and two thousands for our Sharps."

Lieutenant Thomas said, "That's two thousand dollars' worth. I'll have to talk to my colonel, and he'll be here next week. I don't know what he's going to say about ex-Confederate soldiers protecting us from the east."

"No," said Darrell. "Tell him that we're a bunch of farmers who've done the Union a lot of favors trying to protect families in that part of the county. In fact," Darrell pleaded, "let me and Art talk to him!"

Lieutenant Thomas agreed and said, "You can talk to him next Wednesday morning."

The next day, Art and Darrell discussed the information Darrell had received, and then decided they had better make sure they got all the farmers they wanted to meet the colonel next Wednesday to see if they thought they could do the job.

Darrell asked, "Art, will you talk to the Anthony's, McCoy's, Mr. Brundet, Mrs. Lucas, and Mr. Percy, the ferry boat man?"

The next day, Art visited all five people, and they all agreed to be part of a special militia to defend their area of the county. Each one indicated they would try to get one more neighbor to join and help.

Mr. McCoy told Art, "If we don't get a teacher, the school will not open in September. Will you ask if anyone knows a teacher who would be interested, and if so have them contact me?

"I sure will," Art promised.

They all met at the sawmill at 7:00 a.m. on Wednesday. Art told Velma, "There's an opening for a school teacher in Bryans Mill."

Velma said, "There's a lady I know in Naples who lost her husband in the war and may be in need of a job. She was my teacher. Her name is Mrs. Yeiser. She has two girls, Haylee and Katelyn. She taught school for five years and stopped teaching ten years ago because she wanted to dedicate her time raising those two girls."

On Wednesday morning, nineteen farm protectors, along with ten wives and children, met at the sawmill and rode to Naples to confront the sheriff and Union Army leader. The women were really there to shop, except Velma, Sharon, and their sons; they went to see Mrs. Yeiser. The former teacher was really interested in teaching at Bryans Mill.

Art and Darrell's group met with the Yankee Colonel North and explained the need for ammunition to help protect themselves from the mercenaries, rustlers, thieves, and murderers that were able to attack them. They again requested two thousand rounds of metal ammunition for the Henry rifle, and two thousand rounds of metal ammunition for the Sharps carbines. Art also requested some extra ammunition cylinders for the Colt six-shooters. Colonel North was hesitant to give a group of ex-Confederate soldiers this ammunition.

That really set Art and Darrell off, and they asked if they could speak to the colonel in private. He said, "I'll give you a little bit of private time."

The boys told the colonel, "We delivered cattle and horses to Fort Smith and Fort Gibson. We are also responsible for starting the black settlement north of Naples. If you need to verify this, talk to colonels Nance and Phillips."

He said, "Before leaving Naples, I'll telegraph them and have an answer for you by tomorrow."

Art explained to the entire protector group, "I'll make sure each family will have at least a Henry rifle or Sharp carbine to work with."

Everyone left to finish whatever other business they had in Naples, and all met for supper at four o'clock.

In the meantime, Mr. McCoy had gone over to talk to Mrs. Yeiser about teaching in Bryans Mill. They both agreed she was the one for the job. She said, "It will be necessary for me to move to Bryans Mill." Sharon and Velma volunteered their husbands to help move her. Melinda and her daughters would go with Mr. McCoy to see their new home and the school. They all spent the night in Naples.

The next morning by nine o'clock, everyone met. Colonel North told the boys, "We have gotten good reports from Colonel Nance and Colonel Phillips. Everything you asked for has been approved. I'm leaving my Master Sergeant Best with two privates to go to each member of the group and make sure they can all shoot properly and good enough to defend themselves."

Art suggested, "You could use the Yankee firing range today, and that would take care of the training most of them need."

At eleven o'clock, twenty members of the group were out at the range, and everyone shot and practiced until one o'clock. Even

Sharon, Velma, Melinda, and her girls came out to practice. All of the ladies shot the Sharp carbines.

Sergeant Best said, "I'm impressed with everyone's shooting ability." The entire group talked with him about shooting the Henrys. He told them, "The Henry Rifle is only good up to one hundred twenty yards."

The group had also been talking about not discussing with anyone how many cows and horses they had when they were leaving their farms. If they had to leave, they would let the other members know so they could protect the farms. Art also told Sergeant Best, "Someone needs to make a sweep north of the Sulphur River and round up the toughs." This usually meant peace and quiet for everyone for about two months. Sergeant Best promised, "I'll talk to the colonel and get that done next week."

Sergeant Best gave the ammunition to Art and Darrell for them to distribute to the group. He said, "It'll take about a month to get the extra six-shooter cylinders."

Art gave all the Henry rifles or Sharp carbine owners one hundred rounds of ammunition for each gun. He and Darrell told the people, "If you don't have either a Henry rifle or Sharp carbine, we will deliver a repeater rifle or carbine to you sometime in the next two weeks."

Art had taken the Sharp carbines and Henry rifles to those of the protection group who didn't have the repeaters. He made sure each one knew how to load, shoot, and clean their firearms. Art said, "It would be a good idea to keep your guns loaded, and if you have a shotgun, keep it loaded also. Nothing puts the fear in these bad guys like a loaded shotgun pointed at them within twenty yards. If you do not have a shotgun, I'll get one to you as soon as possible." Art also had given three of the carbines to the Anthony boys' wives.

Darrell gathered all the Sharps and Henrys they had distributed and took them to the gunsmith in Texarkana. The gunsmith said,

"I'll have the guns converted for metal ammunition in ten days. It'll cost four hundred dollars."

Art said, "Darrell, the only one of my farms they ever try to rustle from is my homestead. I don't think they know I have these other farms. I think I should move most of my cattle over to Ed's or Louis's. What do you think?"

"If that's a fact," said Darrell, "we need to talk to all our people, including women and children to make sure they don't talk to anyone else."

Art said, "I've got 300 head on Ed's farm and 200 on Louis's farm." Art only had 200 head on his farm and 125 on the old Shaw farm. Mr. Shaw had a few sows of his own. Of course, each of the farms had about 10 horses and two mules on them. Darrell's farm had about 120 horses, and he kept most of his horses hidden. Darrell said, "Don't move the cattle because at least we know where to defend and everyone is getting tired of guard duty anyway."

Art, Ed and Louis met at Louis's house the next day to work the cattle. The crew branded, castrated, and treated the sick ones, and moved them to a close-by pasture that was fenced. At noon, while they were all eating, Art said, "I think it's very important no one knows these places belong to me, because I think that's the reason your farms have not been harmed."

CHAPTER 6

Art and Darrell were operating the sawmill Tuesday through Friday, without a night guard. Art figured they would probably be safe from an attack for about a month. On Saturday most of the crew, except Joe and Jed, went to Naples where Art had rented rooms so everyone could go to the dance Saturday night. The boys finally got to sign all the necessary papers to have the rustlers go to trial. They also told the lieutenant they lost the trail of the one rustler that got away.

Everyone walked up to the dance at seven o'clock that evening and was having a good time. Even Mr. Shaw had found a local Confederate widow and they were dancing. She had fifteen-year-old twin daughters named Ashley and Sarah who were also at the dance. Ashley had been dancing all night with Tommy Brundet. At nine thirty, she came running into the dance hall shouting, "Four toughs said they're going to kill Tommy because he told Art about the rustlers raiding his farm!"

Art and Darrell were the first ones out the door as the four men were dragging Tommy down the street. Art shot one of them and told the rest, "Drop your guns."

When they tried to draw their guns, Art and Darrell killed the other three. Lieutenant Thomas finally arrived twenty minutes later. Tommy told the lieutenant, "Those men wanted to kill me because I told Art they were planning to steal his cattle." After talking to twenty people he said, "Looks like they got what was coming to them." Three men were dead and the fourth went to prison. That pretty much finished the dance for the night.

Mr. Shaw told Widow Lucas, "My son and I will accompany you and your daughters to church tomorrow and home afterward." The Lucas' farm was only five miles from the Shaw's farm. After some discussion, it was decided everyone would meet at two thirty and ride toward Bryans Mill. Art and Darrell and their families ate at Mrs. Hill's after church and then met all the others ready to go to Bryans Mill. Even Tommy was riding with them, but he was still in bad shape.

Mr. Shaw asked, "Art, if we give Mrs. Lucas a repeater rifle, would you show her how to use it?"

Art talked to Darrell about the request, and he said, "That would be okay."

Art gave her a Spencer carbine the boys had captured off one of the raiders. The next morning, the sheriff and lieutenant came by and started complaining, "Seems like everywhere you boys go trouble follows, and we want it to stop!"

Darrell said, "We didn't start any of it, but we are sure going to finish it."

Art said, "The way you're talking, you think we should just give all the thieves everything we have."

The sheriff said, "Some of the people in this county think it's you boys' fault."

"Then arrest us!" said Darrell.

The lieutenant said, "If anything else happens, we will arrest you." Then he walked away.

Art said, "I'll just kill all the rustlers and bury them when they come on my property."

Art and Darrell thought everyone needed to get caught up on chores around their farms, so they went back to the sawmill at nine o'clock the following morning. Art and Darrell knew they

CHAPTER 7

On Tuesday, Art was going to go look for his Indian friends to see if the steamboat that was sunk on the Arkansas was still there, and if the engine was okay. He told Sharon and Darrell, "I think I'll be gone about ten days."

On June 1, Art left Darrell at the Red River, going up to see his Indian friends about helping him get the steam engine out of the sunken Yankee paddle wheeler on the Arkansas River. Art received a friendly welcome at the Choctaw village and Chief Eagle Feather gave his permission for Hawk, Running Bear, and Straight Arrow to help. They left the following morning. It was a two-day ride to the sunken boat. It looked almost salvageable, and after a day, they decided it would be worth trying. They even thought they might be able to float it if it was repaired.

The next day, Art left for Fort Smith, Arkansas, to see Colonel White, the new commander. The Indians were working on repairing the hull. Art told Colonel White, "I want to buy the sunken paddle wheeler."

Colonel White said, "You can have it for a hundred dollars."

Art paid him and got a receipt. Art then asked the colonel, "Who is the best carpenter and blacksmith in town?"

Colonel White replied, "The best carpenter is Steve Hand, and the best blacksmith is Bob Schmidt."

Art proceeded to contact them and try to make a deal for them to come with him and work on the sunken boat. They told Art they would each need a hundred dollars to spend a week working on the sunken boat at its present location.

It was now Friday, and they would not leave until Sunday. They gathered all the necessary repair equipment they thought they might need, and Art got enough food to feed six people for a week. They both insisted that they take six mules and a wagon so they could use them if necessary to pull the boat. They arrived at the sunken boat Monday afternoon. Steve said, "I think we can just jack the boat up eighteen inches and build scaffolding, raising it high enough to repair and seal it."

Tuesday, Mr. Hand and Mr. Schmidt started their work to repair the boat. Art and Hawk helped them while Running Bear and Straight Arrow guarded and cooked for everyone. In two days, the carpenter thought they could float the boat to Fort Smith. The blacksmith never could get the steam engines to start, but he thought he could if they got it to Fort Smith. They re-launched the boat and then poled, paddled, and with the help of the mules, pulled it back to Fort Smith, arriving early Friday morning. The Indians followed in the wagon managing the mules and horses. After two days, the blacksmith finally got the steam engine cleaned up, started, and let it run for over an hour. The question now was how to get it to the Sulphur River. On Monday, Mr. Hand and Mr. Schmidt again worked on the boat.

Colonel White, the Fort Smith commander, requested Art to come to his office at four o'clock that afternoon. When Art arrived, Colonel White introduced him to Carl Ryan. Mr. Ryan said, "I'll give you eight thousand for the boat."

"I don't know if I want to do that. You have to pay ten thousand for a new steam engine for the sawmill," Art said.

"Eighty-five hundred, and that is my final offer.", "Sold."

Mr. Ryan was going to use the paddle wheeler to transport supplies on the Arkansas River from Memphis to Fort Smith. They went to the bank and Art got his money. Art gave the carpenter and blacksmith two hundred dollars each. He just could not thank them enough for what they had done.

Art and his three Indian friends left Fort Smith at nine o'clock Tuesday morning. Art went by to talk to Colonel White before leaving and offered him $250.00 for his help, which he took. Art told Colonel White, "I need and will pay for four thousand rounds of Henry rifle, Sharp carbine, and Colt six-shooter ammunition."

Colonel White said, "I'll sell you the ammunition."

Art had taken an extra horse and loaded all the ammunition on that horse and paid the colonel a thousand dollars. He also loaded two cases of whiskey on the horse.

It took them until Wednesday to get to the Indian village. Art gave a case of whiskey to the three braves that helped him, plus a case to the chief. He also gave the three Indian friends that helped him $250.00 each. Art gave Hawk one half of the ammunition he had purchased. Since Hawk knew Art had a lot of money on him, and the Oklahoma Territory was overrun with mean lawbreakers, he told him, "We're going to ride to the Red River with you to help protect you."

Art said, "I want to thank you and everyone for the help, and I hope to see you soon at Sulphur River."

Hawk accompanied Art to the Red River without incident, and then returned to his village.

It was now Friday, and Art only had forty miles to ride to the Sulphur. Art shot a big white-tailed deer just outside the river. He gutted it and put it on the extra horse. He rode fifteen more miles when someone took a shot at him, which just missed. Art began tracking his assailant and came upon a small cabin, where a husband and wife, Mr. and Mrs. Jenson, their eight- and ten-year-old boys and their nine-year-old girl lived. They looked like they were hungry, and the horse they had looked even hungrier. Art took the ammunition off his extra horse and gave them the horse, deer, horse feed, and the human food he had left.

He left them a pair of homemade deerskin shoes so they could use them as a pattern for making everyone a pair for themselves. All their clothes were ragged. Mr. Jenson said, "We lost our farm and had nowhere else to go when we came to this cabin, which was unoccupied. Art guessed the couple was somewhere in their mid thirties.

Art said, "The forest near the Sulphur River has an abundance of game and, of course, fish in the river." He even left his Henry rifle for Mr. Jenson. Art also told them where he lived, and he might have some work and if they were interested to come see him. He cautioned them to be careful of quicksand and only cross on a well trodden path.

Art had been gone sixteen days when he got home at six o'clock on Friday evening. Darrell and Mr. Shaw were really glad to see him because Sharon and Velma had been after them to go check and find out where Art was, if he was dead or injured. Darrell had promised the women they would start tomorrow. They all said they had been extremely worried about him since he was gone so long. Art told everyone the story about his trip, leaving out the amount of money he had made. He also told them about the poor Jenson family he had met twenty-five miles from there. Sharon and Velma wanted to immediately go and give them food and clothes. The Boys said no, that Art had offered him a job, and if he wanted it, he could come to the house.

Sharon said, "I don't know what I would do if something happened to you. Someone is always shooting at you, and if they're not, you're off on some venture somewhere, putting yourself further in danger for money. You have a family, and you need to stay here so that your family can grow. I'm just sick of worrying about you. I love you, and I don't think all this traveling and shooting would be happening if you just stayed here."

Art told her, "I'm just doing this so that our family can have a better future, and I must have your love and support to make things better."

Darrell and Velma said, "We'll see you tomorrow, and we can talk over our plans at that time."

Art told Sharon. "I'm tired and need some rest."

After she took care of junior, they all went to bed. Sharon only had to get up once during the night. She and the baby were up at six o'clock, but Art didn't wake up until nine o'clock.

CHAPTER 8

At breakfast, Art told Sharon, "I really want you to learn to shoot the pistol and shotgun. You already know how to use a rifle, but I want you to be able to protect yourself." Art then went out and checked all the cattle, horses, and mules. He cut out four cows, a horse that looked bad, and drove them up to the barn, fed and watered them, and put them in the corral. Then he rode over to Darrell and Velma's, and had lunch. He and Darrell talked about how to protect their families, the sawmill, the livestock, and the land. They also discussed their plans for the next few weeks.

Art and Darrell didn't trust banks. Art had found a special large oak tree that had been struck by lightning a hundred yards from his home. Art hollowed it out more and stored his money, papers, and guns in it. That day was the first day Art had shown Sharon his special tree. It took a while for Art to really trust anyone! Art put six thousand dollars from the boat sale, and he then had over eleven thousand dollars, three repeater rifles, three handguns, and three loaded shotguns in his special tree. He kept his ammunition in his house. Art also paid Louis and Ed their wages through December, and Joe and Jed five hundred dollars for previous work. He also usually kept two thousand dollars hidden around the house. Darrell knew about the special tree, and he hid his money, important papers, and extra guns in another tree which Art knew about.

It was now June 30. Jed and Joe had about five more weeks of hauling stones for building Art's and Darrell's new homes, but there was enough stone to begin work on Art's home. Art had hired a man from Texarkana to come and supervise the building of his new stone house. He paid him three hundred to work a month supervising the building of his stone house. This man, Roger Russell, had a lot of experience building stone houses, and the plan was he would show the boys how to build Art's house, and then they would not need his help to build Darrell's house.

Roger was due to be at the site of the new house a week from Monday. Roger was about fifty years old and had developed a great reputation for building stone houses. In other words, he was known as the best.

The Jenson family showed up on Thursday of the following week and said, "We would sure appreciate a job. We do not seem to be getting anywhere and need a chance to earn money to survive. We are used to hard work and are willing to work any jobs you might have for us."

Art took them over to the cabin they had built at the sawmill site. "You can live here until October," Art said. "And you can start working on my new stone home on Monday." Sharon and Velma took Mrs. Jenson and her kids to Bryans Mill to get the necessities for their home.

Roger, the experienced builder, arrived on Monday and Art, Darrell, Louis, Ed, Phil Jenson, Mr. Shaw, and Onnie finally began working on Art's new stone house. Roger got them started. Mr. Shaw, Art, and Roger laid the foundation, which took one week. Roger left after the third day telling them, "I'll be back in three weeks." For the next two weeks, everyone worked on the house, except Joe and Jed, who were hauling stones for Darrell's house. They struggled to get the sidewalls of stone finished so they could get the tin roof on. Roger came back and stayed three days while they finished the tin roof.

Art's house would be a two-story, four-bedroom home with inside running water, a separate bathroom, kitchen, and living room with a covered front and back porch. It had eight windows with one-inch bodark wood shutters that had shooting cross slots for protection. It would take at least two months to get these special glass windows and shutters. Also, the house was to have a two-story stone chimney and a stone fence across the front and back yards. A man who claimed he could put screens on the windows in both the front and back doors would be there on September fifteenth.

After eight weeks, none of the inside of the house was finished, but the outside was all completed. Sharon told Art, "My dad knows a man, Bill Stalworth, in Marietta that could build cabinets and closets, and finish the inside of the house. He thought, with some help, it would take four weeks to finish the inside of our house."

Art replied, "Contact him and offer him three hundred for four weeks to finish the inside of the house."

Sharon hired Mr. Stalworth to finish the inside of their house. Sharon and Velma also hired Ashley Lucas to look after Art Jr and Velma's boy so each woman could be free to supervise the house-building. Sharon also hired Sara Lucas and Mrs. Lucas to help Bill finish the inside of their new house. The following week, Mr. Stalworth began working on the inside of the house. Art also asked Phil, Onnie, and Mr. Shaw to help. Art's new house was completed on September fifteenth, and everyone helped them move in. The man also came and installed screens on the windows and both the front and back doors. This cost Art five hundred dollars, which he thought was well worth it. Of course, everyone who saw them had to have screens for their own homes. The man was happy to get the work and promised to be back in December with enough material to finish screening all the houses in the area.

CHAPTER 9

Jed and Joe had been courting Ashley and Sara Lucas, taking them to church several times and attending dances in Naples. Jed and Joe came to Art and asked, "What can we do to make more money? We are not making enough to keep us going and certainly not enough to get ahead." Ashley and Sara were pretty young girls, fun-loving yet sensible. Their mother raised them to be hard workers and dependable. The boys very much enjoyed their company.

Art told them, "You could build cow traps in areas where there's no obvious owner." That's the way Darrell and I got our start. You could still make three dollars a log hauled to the sawmill."

Darrell said, "You should try to buy some of the land just north of Sulphur River." Jed and Joe each had saved five hundred dollars, which was pretty good for a couple of boys who had tried to rustle Art's cattle eight months ago.

After Jed and Joe had hauled stone for four more weeks in the summer, they were put on permanent guard duty and had experienced no bad trouble from any of the outlaws. In the last month, Darrell was uneasy and did a lot of scouting for signs of people looking over the herd, but had not seen anything. Darrell seemed to have a sixth sense about these things.

On Saturday, everyone was going to Naples for the big dance. Art rented three large rooms in a rooming house for his crew. Darrell, Velma, and their son were going to stay with a friend of Velma's. Everyone was to meet at the dance at seven o'clock. They all went shopping from 2 to 5 p.m. and then went to the boarding house at six. Darrell's dad had stayed home to guard the farm. There was no trouble at the dance, but Art was worried when he saw four men he thought were rustlers. They were not drinking, dancing or looking over the women, which was a little strange. These men had been watching Art, Darrell, and their crew ever since they arrived at the dance. After about an hour, three of the four men left.

Art told Sharon and Darrell, "I'm going to follow those three men. If they go anywhere toward Bryans Mill, I won't return."

After Art left, another suspected rustler left, and Darrell followed him. Darrell came upon the suspicious rustler he was following just outside of Naples heading toward Bryans Mill. He jumped him, took his weapons and dragged him into an empty hut building. He tied his hands and feet and gagged him. Leaving the building, he flippantly said, "Gee I hope there aren't any snakes in here." He then proceeded to try to catch up to Art.

Art was in a hurry and almost ran into the would-be rustlers, but veered off on a path that took him toward Darrell's barn to get Darrell's dad to follow him about two hundred yards behind. Art thought Mr. Stroud could go for help or keep the rustlers covered. Mr. Stroud was glad to do that, and even shoot it out if need be. That, of course, was not in Art's plan. He went over his plan again, and Darrell's dad waited for ten minutes.

When Art got to his place, the three rustlers had already gathered about one hundred cows and five horses. He slowly rode within ten yards of the three riders that were ten yards apart, and he was right on top of them. He shot and told them, "Drop your guns!" The two on either side of him drew, and Art shot one with his six-shooter and rammed his horse into the closest rider, sending him sprawling. The outlaw lost his gun as he fell. The rider sixty yards away cut out thirty-one head of cattle and headed for the river as quick as he could.

Art was not sure what to do and paused. He decided to control these two and proceeded to take their guns. Art had badly wounded one of them, and he probably would not live. He tied up the rustler, he had knocked off his horse, to a tree. As the man struggled, the rope tightened around his neck. Art warned him, "You better not struggle, or you'll hang yourself." He immediately stopped struggling. Art collected all the money, guns, and horses with saddles, and put them all in the barn. He got some bandages and blankets for the wounded man. Maybe he would have some help soon. Art went back out and tried to treat the wounded men. He did finally get the bleeding stopped.

Darrell finally arrived and said, "I sent Dad after Louis, and Ed told him to then go back to my house and stay with Velma, Sharon, and the kids."

Art said, "Let's send Louis to get Dr. Lilly and his wagon, and then go tell Lieutenant Thomas what happened."

Darrell said, "No, you stay here. I am going to track this other rustler down, and I'm going to kill him. I am so tired of this."

Art said, "If you go alone, he'll easily ambush you and you know it." Finally Louis and Ed arrived, and Art told them what to do in Naples with the prisoners.

The boys then took off, tracking the one rustler with the thirty-one head of cattle. They tracked fifty yards apart, so he couldn't easily shoot both of them. Tracking him was not a problem. Darrell said, "Art, we have to catch him before he gets some of his buddies, or we'll be outnumbered."

They were riding pretty fast for the first two hours, but signs told them to slow down and proceed cautiously. They spread to seventy-five yards apart and came upon the thirty-one headof branded cattle. The cattle were in a small five-acre meadow with a stream running through, but Darrell and Art could not find the rustler. They left the cattle where they were because there was grass and water for them. They proceeded cautiously for about another hour when they heard voices arguing. The rustler was trying to talk five others into coming back with him and getting the cattle he left. Art rode up on one side and Darrell on the other and told them, "Drop your guns."

The rustler went for his gun, and Darrell shot and killed him instantly. The others all immediately dropped their guns. Art went over and took the rustler's horse, gun, and money. He told the others, "Bury him."

The men told Darrell, "We had no part in what those rustlers did."

Art and Darrell assured them, "We know no one else had helped with the rustling."

Art asked the leader, "Will you come back with me to where the thirty-one head of cattle are located?" The leader agreed, but he was afraid the boys were going to shoot him. Darrell was wondering, *What crackpot idea Art had this time.*

As they rode Art, told the leader named Tom, "I'd like to make a deal with your gang. I'll give you two head of stock from the thirty-one that was taken. This will keep you and your gang in meat for a month. Also, if you could round up fifty cows or so, I will pay ten dollars per cow, Union money, and if you could find any good English bulls, I'll pay fifty dollars each." Tom agreed.

Darrell and Art drove the remaining twenty-nine headback to his farm where they found the sheriff and lieutenant talking to the one of the four live rustlers. Art told the sheriff, "I think we should go ahead and hang this rustler right now."

The sheriff said, "Now just hold on. Let me hear your story."

Art told his story, and the sheriff was satisfied and took the rustler to jail.

In two weeks, Pete and Aaron and another member of Tom's gang, brought fifty-six cows and four horses. None had brands.

Art gave the men $660.00, Union money, and made them give him a bill of sale. Tom said, "We're splitting up the money, and all five of my gang members are heading home. With this money, their families can easily survive for six months."

CHAPTER 10

After Darrell, Mr. Stroud, and Velma got settled in the new barn, Velma wanted to go to Texarkana and buy some furniture and other necessary items for the new house. When she told Sharon, of course Sharon decided she must go and had sent Art over to Marietta to see if her mother and father wanted to go. Art set up the meeting at nine o'clock the next day at the Texarkana road close to Marietta. He had made arrangements for Haylee Yeiser to take Art Jr. to her house and keep him for three days. The next day, Darrell and Velma drove their wagon to Art's homestead, and Sharon drove their two-seater buggy to meet her parents at the Texarkana highway. Everyone arrived in Texarkana at three o'clock that afternoon.

Late the next evening, Darrell, Velma, and Sharon returned from the Texarkana shopping spree. Each family spent a thousand dollars, and some of the items would have to be shipped later. Darrell said, "We don't even have the house built yet, and she's already buying new items for it. I wish I had stayed home. There's nothing worse than waiting for a bunch of women to make up their minds." Darrell had taken several repeaters and pistols to sell and had received $300.00 for them. He gave Art his share which was $150.00.

The first weekend in July, the election was held, and the Democratic Party won all elected positions in Texas because the confederate soldiers all voted, and they did not let the blacks vote. This was no surprise to Art and Darrell, and they knew there would be changes in Texas as soon as the Republicans controlled the Federal Government and could take charge. The Yankee Army had been occupying Texas within a month after Lee surrendered. Art and Darrell could live with all the local people elected. All the national elections went to the Republican Party, and General Grant was the new president. The South would pay sometime! Texas and other southern states had still not been readmitted to the Union, and Martial Law was still in effect.

The Indians came to fish on the Sulphur the last week in September, and Art spent two days fishing and visiting with them.

Art, Ed and Louis began harvesting the one hundred acres of corn. Meanwhile, Mr. Shaw and Onnie had finished picking thirty acres of cotton and hauled it to the cotton gin in Marietta. They made twenty-five bales and sold it for $190.00 a bale. Art and Mr. Shaw had split the money. Now Mr. Shaw felt like he had enough money and was not beholding to anyone anymore.

Right after that, they began harvesting the thirty acres of corn, and that took another two weeks. Mr. Shaw then went to Marietta and bought twelve sows and a boar. That cost him two hundred dollars. The most fun for everyone was watching the cow dogs trying to drive those hogs. By November first, the harvest was finished. In early fall, all the women had canned as much food as they could for the winter. This really made Velma tired as she was getting close to having her baby.

Art and Darrell knew they had to begin logging and bring more logs to the sawmill. They now had ten orders for barns and two orders for lumber for houses. On the farms that Art owned, he thought there were over fifty logs on the ground that needed to be hauled to the sawmill, but they needed over three hundred logs just to fill their orders. In the last three months, Joe and Jed had bought over 150 logs. Art also had to haul 70 loads of corn to McCoy's grinding mill, and a total of 15 loads of corn to each of the Shaw's, the Parkinson's, Louis's, Ed's, and Darrell's farms. Art assigned Jed and Joe to pull two wagons each and haul all 115 loads. This would take them until Christmas to complete. The boys had Louis, Ed, and Onnie haul all the downed logs into the sawmill, which took about two weeks. Then they started cutting more trees. Darrell took his dad, Mr. Shaw, and Mr. Jenson to begin work on his stone house.

Darrell came running to Art's house and said, "Velma's ready to have her baby." Art took Sharon and Mrs. Jenson over in the buggy when he and Art Jr. were on their way to get Dr. Lilly in Naples. It was a miracle Dr. Lilly was home. Dr Lilly said, "I'll be ready in ten minutes." Art hooked up Dr. Lilly's horse to his buggy so he could follow him. It began to rain and turn colder. Art wrapped his son in a slicker, which he kept in the buggy just for these occasions. Art made a game out of it, and Art Jr. enjoyed having the slicker on.

Art, Art Jr., and Dr. Lilly arrived at Darrell's house at 8:15. Twenty minutes later, Velma gave birth to a baby girl. Dr. Lilly stayed until midnight and said, "Mother and baby are doing well. I will be back to see Velma and check on her and the baby in two days."

Sharon and Mrs. Jenson were going to spend the night, so Art and his son went home at ten o'clock. Art told Sharon, "I'll pick you up in the morning at eleven o'clock."

The next morning, Art left Art Jr. with the babysitter, Haylee, and then went to get Sharon and Mrs. Jenson. He took a saddled horse so he could go on to Bryans Mill and check on the special door and window frames the new blacksmith in Bryans Mill was making for the Logging's and Stroud's homes. Bryans Mill had three businesses: the blacksmith and wagon repair, a gunsmith and leather person, and of course, McCoy's store and mill. It also had a church and school.

CHAPTER 11

Art and Darrell took one week off to work cattle and horses. At Ed's place, Art could see a big difference in the calves from the Hereford bull compared to the Longhorn bull's calves. The following day, they worked cattle at Art's old homestead. The calves from the Shorthorn bull were much better than the calves from the Longhorn bulls. Art wondered if they could withstand the heat and insects as well as the Longhorns. He decided to look into this matter after talking to some other ranchers about what he had seen.

On November twentieth, Hunter Anthony came riding up to Art's farm and said, "We need help because some Yankee soldiers are going to take all our horses in the morning. They said they were going to buy all our horses for twenty dollars each. They're having trouble getting enough horses in Texas because there was a deadly horse sickness that killed about half of the horses." The real good horses could be sold for a hundred dollars each. "They say they're going to take the horses whether or not we wanted to sell," he continued. "My dad wants to know if you and Darrell can help us move all our horses to Fort Townsend, on the Red River in Indian territory?" He also asked, "Art, will you ask your Choctow Indian friends to help keep the horses there for a month or more?"

Art asked Darrell, "Will you get Joe and Jed to go with the Anthony boys and help herd the horses to Fort Townsend? I'll start to find the Indians and check if anyone is at Fort Townsend. Darrell, you better make sure your horses are well hidden, and will you take care of things around our farms?" Darrell agreed.

After talking to Sharon, Art was on the trail with an extra horse three hours before the Anthony horse drive started. The herd was already across the Sulphur when Jed, Joe, and Darrell arrived. It took Art two days to find Hawk and their village. After asking Chief Eagle Feather for approval for the Indians to help, the next morning Hawk, Running Bear, and Straight Arrow all left for Fort Townsend prepared to stay there about six weeks.

In the meantime, Joe, Jed, Hunter, and Chandler drove 160 head of horses. When the herd drivers and Indians arrived at the Fort, there was no one there. It took two days to get the herd settled, and they made arrangements to feed and protect the horses. It was decided the herd would need at least two wagonloads of feed a week. Joe and Jed were to leave and each drive two wagonloads of feed to Fort Townsend right away. They should be back in three days. Chandler and Hunter were also going to bring two wagon loads each of feed for the horses each week. Thereafter, this meant the Indians would be taking care of the horses. Art asked Chandler, "Do you need me anymore?"

Chandler told him no and Art took off back home, which was a hard day's ride.

The army came for the Anthony's herd, and when they arrived there, the herd was gone. They searched the whole place and could not find the horses. Darrell told Art, "I thought the Yankee soldiers were going to put Mark Anthony in jail when they came for the horses."

Art said, "What for?"

Darrell replied, "Gene McCoy, myself, and two others of the protection group were there, which meant Mark had three Henry rifles and two sharp carbines behind him."

Mark told them, "I guess rustlers must have stolen them."

The army captain said, "We'll track them."

Mark said, "Okay, do it."

The captain and his soldiers left, saying, "We'll be back."

Mark was pretty mad about the Union trying to steal his horses for twenty dollars each. Mr. Anthony said, "I think the man who owns the ferry that crosses the Sulphur River two miles south of our ranch told the Yankees about our horses. His name is Bob Horton. He built the ferry and began running it after the war. He also has a wife and two young sons about eight years old. He feeds hungry travelers and sells home brewed whiskey."

Darrell quickly returned to Art's house and guard duty. He made up his mind that he was keeping his horses hidden.

It was hard to cross the Sulphur. From the ferry west to the nearest crossing point was just past Art's farm or nine miles. Crossing the Sulphur east was five and a half miles to a place to cross more easily. The road went north to Clarksville about twenty five miles away. The Sulphur usually flooded at least once a year. The temperature in this area was around ninety degrees in the summer, forty-five in the winter and sixty-five degrees in the fall and spring. The yearly rainfall was over forty-five inches. It snowed maybe once or twice a year, and they had ice about three days a year. The terrain was hilly with a lot of trees, both pines and hardwood. The soil there was mostly red and sandy.

In six weeks the Anthonys made a deal, with a farmer just south of Clarksville, to lease land for the horses for three months. It was a remote farm fifteen miles from the Anthony farm. They brought their herd to the farm, taking special care to be able to hide the horses. In the meantime, Darrell with some help had finished his stone house and had planted one hundred acres of oats. Finally, they got Darrell and his family moved into their new home. Darrell was revamping his barn so his horses could finally use it.

CHAPTER 12

Christmas was a lot of fun for Art and Darrell this year. Art Jr., three, and Darrell's son, Eric, age seven, really made it exciting. Art and Darrell took the kids out and cut a Christmas tree for each house. The mothers spent a day helping the children decorate the trees. Christmas was all they could talk about. Their little faces just lit up with the excitement of the holiday.

In January, Art and Darrell took their families to Naples to pay their taxes and try to plan how they could hold onto their farms and stock. The politicians had made the mistake of offering anyone who would pay their taxes two years in advance the opportunity to not have a tax increase within the next two years. Art paid $425.00 for two years' taxes, and he didn't report his saw mill which was up and running. Darrell taxes were only $190.00 for the two-year period.

During the last week of February, it rained two inches a day.

The Sulphur River was beginning to swell and flood. Art, Darrell, Louis, Ed, Joe, and Jed were busy getting all the cattle, horses, and mules to the highest ground, near the closest barn. The crew had never seen so many animals, including snakes. Within five days, the families killed over sixty poisonous snakes and another sixty non-poisonous ones, which they could make into stew. Art and Darrell were the only ones that would dress the snakes, but all the families had stew for about a week. They shot eight deer and would take each family a deer after the flood. With help, they dressed all of them and put them in Art's old smoke house. This took a full day.

On March first, the entire area received six to eight inches of rain. The ground was already soaked with water. The next day, it rained another three inches. Sure enough, the river flooded the whole country. Water cut off all the stock from feed. All of Art's and Darrell's stock was on higher land and had been fed the day before, plus they had enough feed for this day. They couldn't feed every day because of the flood they couldn't get around to feed daily. Art and Darrell had two rowboats and tried to feed corn to all the cows and oats to all the horses and mules. The severe flooding lasted a week. Then the weather turned spring-like. It was now close to planting time. Art and Darrell were really busy with the sawmill, livestock, crops, and families.

CHAPTER 13

Army Sergeant Best came by and told the boys, "We think a Comanche killing party of about one hundred has attacked farms in the area of Paris and Clarksville, killing over forty white settlers, burning over twenty-five homes and barns, and killing livestock. They're attacking over two hundred miles east from their normal area. Their trail of terror started four days ago. Two companies of troops are trying to catch up with them but haven't done so yet. They'll try to get back to their village, which is 270 miles west of here, and I think they'll strike on their way home. They're in this area somewhere, you better make real preparation for an Indian attack."

Art and Darrell got all their people together and began making preparations. The plan was for everyone to come to the boys' houses if the Indians came. Mr. Shaw, Onnie, and Louis were at Art's house, and Mr. Stroud, Mr. Jennings, and his sons were at Darrell's house. They stocked up on water, food and made sure all the guns were loaded and the nearby stock was well hidden.

The Indians came to the ferry two miles north of Bryans Mill. After crossing the river, they killed the owner and burned the ferry and house. They then went to Bryans Mill. That evening, Chandler came riding into Art's farm and told him, "The Indians have attacked in Bryans Mill. The people in Bryans Mill need all the help you can provide."

Art sent him on over to Darrell's and told him, "Bring Darrell back to my house, ready to ride."

In the meantime, he had Chandler get another horse because his horse just plumb gave out. Art knew they had to plan to defend their own homes. He quickly rode over and got Onnie and Mr. Shaw to come back to his house. By that time, Darrell and Chandler had also returned to Art's house.

Art asked, "How many Indians are attacking?"

"Looks like about seventy," said Chandler.

Art also asked, "Do we need more ammunition in Bryans Mill?"

"We sure do," said Chandler. Art sent Sharon to get five boxes of fifty shells each for the Henry's, and Art gave Chandler three of those. Darrell and Art put another one in their saddle bag. Art also loaded up six more boxes of shells for the six-shooters. Everyone had already discussed how they could protect their families if Art, Darrell, and the group went to help in Bryans Mill.

Chandler was really anxious to get started back to Bryans Mill to give them help. Art sent Onnie to get Joe and Jed, and have them get Ed and also Louis and his family to come back to Art's house. Joe and Jed were to come to Bryans Mill and help Art and Darrell. He told Onnie, "After you've had done that, ride as fast as you can to Naples and get the soldiers, and also tell the Sheriff. Tell him that Bryans Mill is under attack by a large number of Indians and they're trying to burn down the town."

Art asked Mr. Shaw, "Can you hide along the road and monitor if the Indians are coming down the road, and warn Darrell's and my house?" He assured Art he could and would be glad to do that. Art then asked Mr. Shaw, "Will you go get the Jenson family and bring them to Darrell's house fully armed and ready to help protect that household?"

Mr. Shaw said, "That'll take me about fifteen minutes."

Art told him, "The plan is for Ed and Louis to stay in my house, and for Mr. Jenson and his family to stay in Darrell's house to make sure we have at least three people in each house able to shoot if the Indians attack."

Sharon and Velma said, "We'd rather go to Marietta and stay with Sharon's parents."

Darrell told them, "We can't risk you out on the road right now because we don't know where the Indians are, so we're just going to have to make do with y'all being able to protect yourselves."

Art told Mr. Shaw, as he, Darrell, and Chandler were leaving, "I want you to go back to my house after you've warned everyone that the Indians are around."

The boys and Chandler rode as fast as they could to Bryans Mill and cautiously entered from the south side because it seemed to be less protected by the Indians. They hid their horses and decided they needed to try to shoot as many Indians as they could before the Indians knew they were caught in crossfire.

At that time, there was very little firing coming from the Bryans Mill people, probably because they were low on ammunition. The boys slowly moved into position without the Indians knowing they were there. Art, Darrell, and Chandler each had three Indians as good targets and when they opened up, they either killed or wounded six Indians and shot two other Indian's horses.

At that time, Art told Chandler, "Get to the Bryans Mill people and tell them that we're out here, and we'll be shooting from this side because the Indians don't know who or where we are."

As Chandler was making his way to the Bryans Mill people, Art and Darrell emptied their Henrys into the Indians' ranks to give him cover. In the process, they wounded two more Indians and shot two more horses. They quickly reloaded and Darrell said, "Let's try to find their horses, they're bound to have some around here close by." In five minutes, the boys had located three Indian guards and over thirty Indian ponies. They shot the three guards, scattered the ponies, and then returned to their old south side position in Bryans Mill.

The fight continued without many shots or casualties in the next ten minutes. The Indians were trying to start burning the town. At that time, the boys were joined by Joe and Jed along with four people from Marietta, Charles, Ace and one of his friends, Jim and one of the preacher's sons, Clay and his bunch should go on the north side of town, and the boys would stay on the south side and then the townspeople were in the center of town to try to convince the Indians that they were up against a larger force.

In the meantime, an army squad came down the Bryans Mill Road close to Art's home, and Mr. Shaw stopped them by telling them what he knew about what was happening in Bryans Mill. The army squad arrived in Bryans Mill about two hours after the boys had been told the Indians were attacking.

Art asked Lieutenant Thomas, "Will you attack from the west side?" As soon as they started firing from all three sides, the Indians decided they would surrender. Art and Darrell did not see twelve Indians that rode off on the road toward their farms and did not find this out until twenty minutes after the Indians had surrendered. Art got Joe, Jed, Charles, and Ace to ride with him and Darrell as fast as they could to their homes on the Bryans Mill Naples road. He told the army lieutenant, "I'm afraid the Indians are heading for my farms so we're leaving."

The Lieutenant said, "We'll try to mop up everything in Bryans Mill. We'll come to you as soon as we can."

Mr. Shaw had told Louis, Ed, and Onnie, "I'm going to hide outside and check to see who was coming down the Naples Road." He had been hidden for two and a half hours when he saw flames coming from his home, but knew he couldn't do anything about it.

In twenty minutes, he heard many horses with Indians coming past his position. He counted twelve Indians going toward Art's new house. Then six of them went for the old Logging barn and house, and six went on toward Art's house. Mr. Shaw fired three quick shots at the six Indians going toward Art's new house. He didn't hit any of them but warned the defenders in the house that the Indians were there. He hoped they could protect everyone at Art's house. Mr. Shaw then quickly went to the backdoor of the Loggings' house, and Onnie let him in.

It took the boys about twenty minutes to get to Mr. Shaw's house, which was already blazing along with his barn. All of his hogs had been shot. Art hoped that Mr. Shaw had not tried to protect that farm because he would be much safer at his house. Art's house was built of stone with a tin roof, and it had one-inch thick bodark shutter covers with shooting slots. The house had four windows on the ground floor with gun slots. Also, the thick bodark doors at the front and back had gun openings and bolt locks on them. Manning those were Louis, Ed, and Onnie who had returned from Naples, and finally Mr. Shaw, with Sharon and Art Jr. helping load and reload guns. All the other women and children were upstairs where they had a shotgun, a pistol, and a Henry rifle all loaded, ready to protect themselves if necessary. Two Indians approached the northwest corner and two to the southwest corner of the house with torches. They were shot and killed by Louis and Ed. The other two Indians with them had retreated to the barn, and six other Indians had gone over to burn the old logging's homestead house and barn, and kill the cows and horses. After about ten minutes of exchanging gunfire, the Indians in the barn decided they would be better to start killing stock around this farm and proceeded to kill ten head of Art's cattle. By this time, Art and Darrell and the other four men with them had arrived, shooting two more of the Indians before the others said they had had enough and threw up their hands and surrendered.

Sharon and Louis were wounded, and Art asked Onnie, "Will you go out on the road toward Naples and see if you can see Dr. Lilly coming to the aid of the people in Bryans Mill? If you see him, divert him to my house to treat Louis and Sharon before he goes on to Bryans Mill."

Sure enough, it wasn't five minutes until Onnie found Dr. Lily on the road and brought him to Art's house. Dr. Lilly quickly treated the semi-serious wounds. He told Art and Darrell, "I'll be back after I finish in Bryans Mill to further treat Louis and Sharon." Everyone understood there were probably more serious injuries in Bryans Mill, and he would be better off to go on and take care of that battle and come back to treat the less seriously injured. Darrell and Charles had disarmed all the Indians and put all of their material, including their horses, in Art's barn and corral. They hitched up four mules to take the twelve Indians back to Bryans Mill. Art and Darrell were guarding the prisoners, and Dr. Lilly was in his buggy leading the wagons.

It was decided everyone in Art's and Darrell's homes should stay there until they returned with an all clear. Everyone was advised to post one guard inside each house and stay locked down until the boys returned. All the others were to go to sleep. Meanwhile, the boys took their Indians back to Bryans Mill.

Art asked, "Can I just kill all the prisoners, wounded or not?" They had over twenty prisoners. He told Lieutenant Thomas, "It's a good thing we had our entire protection group. I expect plenty of free ammunition for us doing the army's job of stopping the Indians cold."

There happened to be a reporter from Texarkana who came up to Art and Darrell and said, "I'd like to talk to you."

They said, "You also need to talk to the Anthony boys and Gene McCoy."

"Let's get them together."

The facts were, seventy-five Comanches had crossed the Sulphur River, killed the owner of the ferry boat, and burned the ferry and his house. The owner's wife and children had escaped. The Indians then traveled the two and a half miles to Bryans Mill where there were five local residents killed and four wounded. Art, Darrell, Joe, Jed, Charles, Jim, Ace, and Clay came about an hour after the Indians attacked Bryans Mill. They set up a cross fire between

Art's group and the townspeople, and in fifty minutes, they had killed or wounded forty Indians and twenty more Indians were without horses. Darrell, Joe, and Jed had captured forty Indian ponies. All the other Indians, except twelve, surrendered.

The twelve tried to get away by going on the road toward Art and Darrell's farms. They tried to burn Art's old homestead house and barn, and did burn the old Shaw house and barn. The Indians had already shot ten cows and fourteen hogs. The boys killed six, wounded four, and two surrendered at the boys' farms. Art and Darrell brought all of the Indians back in Art's wagon. The Union squad came at the end of the battle, and they could not say anything different. Lieutenant Thomas witnessed the entire interview and said nothing.

Darrell said, "I don't think you'll publish the truth. How do we let the Indians know that when they came to Bryans Mill, we kicked their butt and they better not try it again?"

Lieutenant Thomas said, "We'll probably let one Indian escape when we take them to Fort Worth so he can go back and tell the others what happened."

The lieutenant filled in the reporter on the fact the Comanches had raided and burned farms in Paris and Clarksville before coming to Bryans Mill. They killed forty-five men, women, and children and hurt over fifty others. Over twenty-five farms, homes, and many barns were burned, plus over two hundred cows and horses were killed. The lieutenant said, "My superiors, including General Young, will be in Bryans Mill day after tomorrow and would like to issue a statement to assure the people in Central and East Texas that an incident like this will never happen again." The lieutenant continued, "He wants to thank the people that stopped the raid and tell them about the precautions the army will take to stop the Comanches from wanting to come to East Texas again."

On the second day, they dressed the last of fourteen hogs and ten cattle. After all the dead animals were butchered, Art and Darrell and Darrell's group went to Bryans Mill to attend the funeral of all the people killed during the raid. Among the dead was Mrs. Yeiser, the school teacher. Art, the Jennings, Louis, Ed, Mr. Shaw, and Onnie were all busy dressing out all the dead cattle and hogs.

Art decided these dead animals' meat could be sold and there would be less of a loss. Art donated a steer for the celebration. General Young was coming, and someone had to feed the entire crowd. Gene McCoy was going to cook the steer and also a butchered hog from Mr. Shaw. After butchering the dead animals, Art and Mr. Shaw sold all the animals the Indians killed to neighbors, people in Naples, Marietta, and Bryans Mill.

Sure enough, the general came with ten of his staff, plus the Union squadrons stationed at Naples and Clarksville. There were also ten reporters. After a few speeches, including one by General Young thanking the people of the Bryans Mill area, Art and Darrell wanted to talk to General Young privately. General Young told the boys, "I know of your contribution in stopping the Indians."

Darrell asked the general "Is it possible for you to replace the ammunition?"

The general ordered Lieutenant Thomas to give them six thousand rounds of whatever ammunition they needed. Art also asked, "Could we also have help to replace the ferry the Indians burned?"

The general promised, "I'll get one built and brought to the village within two months."

"Can anything be done for the widow of the ferry owner?" asked Art.

The general then proceeded to take up a collection from everyone there and collected $140.00.

"I'll get a hundred dollars more," said the general. Art and Darrell made up their minds to each give her seventy-five dollars.

Art asked the general, "May I have a letter of introduction to General Sheridan in New Orleans?"

"Why do you want that?" asked the General.

Art said, "I want to salvage some sunken boats on the Red, south of Shreveport."

"I'll see to it you have the letter in two weeks," he said.

The boys thanked General Young for coming and helping. General Young talked to the boys about ten more minutes, asking about what they did in the war and why they were so favored by Yankee Colonel Nance and White. The boys told him, going into detail. The general did not know Sharon and Louis had been shot. He immediately sent his surgeon to check on them. They were both feeling bad two days after being shot, but in six weeks their wounds had healed.

The ferry owner's widow said she wanted to live in Bryans Mill. Before the boys left, they decided to have a house raising for her and the children on Tuesday. Mr. Brundet told Art, "I have a small farm outside of town I would sell her for a hundred dollars."

Darrell said, "How about seventy-five?"

"All right, seventy-five," Mr. Brundet said.

She still owned five acres outside the ferry docking area, but the house had been burned, and she and the children had been lucky to get out alive and away from the Indians.

The next morning, after the celebration in Bryans Mill, Art and Darrell's ex-slave friends, Sherman, Robert, Mae, and Trixie, came to do what they could to help the boys. Art asked, "Would you try to clean up the old Shaw cabin and barn?" After a full day, there they went to Art's old house to spend one more day helping.

Each newspaper sent several copies of their write-up on the Indians and Bryans Mill to McCoy's general store. Art had paid each reporter two dollars, and they were to send him and Darrell ten copies of their paper's article about the incident. It was evident the protection group had skill and luck defeating the fearsome Indians.

Art and Darrell had gathered as many tomahawks, guns, knives, feather lances, and shields from the Indian attackers as they could. Art had stored them in his new barn. He had talked to a Washington paper reporter and asked, "Do you know anyone that would be interested in any of the Indian's lances, tomahawks, knives and shields?"

The reporter said, "Pack the Indian's material and I'll take them with me on the train. I assure you I will get at least one thousand dollars for the items." He did much better than he thought. All of it was sold to one person for forty-five hundred dollars, and the reporter sent the boys a check for thirty-five hundred dollars.

The boys could not cash the check because they did not have a bank account. Lewis Rogers convinced them to open an account at the Naples bank. Finally, Art and Darrell opened accounts.

After a month, the bank finally deposited $1,750.00 in each of the boys newly opened accounts. They promptly withdrew $1,650.00 each and hid it at their secret storage tree on their own farms. The Naples bank had been robbed three times since the end of the Civil War and several times during the war. Lewis Rogers, Art's father-in-law, was always trying to get the boys to put their money in the bank, but neither Art nor Darrell thought it was safe. Now maybe Mr. Rogers would stop harping on putting their money in the bank!

CHAPTER 14

Art now had over six hundred cows, but after talks with some of the more experienced farmers and ranchers, he decided to purchase thirty real good English bulls. That would get him better livestock in about three years. He would buy fifteen Whiteface bulls from Mr. Parkinson, who lived south of Shreveport, Louisiana. Art was still looking for fifteen good Shorthorn bulls and did not know where to go to buy them. He had bought one two years ago from a farmer in Linden. Art knew he had several Shorthorn cows and decided he would go visit Doc Ellis and find out where he would go to buy fifteen Shorthorn bulls.

Art and Sharon were talking one night, and Art said, "I'm so sick and tired of the fighting I've had to do the past two years just trying to hold on to our farms and livestock. I've killed and wounded a lot of people, and that's beginning to worry me a lot."

Sharon said, "You've never shot anyone who was not threatening to kill or hurt you."

"I know," he replied. "First it was Lassiter and all the raids he had made on our farm, and now this raid of a local boy trying to steal my stock."

She answered, "The shooting competitions you and Darrell have decided to enter should show the locals you two are not to be pushed around or confronted."

Art said, "But that might not be doing any good because some people think they can just take whatever they want from anyone. We do enjoy competing, and it certainly can't do any harm."

Well, here they were again on a Saturday morning in Clarksville, at another shooting contest. The boys entered the rifle and pistol contest. Art was the first shooter in both the rifle and pistol contest. At a hundred yards, he had put five shots in the bull's-eye with his Henry. There were sixty-six contestants, and only one other shooter had matched that. The judge said, "We can split the winnings."

Art said, "That's okay with me."

The other man said, "I don't want to split. I'm not going to let some smart aleck kid outshoot me."

The judges put the target back a distance of 125 yards. Art shot first and put five shots in the bull's-eye in ten seconds. His competitor put five shots in the bull's-eye, but it took him thirty seconds and Art was declared the winner and received the one hundred dollars. The other man came over to congratulate him and asked, "Where did you learn to shoot a Henry rifle like that? You're the best shot I've seen around here."

"In the army," replied Art. The man had a wife and four kids that looked like they needed something to eat, and a rickety old wagon. You could see the wanting and pleading in eyes of his children. He said, "Here's your fifty dollars. It really was a tie you know."

The man wouldn't take it so Art took it and gave it to his wife. He told them, "I run a big farm near Bryans Mill, and if you ever need work, come see me." Art noticed when they left town their wagon was loaded with groceries, and the kids all had a stick of candy.

Darrell had shot in the first rifle contest and had two of his shots just outside the bull's-eye. Now it was time for the pistol competition at twenty-five yards. Art shot first and only had two in the bull's-eye and four just outside the magic circle. When Darrell shot he put all six in the bull's-eye along with two others. They then moved the target back to fifty yards, and Darrell put six bullets in the bull's-eye in twelve seconds. The other two shot six times, and two bullets were outside the bull's-eye. Darrell also split the hundred dollar winnings with the other two men.

All the Anthonys, Jensons, Louis and family, Ed, Onnie, and Mr. Shaw had competed. There were several other people there from Bryans Mill. The women had prepared a picnic, and they enjoyed fried chicken, deviled eggs, potato salad, and pecan pies. They also brought along tea, and Darrell had been in charge of the ice so they could have cold tea to drink. There were foot races for the kids. Art estimated there were about three hundred people there.

They left at about four o'clock in the afternoon and arrived home at seven o'clock that night. It was a very long trip, and the group decided if they took a long trip like that again, they would plan to spend the night. All the group was discussing the horse races which the Anthony's won. They won the championship race. There were four races, and the winner of each of those races competed for the championship.

The following Sunday, Art, Sharon, and Art Jr. took off in the buggy with Art's favorite horse, Dick, tied behind, and also the two cow dogs. Art told Darrell, "We're going on a trip and might be gone for a week." They had packed enough clothes so if time permitted, they would go see Art's mother and sister.

When they reached Doc Ellis's farm in Linden, Doc Ellis said, "The only Shorthorn bulls in two states are in Marshall, Texas, which is about twenty-five miles south."

There was two hours of sunlight left and Art wanted to push on, even if he could not get there until eight o'clock. He said, "We could get a room about dark and look at the Shorthorn bulls in the morning." They arrived in Marshall at eight o'clock and got a room at a boarding house, ate supper, and went to bed. The dogs had ridden in the buggy, all except for five miles. They stayed all night at the stable with the horses and buggy.

After breakfast the next day, they went to the ranch and told them, "We're interested in buying some bulls. We were thinking about fifteen."

Now that got their attention! The owner came out and talked to Art. He said, "I have a number of good twenty-month-old bulls. I'll sell fifteen of them to you for a thousand dollars, cash."

Art picked out the ones he wanted and told Mr. Goodman, "I'll return in four days to drive them home." He gave him five hundred dollars, and they agreed he would give him the remaining five hundred when he returned.

Mr. Goodman was really interested in Art's cattle and sawmill operation. He was amazed at how the cow dogs worked and asked Art, "Where can I get a pair of cow dogs for myself?"

Art said, "I got mine from the Martins in Red Oak, Louisiana, which is only thirty miles from here. That is where we're going now."

Mr. Goodman said, "Here is two hundred dollars. Will you buy me a pair and bring them to me when you return?" Art agreed.

Art and his family left for Red Oak to see his mom and sister. They had not seen Art Jr. and were in for a real treat. The Loggings arrived in Red Oak at seven o'clock that evening. The Martins were so happy to see the family and were disappointed when young Art Jr. fell asleep at nine. Art and Sharon were also tired from their travels, and after another hour of talking, they went to bed. Sharon got up at six o'clock with Art Jr. After dressing him, Art's mother took him for breakfast. Sharon went back to bed, and she and Art finally got up at ten o'clock.

That afternoon, Abe and Art had a talk about going to the Parkinson's ranch to buy fifteen Hereford bulls and what Art planned do to improve his cattle. Abe was in full agreement and asked, "What can I do to help get the bulls?"

Art said, "If you could send a cowboy to help, that would be great."

"Done," said Abe.

"Also, take care of Sharon and my son while I go get the bulls."

"Of course," said Abe.

Art said, "I plan to leave early in the morning."

"I'll have my neighbor Ted Wilson, who helps about one week out of each month, come over about six o'clock this evening and meet you," said Abe. "You can discuss your trip then."

Art spent the rest of the afternoon talking to his mother, sister, and Abe's daughter, Cynthia. Sharon had already given Cynthia the two hundred dollars for the two cow dogs from Marshall that Mr. Goodman wanted.

Art and Ted left with three horses. The spare horse was carrying the two cow dogs. They weighed fifty pounds each, and it was a funny sight to watch them ride in two side bags on the horse. Everyone in the Martin and Wilson households came to see them off.

Art asked Ted, "How long have you had this farm?"

Ted said, "It has been in the family about ten years but no one has worked it. I was going to raise cotton, corn and hogs. When I got married we built a new cabin and barn and moved here from Hope, Arkansas." Ted was twenty two years old and had been in the confederate army.

Ted seemed to be all right so Art took a chance and asked, "Do you know a couple of men by the name of Alton and Bixsby?"

"Sure, everyone around knows them. Alton was a big farmer. Then about a year after Lee surrendered, two companies of Yankee troops came to town looking for Major Alton. They went out to his farm and confiscated two hundred fifty horses, two hundred mules, over one hundred wagons, more than two hundred rifles and pistols, three hundred head of cattle plus all kinds of equipment and arrested Alton and Bixsby for theft. They were finally released after they told their story that fifteen confederate generals came by after the war and took livestock and equipment worth ten thousand dollars for each general. This was all confederate equipment many of them had stolen from the confederacy. Before they were released, a group of ex-confederates came up from Texarkana and burned his home and barn. After their release by the Yankees they came home and were badly beaten several times by local ex-confederates before they decided to leave Hope."

Art said, "When I was first drafted into the confederate army we stopped there and they completely outfitted our company with good equipment. About a year later we delivered over seventy Yankee wagons there that we had captured."

Ted said, "I'll tell you they were lucky to get out of town alive. Folks were pretty mad because many of those men did not have boots, socks, and some didn't have enough food or ammunition."

"Right now my wife is pregnant and I kinda hate to leave town but she said it would be at least a week before the baby comes and we need the money"

They arrived in Shreveport at 9 a.m., and Art went to the hotel where Mr. Parkinson played dominos. Art was informed Mr. Parkinson probably would not be there until the next day.

Art and Ted then left for Mr. Parkinson's ranch, arriving about two o'clock. Mr. Parkinson remembered Art and visited with the two young men for about an hour. Then Art selected fifteen Whiteface bulls that Mr. Parkinson had used in his herd for two years and was now ready to sell fifteen of the four-year-old bulls. Art paid him nine hundred dollars for the lot, and they put them in a pen. The boys planned to eat supper and spend the night at the Parkinson's ranch. Mr. Parkinson was even going to help them herd the bulls all the way to the Martin plantation because he wanted to buy four cow dogs to try on his ranch. After a great breakfast, they left at six o'clock. Everyone pushed hard because they had forty-eight miles to cover. They were around Shreveport by eleven o'clock and arrived at the Martin plantation at five o'clock. They put the bulls in a holding pen. Mr. Parkinson stayed two nights and one day. He left the same day Art, Sharon, and Art Jr. left with fifteen Whiteface bulls and four cow dogs.

Art was always down in spirit after leaving his mother and sister, but was glad they got to see Art Jr., and they had promised to come visit at Bryans Mill. Sharon had some ear corn in the buggy, and every four or five miles she would scatter fifteen ears of corn, and they were able to drive the bulls to Marshall and Mr. Goodman's shorthorn ranch. This scene gave Mr. Goodman and his ranch hands a really big laugh, but Mr. Goodman was happy to know two of the cow dogs were his.

Mr. Goodman said, "Art, you and your family should stay at my home tonight. I would like to send one of my hands at least part of the way to help drive the thirty bulls. You should leave early in the morning." Art paid Mr. Goodman the additional money he owed for the shorthorn bulls and Mr. Goodman thanked the Loggings for bringing his two cow dogs.

Mr. Goodman had his seven-thousand-acre ranch for twenty-five years. He was about fifty-five years old. His wife had died five years ago. He had three sons, two were killed in the Civil War. The one living had a two-thousand-acre ranch next to his. He was married and had three children. Mr. Goodman and his crew worked at the ammunition factory in Marshall during the war, plus worked his ranch after work and weekends. He was a tough old guy who fought hard for his ranch and family.

At seven o'clock the next morning, the family left with fifteen Shorthorn bulls, fifteen Whiteface bulls, their two cow dogs and a cowboy, Henry, who worked for Mr. Goodman. Sharon's wagon was loaded with ear corn to keep the bulls following the wagon. Several families came out to see this very amusing sight. Mr. Goodman had convinced Art to take a new road that went to Hughes Springs and was forty miles away. It was then only nine more miles to Marietta where Sharon's family lived. Art thought they could make it by seven o'clock that evening. They would only have to average four miles an hour.

When they got to Hughes Springs, Henry said, "I have relatives living here." He helped Art until they were about four miles past Hughes Springs and five miles from Marietta. He then left the Loggings family to return to relatives in Hughes Springs. Art thanked him and gave him five dollars. Henry was grateful, and he said, "I learned a lot about how the cow dogs work."

Sharon had taught Art Jr. how to throw the ear corn evenly to each bull and by the end of their trip he knew the different bulls. He made sure each bull got close to the same amount of ear corn. He was proud of himself because he knew he was helping, and everyone bragged on him. Art also warned him, "The cattle, especially the bulls, can be dangerous, so always be careful when you're working with them." Throughout the trip, Art had given Art Jr. thirty-minute rides with him on his horse. Of course, he wanted to ride more and more.

The Loggings family arrived at Sharon's parents' home in Marietta about seven thirty. Everyone was tired, including the animals. After putting the bulls in a small pasture, which was close by, for the night Art fed the bulls, horses, and dogs. He didn't think there would be a problem since they were all tired and needed rest.

The family had eaten supper and was in bed by nine thirty. The next day, they visited and rested. They told Sharon's parents about the trip. Art, Sharon's dad, and her older brother, Charles, spent about two hours looking after and feeding the bulls. Charles and Lewis were impressed with the bulls Art had bought and agreed he would have a much better herd in three years. Lewis asked Art, "What kind of trouble did you have while driving the bulls?"

Art said, "The only trouble we had was dogs around farm houses. We just tried to go around the houses. We would circle the houses at least 250 yards or more, and Sharon would stay on the road. We had one incident in Louisiana where the farmer rode out and said not to go around. He would put his dogs in the barn. We also had about twenty or thirty people look over the bulls and comment on how good they were. Several wanted to buy one or two. I told them where I bought them. Art Jr. was the biggest surprise of all, how he had so quickly learned to feed the bulls."

Lewis said, "I'll help drive the herd home tomorrow."

That afternoon and evening, Sharon's mother said, "I'll take care of Art Jr."

It was a pretty warm afternoon so Art and Sharon went swimming down at the creek where they always swam. Someone had rigged a rope to a large Oak tree with a big branch hanging over the water. It was a lot of fun to swing out over the creek, but they had a lot more fun than that. They would swim awhile, then lie in the warm sun discussing their dreams and sharing their love for each other. It was a fun, relaxing afternoon. They got home in time for supper and afterward went to bed in Sharon's old bedroom.

The Loggings family, bulls, cow dogs, and Mr. Rogers got underway at nine o'clock the next morning. They arrived at the old Loggings homestead at one o'clock. Art cut out five Hereford and five Shorthorn bulls. He and the dogs drove them over to the farm Louis ran for Art. They took the one Whiteface bull he already had, plus ten Longhorn bulls, and drove them to the Loggings farm. Art took five Hereford and five Shorthorn bulls, and drove them to the old Parkinson ranch. Art, Ed, and the dogs drove the eleven Longhorn bulls back to the Loggings farm.

Art now had thirty-one Longhorn bulls he had to sell. He had put a FOR SALE note at McCoy mill, a store in Bryans Mill, Smith's store in Marietta, and the restaurant and Hill's General Store in Naples. There had been eight of the bulls spoken for at twenty dollars each, and Art had to get them delivered. He got Joe, Jed, and the dogs to deliver them throughout the area. By the time they got those eight delivered, they had orders for eight more Longhorn bulls and proceeded to deliver them. Art also put the Shorthorn and Whiteface bulls from the Louis farm to the Shaw farm and picked up two more Longhorn bulls. Art only had eighty cows at the old Shaw place.

There were still fourteen Longhorn bulls to be sold. Charles came over and begged him to let him buy one Shorthorn and one Whiteface bull plus he wanted two of the Longhorn bulls. Art made the deal for Charles to help him sometimes, which pleased Charles. Sharon's dad wanted the same deal, so Charles had to drive all eight bulls back to their two farms in Marietta. Of course, he had his own two cow dogs to help him. That left Art with only three Shorthorn and three Hereford bulls for his own farm, which had 250 cows. He would have to take back a Shorthorn bull from the Louis farm and a Whiteface bull from the old Parkinson farm.

Meanwhile, Darrell and Art talked about what was happening at their places. Darrell said, "The land on the north side of Sulphur River that borders your old homestead is for sale, twenty-five hundred dollars for five thousand acres."

"Who owns it?" asked Art.

"Lawyer Lassiter," said Darrell. "And if you want to buy it, you will have to go through Lawyer Hastings in Naples. Also, I have heard several other people are interested in some of your Longhorn bulls."

Art and Darrell decided they would check on things in Naples and everyone should go to the dance Saturday night. They could buy the acreage Saturday morning, and maybe sell some more Longhorn bulls. Art related his conversation with Ted about the secret confederate ranch to Darrell. Darrell couldn't believe it and responded, "Wow we should have made a raid on that ranch after the war."

There was quite a crew that went to Naples: Darrell, Velma, their son and baby, Art, Sharon, Art Jr., Louis, his wife, son and two daughters, Ed, Joe, and Jed, who were to meet the Lucas girls, Ashley and Sara. Mrs. Lucas also came along and was to meet Mr. Shaw and Onnie. On Saturday morning, Art bought and recorded the five thousand acres north of his farm on the other side of the Sulphur River. Both Darrell and Art felt good about buying the land because this could better prepare them to defend their property. Joe and Jed had also bought six hundred forty acres each for four hundred dollars, which was on the South side of the Sulphur, next to Art's old Parkinson farm. They told Art and Darrell they wanted to buy enough lumber for one of those barns everyone was ordering.

The boys went to town, mainly Mr. Hill's General Store, and Mr. Hill said, "I have nine farmers wanting Longhorn bulls." By the time they made their way back to the boarding house, they had sold over fourteen bulls. Art told most of the buyers to come to the Hills' corral in Naples on Monday to pick out their bulls. The buyers thought that was a good idea and agreed to be there.

Darrell had named Art's buying thirty new bulls and selling the Longhorns "The Great Bull Event". All twenty members of the group attended the dance and had a very good time. Haylee Yeiser had babysat with Art Jr. and Darrell's son and new daughter. Darrell drove the fourteen Longhorn bulls to Naples on Monday. All were sold within two hours. He came home and gave Art $280.00. Finally, Art's plan to upgrade his herds was beginning to take place.

Art knew he had to get his crops in before trying to find a steam boiler for the sawmill. Right now he was going to spend most of March planting and calving. He now had 860 cows. He only had 145 calves in January and February, but lost 14 calves. It always made Art sick when he lost any animal. He decided to bring all the cows that were close to calving up to a fifty-acre pasture just north of his barn. That meant Ed, Louis, and Art riding every three days and bringing those cows and heifers to the special pasture.

In March, over 200 cows and heifers had calves, and Art only lost seven calves. Sharon had helped Art with at least twenty calvings, and she was getting pretty good at it. Art would go out at seven o'clock in the morning and again at four o'clock in the afternoon. Sharon inspected the cows at noon. She would then get Art if necessary.

Art and Darrell continued sawmilling for three weeks, and on the fourth week, Art, Joe, and Ed started planting his one hundred acres of corn and thirty acres of cotton. Mr. Shaw and Onnie started planting thirty acres of corn and then thirty acres of cotton. Everyone was finished with their planting by April 20. Two hundred more cows had calved this month.

CHAPTER 15

Art had been talking to Darrell about a steam engine to improve their sawmilling operation. Finally, Art thought it was time he went to Louisiana and the Red River to try and salvage any of the Yankee steam boats that had been sunk by the Confederates during the Red River campaign of '64. Darrell said, "I bet someone's already salvaged the sunken boats." Art had sent a letter to his mother and said he and his family would be arriving in about a week. Darrell said, "Art, you should take Joe and Jed with you."

"No," said Art. "I'm first going to see if there are still sunken boats on the Red below Henderson Hill, Louisiana." Art knew he could count on the ex-slaves Amos and Lenny to help him if he could find them. They had been real helpful to the boys when they were Confederate soldiers serving in the Red River Campaign.

On April twenty-eighth, Art, Sharon, and Art Jr. started to his mother's. Art had a string of four mules, his heavy-duty working wagon and two horses tied to the back of the wagon. Art, Sharon, and Art Jr. would ride the horses every two hours. He took plenty of ropes, chains, pulleys and tie-downs. The Loggings family began the journey at 5 a.m. They had a couple of blankets and a pillow in the wagon. Art and Art Jr. slept for about two hours until they were a mile past Marietta. By eleven o'clock, they had reached

Linden. They ate and rested the horses and mules for about forty-five minutes. They then cut across the Louisiana border through to Red Oak. They arrived at Art's mothers at six o'clock. At supper, Art talked over his plans to try and get used steam engines from some of the Yankee boats that were sunk during the Red River Campaign. Art said, "Day after tomorrow, I'm going down to the Red and first see if there are any of those sunken ships left." Sharon and Art Jr. stayed at Red Oak while Art went down to the Red River between Mansfield and Natchitoches, Louisiana.

On the first day, he stayed in a room over a saloon in Mansfield. It was a pretty rough place. There was a lot of cussing and fighting until midnight. A man came to Art's door. As Art opened the door, he stuck his six-shooter in the man's face and marched him straight down to the desk clerk and said, "The next person who disturbs me will get shot!"

After breakfast the next morning, Art rode out to Ernest Albright's farm, where General Taylor stored the three million dollars' worth of equipment he had captured from the Yankees. Art thought whatever was still there would be available for purchase, but decided he would take care of that later. Mr. Albright said, "I'll go and help you look for sunken boats in the Red River. You better get permission from the Yankees," he cautioned, "or they'll just confiscate whatever you take." Art and Mr. Albright began their search, covering twelve miles the first day and found no boats.

Mr. Albright invited Art home to spend the night and eat supper and breakfast with them. Mr. Albright had two daughters, one eighteen and one nineteen, named Paula and Virginia. The girl's boyfriends were also having supper with them that night. Art was sure these young ladies and men were pretty serious, and it would not surprise him if they were married soon. During his discussion with Ernest, Art said, "General Taylor still has a lot of equipment left, and if I wanted to buy some, I'll bet I could get a good price. I sure would like to see if it's possible to buy some of the equipment."

The next day, Art and Ernest covered twelve more miles and located two boats. The two men looked the boats over the best they could. It looked like they could salvage both the engines and the boats. Art told Ernest, "I need to locate a good blacksmith and carpenter to see if the boats will float or can be loaded."

Ernest said, "I can get people to help jack the boats out of the water. Then I think you need to take them to Shreveport where they have a big shop that could work on the engines and do the necessary repairs to the boats."

Art and Ernest found six people with jacks. It took three days to get the boats out of the water. They then started plugging holes and seams on the boats.

Ernest told Art, "I'll watch the boats eighteen hours a day while you're gone so no one will steal the engines."

The next morning, Art left for Shreveport by a paddle wheeler. It cost an extra ten dollars to take his horse. The boat arrived at noon, and Art went directly to the Ardmore Shop to check on repairing the two engines and boats. Mr. Ardmore told Art, "I have a heavy-duty block and tackle that will lift the engines from the boats. I can have my boat ready in two days and can leave at eight o'clock that morning along with two crew members."

When Art and Mr. Albright first located the sunken boats, they found eight skeletons. They took eight blankets, putting a skeleton in each blanket, along with any items they had with them that might identify the man. Art had transported the skeletons in a wooden box to General Bond's headquarters in Shreveport. He explained what he had in the wooden box to the Union sergeant major, and then again had to explain the situation to General Bond. General Bond told a young lieutenant, "Get some men to identify the men. And Art, I also want to thank you for taking the time to respect those soldiers."

Art had also shown the recommendation letter General Young gave him after the Indian attack. After reading the letter, General Bond asked, "How can I help, Art?"

"You can contact General Sheridan," he replied, "and ask him to sell me those two sunken boats at a reasonable price."

"I'll contact General Sheridan," said General Bond, "and get him to sell the boats to you." General Bond then asked about Art's service during the Civil War, and his family. This conversation lasted several minutes, and it was two thirty when Art left for Red Oak to see his family.

Art arrived at six o'clock and received a warm greeting from all his family. Supper was great, and Sharon's special greeting was fantastic. At breakfast the next morning, Art told them everything that had happened since he left home a week before. He also told them, "I plan to leave day after tomorrow, about four o'clock in the morning, and if we get the two steam engines, I'll be back in three to five days."

Art left as planned, and he and his horse were on Mr. Ardmore's boat at eight o'clock, ready to go down the Red. They arrived at the sunken boats at one o'clock and found Mr. Albright waiting. Ernest told Art, "A Yankee patrol came by and checked on me and the boats yesterday. They looked through the boats, thanked me for treating the dead men with such great respect, saluted me then they left."

Mr. Ardmore and a man named Jack began looking over the two steam engines. Mr. Ardmore told Art, "I know I can fix one engine, but I'm not sure about the other. If I can get the best one working, maybe the other one could be used for spare parts."

They all decided it was worth a try. Art then asked Ernest, "Will you show me all the Yankee material that was captured that you have for sale?" Mr. Ardmore and Jack also went along to look at the material for sale. Art bought a heavy-duty wagon, six-shooters and holsters, six saddles that needed repair, some medical supplies he thought Dr. Lilly might need, repair parts for the wagon, four mules, two horses, and a set of wagon cooking pots and pans. Mr. Ardmore and Jack also bought a heavy-duty wagon and parts, several guns, ammunition, and four saddles. Art paid Mr. Albright five hundred dollars for the equipment plus three hundred dollars for his help. Mr. Ardmore paid two hundred dollars for the equipment he purchased. It was decided Art would drive the two wagons loaded with the equipment Mr. Ardmore, Jack, and Art had purchased from Ernest Albright. Ernest and his two future sons-in-law would help Mr. Ardmore and Jack load the two steam engines onto Mr. Ardmore's boat. Art had already paid Mr. Ardmore $250.00 for his time and getting the two steam engines back to his shop in Shreveport. Art had already decided he didn't want the boats, and when Ernest's future sons-in-law said they wanted them, Art gave the boats to them.

Art began his trip innocently enough, not having any idea what problems lay ahead of him. He traveled about ten miles the first day and made camp. During the night, three men approached the camp. They hollered, "We're coming into your camp for coffee and to spend the night."

Art warned them, "Don't come into my camp. Just keep moving and make your own camp."

They did not heed his warning, coming into camp drawing their six-shooters. Art was fast enough to shoot one man and get out of the way of the hail of bullets the other two outlaws shot at him. The gun battle continued until about one o'clock when a Yankee squad showed up. A nearby farmer had gone to get the law and ran into the Yankee patrol. They came in and disarmed everyone. The outlaws claimed Art should be hung for murder. Art explained to the Yankee Lieutenant what had happened. He showed him the letter from General Young and a bill of sale along with the permission letter from General Bond.

Art said, "I'll be glad to go back to Shreveport with you to see General Bond." Art thought they believed him, but everyone camped at his camp until after breakfast. At about seven o'clock, the group began leaving for Shreveport. It was a three-day trip to Shreveport. Upon arrival, the group immediately went to see General Bond. He cleared Art and locked up the two outlaws.

Art took his two wagons over to Mr. Ardmore's shop. Even though it was six o'clock, they were still working, and had already started on the two steam engines. Jack had taken all the articles he had bought from Mr. Albright to his house and was through working for the day. Mr. Ardmore said, "Art, why don't you have supper at my house and spend the night?"

"I need to clean up," said Art.

"You can do that too," said Mr. Ardmore. "And we can discuss the steam engines. I think both steam engines can be fixed for about eighteen hundred dollars."

Art said, "Please go on and finish the job. I only have six hundred dollars left, but I'll bring the other twelve hundred dollars when you finish the job."

Mr. Ardmore said," That's fine."

While they ate, Mr. Ardmore said, "Art, you should get a steamboat to take your engines back home.

"Where and who should I contact?" asked Art.

Mr. Ardmore told him who to see.

"I'll go by and see them in the morning," he replied.

During the meal, Art told everyone about the outlaws who tried to rob him south of Shreveport and how he had to kill a man. They were all ears. Art also told them about the Indian raid, his family, the war, his ranching, sawmilling, and his intentions of taking his herd north to get money for his beef. In turn, the others told about their lives. Art felt good when he went to sleep around ten o'clock. Everyone was up and had breakfast by five thirty. The workers had gone to work, and Art left to go to the steamboat company after he thanked the Ardmore's for their hospitality.

Art went to see the owner of a paddleboat about the steam engines being taken to Bryans Mill and maybe to Bare Creek by boat, which would be five miles from the sawmill. He told Art it would cost five hundred dollars each to ship the steam engines to Bare Creek. After about an hour of discussion, he reduced his price to four hundred dollars each. Art then went over to see the

Union General Bond, and he said General Sheridan would sell the two boats for four hundred dollars total. Art wrote a check and got a receipt from the General. Art said, "Don't cash the check for a week."

Art left Shreveport at ten o'clock that morning, knowing he had a hard drive to his family at Red Oak. Art's wife and Art Jr. had been staying with his mother, sister, and his mother's new husband with his daughter. Art's mother and Abe had treated Art's family great, but three weeks is enough to stay in another person's home. *Enough is enough, if you know what I mean. It's time to be back with your own family and home.* Art arrived around six o'clock that evening, with his new wagon and goods, to a great reception from all the family. After supper, they all went to bed at ten o'clock.

When Art woke up, Sharon had already been up since seven o'clock. Art's mother and sister had taken every opportunity to enjoy and take care of Art Jr. During the day, Art related all that had happened to him during the last week and that they were working on the two used steam engines at Ardmore's in Shreveport. Abe Martin was particularly interested in the captured equipment Ernest Albright was selling. He said, "I'll go to his farm and buy some of the captured Yankee equipment and also visit the Ardmore Shop to check on the progress of repairing the steam engines." Art gladly accepted Abe's help.

Art's family prepared to leave Red Oak for Bryans Mill. Art had eight mules to pull both wagonloads and tied his horses to the tailgate. They left Red Oak at 6 a.m. Sharon and Art Jr. slept in the wagon until nine o'clock when it got too hot. They stopped for about thirty minutes at a small, shaded stream to have a drink, water the animals, and rest. The next time they stopped was about noon, and again at three o'clock. The last stop to rest was around six o'clock, and they arrived at Sharon's parents' home by nine o'clock and went straight to bed.

The next morning, the Rogers family and anyone else that came by the farm wanted to know if the wagon was a new style and where they could buy one. Art and Sharon spent all day telling her family about the trip and future plans for the steam engines. Charles and Mr. Rogers said, "Art, if you go down to Shreveport again, we want to buy some of Ernest Albright's Yankee captured equipment." After a day of rest at Sharon's parent's home, Art and his family finally returned to Bryans Mill. It seemed like they had been gone a very long time, although it had only been three weeks. It really felt good to be back in their own home.

CHAPTER 16

The northern politicians had finally gotten their act together, and in the election of 1868, no Confederate soldiers could vote. The blacks and carpetbaggers who permeated the ex-Confederate states and the Republicans won all the state and local elections in Texas. They set about the tasks of punishing the states that fought the Union. General Sheridan had already declared Martial Law in Texas.

Their first act was to raise taxes on present landowners, both state and local. Art and Darrell figured they had at least survived the first year of the 100 percent increase in taxes. On their way to pay their taxes, they could not believe their eyes. Jesse Lassiter was talking to everyone in the courthouse. Lassiter was a sharp dresser, about forty five, very distinguished looking, and smart. He was also responsible for no less than seven attempted raids on the boys. When he saw Art and Darrell, he came right over to the boys and said, "I received a full pardon from the previous governor and I'm returning to manage the twenty-five thousand acres I still own in this area. Also, I'm expecting to be appointed the county judge." He continued, "I hope we can get along."

Darrell had enough and said to Lassiter, "We'll get along if you'll keep your toughs away from us, but it won't be the same as it was three years ago because I will kill you. Art and I are some of the fastest, most accurate gunmen around." The boys then turned away and went to pay their taxes.

While talking to several Naples residents, Art was shocked to learn that Ion Shaw was married to Lassiter. Ion was Art's first girlfriend. A cute little redhead matured beyond her years. She learned early how to use her feminine charm to get what she wanted and did not hesitate to use it to satisfy her selfish desires. Ion was only seventeen years old, and Lassiter was at least forty-five. This bothered Art, and he said, "Darrell, she'll be vindictive against this area."

The boys knew if Lassiter was appointed county judge, there would be more hell to pay than when Lassiter and others were convicted of forgery and sentenced to four years in prison. Art and Darrell talked it over with Mr. Hill. They went over all the previous illegal activities of Lassister. Mr. Hill said, "You boys should have a lawyer write up a petition for the people of the county to sign against appointing Lassiter as county judge. Have it addressed and send it to the governor."

Art and Darrell thought the petition was the only way to stop the judge appointment. Art said, "Darrell, we need to go to another town and get a lawyer to write the petition." They were told there were probably two thousand people in Morris County.

Art and Darrell went to Mount Pleasant and hired a lawyer named Tom Downing to draw up the petition. This project took all day. They had several pages of the petition to stop the Lassiter appointment, also several copies of the conviction of Jess Lassiter two years ago. For the next two days, the boys rode to every person, collecting signatures of those they thought would sign to oppose Lassiter's appointment as judge in Naples. The petition stated to appoint a man convicted two and a half years ago, for ten stated reasons, was violating the law in this county. Tom Downing said, "If you can get over one thousand signatures, I'll take the petition to the governor's aide next week when I go to Austin, the state capital." Mr. Downing charged Art and Darrell a hundred dollars and said, "If I have to bribe someone, it might cost a lot more."

The boys told him, "We think Lassiter is strapped for cash at this time."

The boys were extremely committed and wore out several horses collecting signatures. There were also six others collecting names, the Simmons brothers and Mr. Hill in Naples, Lewis Rogers and Mr. Smith in Marietta, Gene McCoy and Mark Anthony in Bryans Mill. For a week, Art and Darrell and all the others collected many names. There were also a lot of others helping as the people understood Lassiter was going to be appointed as judge, so they began to help gather signatures. Art and Darrell took all the signed petitions to Mr. Downing to take to the governor's aide to try and stop the appointment of Lassiter to the judgeship. There were twelve hundred signatures, which was more than one half of the adult males in this area. Art had even had Robert and Sherman, the boys' black friends, getting signatures. They had gotten over seventy-five names in their black community.

Art and Darrell told Tom, "We might be able to get five thousand dollars for the governor, but not much more, if he wouldn't appoint Lassiter to be judge."

The lawyer told the boys, "I should be back in about two weeks, and if I need money from you, I'll send a telegram."

Sure enough, the lawyer sent a telegram in a week, saying he needed two thousand dollars within two days, and he thought the governor would not appoint Lassiter as judge. The boys discussed it and decided Art would catch the stagecoach for Dallas in four hours. Darrell would send a telegram to Tom Downing, informing him Art had the money, but couldn't get there for three days. This was the best they could do.

Art arrived in Dallas at noon the next day. The Austin stage had left about an hour before Art's stage arrived. Art bought a horse and rode hard for the first stage stop, which was fifteen miles away. The stop was scheduled for two fifteen and would leave at two thirty. Art had paid seventy dollars for the horse and intended to leave it at the stage coach stop until he returned from Austin.

He made ten miles the first hour; and trying to save his horse, he slowed down and arrived at the stage stop at two thirty, stopped the stage, watered and boarded his horse, paid for a round trip to Austin, and boarded the stage. He traveled another sixty miles that day.

As Art was sleeping at the stage stop, a man came up and tried to steal the $2,300.00 Art had. Art marched him to the stage driver and told him the story. The driver worked out a deal where the robber would work for the stage company for one month; and if anyone was robbed or lost something, he would have to pay for it. A hard drive that day got Art to Austin at eight that night. He met his lawyer and confirmed a ten-minute appointment with the governor at 11:45 the next morning.

While eating supper, Art and Tom ran into Colonel Nance, who had been the Yankee Officer in charge of the Naples area two years ago. Art had sent him a telegram asking him for his help. He had told him when and where he would be staying. After explaining everything to Colonel Nance, he was more than willing to help and said he would meet Art and Tom at the Texas capitol building at eleven thirty the next morning. Art stayed in the room Tom had gotten him, had a bath, haircut, and clothes cleaned, and pressed for his meeting with the governor.

The threesome met the next morning as planned. The governor's aide met them and was shown all their petitions. Colonel Nance explained everything he knew about the incident with Lassiter. The aide also took the two thousand from Art's lawyer, and then ushered them into Governor Pease's office, where they pleaded their case as to why Lassiter should not be appointed judge. In addition, the governor told Colonel Nance, "I didn't know all the particulars."

Governor Pease said, "I assure you, I will not appoint Lassiter as Judge. Tom," he asked, "Do you know anyone that would make a good local judge in the Naples area?"

Tom said, "I believe I would be. I would also be the fairest man for the blacks."

At that point, Governor Pease dismissed Art and Colonel Nance and asked Tom, "How about going to lunch with me?"

When Art and Colonel Nance met up with Tom later, Tom explained, "Governor Pease appointed me as judge of the Naples area beginning immediately. It will cost me twenty-five hundred dollars, which I will pay when I return home."

While they were eating, Art asked, "Colonel, where could we get a good price for our horses?" Everyone in the state knew there was a shortage of horses because a disease had killed one third of the horses in Texas, Louisiana, and the Indian Territory. Good horses that had been broken were selling for one hundred dollars each.

After lunch, Colonel Nance took Art to see the Yankee general Mays, who immediately told Art, "I'll buy four hundred good, sound horses for one hundred dollars each, delivered to General Bates just west of Fort Worth at an army post located there."

General Mays, Colonel Nance, and Art had a long conversation about the war, what they were doing prior to it, and what they were doing now.

Art said, "General, I need two letters stating that the US Army has purchased these horses so they won't be confiscated by anyone. These letters will stay in the hands of Darrell Stroud and be given to General Bates in Fort Worth when he pays Darrell forty thousand dollars in cash for delivery of the four hundred horses." The letters also stated the horses were to be delivered within the month.

Art was able to catch the three o'clock stage going back toward Dallas, and left Colonel Nance and Tom Downing a happy man. The stage was full, but Art could ride free if he would ride shotgun. Art had his saddle, saddle bags, six-shooter and Henry rifle, but he didn't have a shotgun. The man who ran the stage office gave Art a brand new double-barrel shotgun, eight shells, and told him to keep the gun when he arrived in Dallas. After getting things settled, the stage left thirty minutes late and didn't arrive at the stage station outside of Waco until eight thirty. They still had covered sixty miles when they stopped at the stage station for the night. A boarding house had arrangements with the stage company to provide food and beds.

The next day, the stagecoach driver was sick and couldn't leave. The stagecoach company made arrangements with Art for him to drive the stage without anyone riding shotgun. They covered seventy-five miles and changed horses twice that day. When they stopped in Hillsboro, there was a driver and a man to ride shotgun ready to take the stage on to Dallas. This was the station where Art had left his horse. The stage would arrive in Dallas about one o'clock the next day.

Art was going to cut across on a road from Hillsboro to Fort Worth and talk with General Bates about the delivery of the horses. It took him all day to get to Fort Worth, and he could see immediately it was a rough town and stayed at the safest place he could find. The next day, Art rode out to see General Bates. He was assured that the general was in agreement with the delivery time and money to be paid for the four hundred horses. After selling the horse he was riding to the army for eighty dollars, Art took the stage through Dallas and arrived at Naples two days later around noon. He borrowed a horse from Mr. Hill and rode on home to a grand reunion with his family.

CHAPTER 17

The next morning, Darrell said, "Glad to see you. There are all kinds of signs that they're going to try to steal your cows."

Art told Darrell, "You have twenty two days to deliver four hundred good broken horses to the Union Army on the west side of Fort Worth. Where in the hell am I going to get four hundred head of good horses? I've only got one hundred fifty."

Art said, "The Anthony families have between one hundred twenty-five and two hundred fifty head. We can get the remaining from some farmers in the surrounding area."

They got eight horses from Art's farm, and then Darrell went to see if Mark Anthony wanted to sell his horses. He met with the Mark, Chandler, and Hunter families, and they decided they would sell 175 head. Darrell said, "You'll have to help me drive them to Fort Worth, and we're leaving Monday morning."

Art had gone to Marietta with his family on Friday, and talked to Charles and Mr. Rogers about horses and where to get more. Each of them had seven good horses they wanted to send.

Art told Charles, "I would like for you and your friends to go with Darrell and do the scouting. Each one will receive fifty dollars for the ten days work. I won't be going." Sharon was so happy she went over and gave him a really big kiss! Art asked Lewis and Charles, "Will you try to find about fourteen head of good horses and put them in the pasture with yours? The drive will start next Monday."

Charles said, "I think I can get at least that many good horses, and I'm sure that Ace would go on the horse drive on Monday."

Art told Mr. Rogers and Charles, "Remember they won't be paid until the drive is over, and everyone needs to keep this quiet."

Art then went south of Naples to a group of farmers who had helped him in the past. Ed Wright told Art he had four good horses, and when Art looked at them, he agreed. He asked Ed, "Will you get as many good horses as you can find from six or seven of your good friends? They'll get paid ninety dollars each in seventeen days. Bring all the good horses back to your farm, and I'll pick them up there. I'll meet you at your house by eight o'clock tonight, spend the night at your house, and you can help me drive the horses home." Art then left to see the Simmons Brothers to check for horses. He got to the Simmons' farm at ten thirty and told them all the facts about the horse sale. Bob and Ralph discussed Art's proposition and thought they had about thirty-two horses that would qualify to be sold for ninety dollars each.

Lane said, "I'll even go on the drive. We'll drive our horses to just across Sulphur River and meet the rest of the herd north of Naples, Monday by ten o'clock. After having lunch with the Simmons, Art returned to Ed Wright's farm.

The next morning Art, Ed, and the dogs herded thirty-eight horses to Art's farm, arriving about one o'clock. Ed had lunch with Art's family and headed home about an hour later. Art assured Ed he would get his money in about nineteen days. Money was so scarce in the area most of these farmers would jump at the chance to get ninety to one hundred dollars for a good horse. It was decided they would buy eating supplies along the way as they drove the horses, but the chuck wagon would go and hopefully not slow them down.

The herd was beginning to come together. Darrell's crew would consist of Darrell, Joe, Jed, Onnie, Chandler, Hunter, Mark,

Charles, Ace, Bob, and Mr. Jenson's oldest son, Paul. Paul was only twelve, but Darrell decided he could take care of the chuck wagon mules and purchasing supplies as they went along. Mark, Charles, and Ace were to be the scouts because with a herd of over four hundred horses, they could run into a lot of trouble with local farmers, going across their crops or with the women folk, messing up their yards and what they had planted.

Everyone but Darrell, Jed, and Joe went to church on Sunday at Bryans Mill and picnicked afterward, returning home by four o'clock. Darrell said, "I saw five riders cross Sulphur River about ten o'clock, but when they saw Jed, Joe and I were heavily armed they rode on toward Naples. They were probably trying to steal whatever stock they could find along the way. I trailed them two miles past the sawmill and then turned back to join Joe and Jed."

Joe and Jed told Darrell, "We saw three men driving thirty plus horses from south of Art's farm toward Sulphur River." Darrell, Joe, and Jed proceeded to stop the three men and horses.

Darrell said, "Show me a bill of sale because these horses look like mine." The three men did not have a bill of sale, so Darrell, Joe, and Jed disarmed them. Joe and Jed held them at gun point until Darrell went over and counted his horses. Lo and behold! He was minus thirty head. Darrell told the three men, "We just hang horse thieves around here." The three men begged Darrell "Please don't to turn us over to the law. Can we just work for you and not go to jail?"

All three of them were married and from the Hughes Spring area.

Darrell asked, "How good are you at breaking horses?" Two of the men said they rode pretty good and broken many horses before.

Darrell said, "Then you're going on a horse drive tomorrow and will be gone for eleven days. You might get twenty dollars when the drive is finished. You'll spend the night in my barn and work harder for me than you've ever worked before. Eat a good breakfast in the morning because you won't eat for another twelve hours."

When everyone returned from church, Art had a fit. "You'll regret making this deal," he said.

"We'll see," replied Darrell.

Everyone was up at five O'clock for breakfast, and by six o'clock, they were gathering the horses. Paul was still going to drive the chuck wagon and take the food. They had prepared canned food, three smoked hams, water, baked bread, biscuits, and cakes. They had cornbread and cooked black-eyed peas for this first night. All the men that worked for Art and Darrell were on hand to help with the drive until noon. At that time, the hands that were not going on the drive would return to Bryans Mill. Before they left, the Simmons Brothers showed up with thirty two head of good horses. That made the count 175 for the Anthony's, the Simmons brothers 32, and Art 8, for a total of 431 good horses.

Both Bob and Ralph were going with the herd and were returning home in the morning. The next morning, Darrell thought he almost had too much help and told Bob and Ralph he thought he had enough. The Simmons brothers stayed all day Tuesday and helped with the drive, spent the night helping guard the herd, and left Wednesday morning. They thought the herd had traveled about fifty miles from Darrell's farm. The herd had camped north of Sulphur Springs and was moving out by seven o'clock in the morning.

About ten o'clock, two squads of Union cavalry stopped the drive and demanded to know who owned these horses and where they were going with them. Darrell and Mark Anthony told the captain, "The horses belonged to us, and we're taking them to the Union camp in Fort Worth."

The Captain said, "Do you have any proof of that?" Darrell showed him the letter signed by General Mays. This seemed to satisfy the Captain, but he tried to keep the letter. After some tense discussion, the captain finally returned the letter. The captain told Darrell, "The army is so short of horses, I would have confiscated all of these horses and only paid twenty-five dollars each."

The rest of the day was about as bad because the herd ran into seven rattlesnakes, which were killed. However, one had bitten a horse, and Darrell had to put the horse down.

Paul Jenson had been driving the wagon. For the main supper meal, he would go to a local restaurant or farm, ask them to cook a meal for fifteen men, and he would pay them twenty dollars to cook it. He would then drive as fast as he could to the campsite, which Charles the scout had designated. He would build a fire to keep the food warm and make coffee. He had to keep the fire going all night and help cook eggs and bacon for breakfast. Paul also had to buy three dozen eggs each day for breakfast.

They camped that evening about twenty miles from the town of Dallas. Everyday Darrel had each man ride two different horses to make sure at least one-third of them had been ridden recently. He realized he really didn't know about eighty of the horses, so he made sure all of those were ridden.

The second day of the trip, Darrell left the drive and went to a farm where he had seen about twenty-five mares that looked pretty good. The farmer was not anxious to talk because he didn't want the army to come in and take his horses for twenty-five. Darrell said, "What if I give you fifty dollars each for the mares?"

The farmer replied, "If I still have them in a week, bring the cash and they're yours." They shook on the deal.

Darrell knew he needed to start rebuilding his horse herd. Mark Anthony and his two sons were going to go to Longview on the way home to buy some horses.

Darrell was going north to Sulphur Springs and Bryans Mill to try and find some phillies or mares on some of the small farms between Pittsburg and Bryans Mill. They would be covering two different routes on the way home.

The next day, they drove the herd one mile north of the town of Dallas and on to the Fort Worth army post. They arrived around seven o'clock that evening. The general ordered a count of the horses before anyone could eat or go to bed. The count was 430 horses, and he told the crew, "I'll buy the horses you're riding for seventy dollars each." The three men from Hughes Springs, Joe, Jed, Charles and Ace all sold their mounts but not the mules and wagon. Then they asked Paul for a ride to the stage. They could take a stage from Dallas to Naples for six dollars and go home to their families. Joe and Jed planned to ride all the way home in the wagon. They all had horses at home, but not as good as the ones they sold. That meant the only ones left with horses were Darrell, Onnie, and the Anthony boys. It turned out all the men rode in the wagon all the way home and didn't catch the stage.

The next morning, the Anthony family took off outside of Dallas toward Longview with their $17,800.00. There were eight men in the wagon, which was too much for the four mules to pull. Therefore, four people had to walk while four rode in the wagon.

The going was slow for the wagon. After spending the night with the crew in Dallas, Darrell and Onnie took off, leaving the slow-moving wagon, which would arrive in Bryans Mill in about four days.

They arrived at the farm where Darrell had bought twenty-five mares. The farmer was glad to see him and said, "I have fifteen more mares for you to look at." Darrell only took ten because the other five had problems. They spent the night at Mr. Case's farm, had supper and breakfast with them. Darrell hired Mr. Case's son to help drive the new herd, which took two days. He paid him ten dollars, and he returned home starting at noon on the second day. Darrell and Onnie arrived in Bryans Mill the following day. Mark and his boys arrived the following day with thirty-two mares they had bought from farmers west of Hughes Spring and Longview.

The next day, Art had Onnie take three horses for Joe, Jed, and Paul to Naples so they could get home quicker. Ace was to take himself, Charles, and the other three men Darrell had hired to Marietta and return the wagon later. Ace lived five miles from Hughes Spring and ended up taking the three horse thieves all the way and left them in town. Darrell had paid the three men twenty dollars each. They sold their horses for seventy dollars each so they each had ninety dollars. Their families could live comfortably for at least six months on ninety dollars. Maybe they would follow the straight and narrow path from now on.

Art went over to his farmer friend, Ed, to pay him for his horses, and then on to the Simmons brothers to pay them. A lot of the people in the area were financially better off because of this horse herd. Just for safety's sake, Art had Joe trail him about one hundred yards back. There were a lot of bad people in most of this area in the south. They would rob, kill, or steal any chance they got.

Darrell came home with over $12,500.00. The Anthonys came home with over $16,000.00, but they would both have to work hard to rebuild their horse herds. Even Art had made over $1,420.00 and didn't have to go on the drive. Art's cowherd had built up to over nine hundred head plus six hundred calves. He would need to start selling to keep things manageable. The trapping of wild Longhorns had only netted him twelve head this last year. Joe and Jed had only caught fourteen, but their own cow herd was over ninety cows.

CHAPTER 18

Robert, Sherman, and their families had come over to see Art and Darrell on Sunday when there was no church at Bryans Mill, and Darrell's Dad always cooked a steer on a spit. All the Anthonys, Strouds, Loggins, Jensons, Shaws, the Louis family, and Ed came. Also Joe and Jed had brought the girls, and Mr. Shaw brought Mrs. Lucas. The families getting together was always enjoyed.

On this day, there were thirty people. They all ate a fantastic meal, then Robert and Sherman wanted to talk to Art. They said, "We each had thirty Longhorn cows and need to start improving our calves. Could we buy some of your great bulls?"

Art said, "I can't sell any of my prize bulls, but I have some fifteen-month-old bulls which are a cross between Shorthorn and Longhorn or Hereford and Longhorns."

At three o'clock, when they were ready to go home, Art, Robert, and Sherman rode out to look at the twelve bulls Art had been saving. They picked out three and wanted to pay him, but he refused and said, "We'll trade out some work or something." Art loaned them two horses and asked, "Will you return them to Mr. Hill in Naples?"

After all that had been happening, all attention was turned on the crops, harrowing and chopping out the weeds. Everyone had to be careful of deer eating the corn. Art had been training his cow dogs to drive the deer away from the corn. This time of the year, Art and Darrell went out in the early morning and late evening when the deer were out looking for food. In six days, they had shot ten deer. They proceeded to save two for each of their families and gave one each to the Shaws, Jensons, Louis, Ed, and Joe and Jed, who were no longer living with Ed but on their own property in their new barn. Joe and Jed spent at least a day and half a week trying to improve their own twelve-hundred-acre farm. They had only had their farm a little over a year. However, their plans were to build stone homes like Art and Darrell, and get married. That would take another two years at least. Not bad for young men who had tried to steal cattle from Art eighteen months ago.

The economics of the area was bad, and the sawmilling had slowed. The boys only had orders for two barns and one house, which they wanted by the first of September. Art was beginning to worry about horses to help on his farms. At the present time, he only had one per cowboy, and that wasn't enough. He had to find more horses just to work all his cattle. Art knew he had to find an answer.

CHAPTER 19

Art had received a letter from Mr. Ardmore in Shreveport telling him both steam engines were finally repaired and ready to be picked up. He also said he had a man that wanted to buy one of the steam engines for three thousand dollars. Art sent a telegram back to Mr. Ardmore, telling him he would take four thousand dollars for one of the engines. He received a telegram back stating the buyer would pay a final offer of thirty-five hundred dollars. Art telegraphed back telling Mr. Ardmore to sell it for $3,500.00 which he did.

Darrell wanted to go to his old ranch home in Jefferson. Art gave him two thousand dollars and asked, "Will you try and buy fifteen young mares with a good stud, and also about fifteen good cow horses?" Art wanted either Joe or Jed to meet Darrell in Jefferson in three days to drive the horses he bought back to Bryans Mill. Darrell's dad was also going to go and help Darrell contact the horse ranchers in the Jefferson area. Two days later, Darrell and Mr. Stroud took off for Jefferson. Mr. Stroud drove a two-horse, two-seater buggy, while Darrell had his horse tied behind. Mr. Stroud talked to three farmers that day and bought fifteen young mares for Art.

The next day, Darrell went to see six farmers in the area, and Mr. Stroud went to see some of his old buddies. Between the two of them, they picked up twenty good horses and ten more good, young mares. Darrell also bought a great older stud for Art. The stud was eleven years old and Darrell paid six hundred dollars for it, knowing Art would like this as it would give him great horses in the future.

The next day, driving their horse herd back to Bryans Mill they stopped at three farms, and Darrell bought ten head of phillies. They trailed forty-six head, and thirty-six of them went to Art. This meant Art owed Darrell another $850.00, but he thought his lack-of-horses problem was solved.

Mr. Ardmore had told Art that next Tuesday, the steamship company was ready to ship the steam engine to Bryans Mill. Art had asked Abe Martin, his mother's husband, to go pick up the money for one of the steam engines, and pay Mr. Ardmore and the shipping company what was owed and send him the rest of the money. He also wanted Abe to supervise the loading of the steam engine on Monday afternoon. Art's plan was to load the steam engine off the steamship, around noon Tuesday, onto the better of the two special heavy-duty wagons he owned. The steamship would come as close to Bare Creek as possible. Art had gone to Naples to talk to Andrew, the blacksmith that had helped him set up the present sawmill. Andrew and all of Art's farm help were to be there all Tuesday afternoon and try to figure out exactly how to hook the steam engine into the present sawmilling operation.

Sure enough, after they had all been waiting about an hour, the steamboat arrived. The boat's boom was able to swing the boiler onto Art's awaiting special heavy-duty wagon. It took six mules to pull the three thousand pound boiler the five miles to the saw mill. Andrew had determined where he wanted to set the boiler so it wouldn't have to be moved again. After a day and a half, Andrew left and said, "I'll be back next Sunday afternoon, and I feel we could fire up the boiler and begin sawmilling again." As planned by the following week, the sawmill was back in business beginning to cut enough for four barns and two houses. Art had begun compiling house plans along with his new barn plans that he gave to customers that bought lumber and brick from the boys. After one week of operation, they were out of logs.

CHAPTER 20

It had been a terrible, dry summer, and all the crops in the area were nearly burned up and wouldn't produce much. Art decided to start harvesting his corn the first of September. With the help of Paul Jenson, they had finished in two weeks. The yield was about 20 bushels per acre for a whopping total of 2,000 bushels. Mr. Shaw who had 30 acres, got about 15 bushels per acre, for a grand total of 450 bushels. Art would need three times that much corn to feed all his livestock. Art always had about 2,000 bushels left over at his place, and there was another 1,000 bushels at the other barns. He needed to buy 2,000 more bushels or his herd would become weak and sick this winter. The grass was burned up, so he would have to start feeding his livestock now. Art was lucky he had put up a lot of hay in the spring and early summer. He began light feeding of corn and hay the sixteenth of September.

Meanwhile, Art, Paul, Mr. Shaw, and Onnie began picking a total of sixty acres of cotton. The harvest yielded thirty bales. They sold the cotton for $250.00, a bale for a total of $7,500.00, which was split with Art for his part of the sharecropping. Art paid Paul $120.00, which was more money than he had ever had. He had made $50.00 on the horse drive and $75.00 working two months at the sawmill. He had now made and saved $245.00. He thought he was rich! Art urged him to save his money until he could buy a farm of his own. Art also wanted him to find a secret tree where he could hide his money as he did not trust banks. This really set well with Paul, and it became his goal for several more years. In fact, he asked, "Art, can I cut trees for the sawmill on your property?"

"Only the ones I mark," Art replied. "And if you use Joe or Jed to help you on the first ten, I mark." Art then promptly marked twelve trees in that area. Art then sent Paul to get Joe or Jed. Paul returned in forty-five minutes. Art told them, "I want you to show Paul how to cut these trees safely. And Paul, you are always to have someone present when you are logging." Paul quickly found out he was not strong enough to do much logging and vowed he would get stronger. Paul thought *maybe he could log next year for more money.*

After the harvest, Sharon went into labor, and Paul took off for Dr. Lilly in Naples. He arrived in four hours, and within thirty minutes, Sharon had a little girl. Sharon and baby were doing fine so Dr. Lilly left after breakfast the next morning. He said, "I'll be back tomorrow afternoon."

They named the baby Patricia after Art's sister and Sharon's mother. Art Jr. was getting used to his sister and seemed to be proud of her. Sharon's family, including Charles, came over to see their new granddaughter. They stayed two days and one night, helping and having fun with their grandchildren.

Art went over to see his friend Ed, to see about buying corn from him and some of his farmer friends. He was lucky and was able to buy 350 bushels from each of nine different farmers for a total of 3500 bushels. Art paid 50 cents a bushel. Art said, "I'll be sending two large wagons that will hold 150 bushels each, but it will take four mules to pull each double set. We'll start Monday, hauling two loads a day."

He then rode back to McCoy Mill and General Store to negotiate a better price because of the shortage of corn. Art liked being able to sell him two thousand bushels each year. However,

Mr. McCoy told Art he would only pay 50 cents a bushel. Art said, "Forget it. I don't have enough corn anyhow."

Then Mr. McCoy said, "Come back, I'll pay 75 cents a bushel for two thousand bushels delivered to me within two weeks. Right now, I'm out of corn."

Art rode home and told Charles, "I need corn badly. I wonder if those three young men that tried to rob Darrell have any corn."

Charles said, "Ace lives near us, and I'll talk to him in the morning and see if they do have corn, and I'll get in touch with you."

Art said, "I'll pay 50 cents a bushel."

The Rogers family left that afternoon to go back to Marietta. Sure enough, Charles found Ace, and he rode over to see the three young horse thieves about the corn. One of their fathers had gotten good rains and made a great crop. After the son talked to his father, he said he would sell Art two thousand bushels of corn for 50 cents a bushel if Art would haul it and pay him within a week. Art found out what the deal was in just a couple of days. He sent his two large double wagons with Joe and Paul, and told them not to come back until they had each hauled one thousand bushels to Mr. McCoy. Art gave Joe $1,000.00 to pay Mr. Ellis for his corn. The boys were told to thank the farmer a lot. The hauling of the corn took four days. Mr. McCoy credited Art's account for $1,500.00 along with his existing credit of $250.00. Art now had a total credit of $1,750.00 at Mr. McCoy's General Store. Art sent Jed over to tell his farmer friend Ed he couldn't get the corn until the following Monday. He had Jed and Paul haul 1500 bushels each to the Parkinson's and Ed's farms, which of course he owned, and another 500 bushel to Louis's barn. Art warned everyone to just keep the livestock on minimum feed for all this winter.

CHAPTER 21

Sheriff Bass, who knew Darrell, had ridden out to see the boys. He said, "I need some help in the Bryans Mill area and would like to appoint you two as my deputies so I can cover the eastern part of the county better."

Art said, "Darrell would be a great man for the job, but in place of me, you need to get one of the Anthony boys. If you don't like that idea," he continued, "you could get Gene McCoy or his son in Bryans Mill, but not me."

Darrell and Bass rode over to Bryans Mill and talked to Gene McCoy and his son about the deputy job, and they both said, "Get one of the Anthonys. They would be so much better at the job." After that, Darrell and Sheriff Bass rode over to the Anthony complex, and none of them were really interested. Leaving the Anthonys, Darrell asked, "Sheriff, are you interested in appointing a deputy from the Marietta area?"

"I sure am," replied Sheriff Bass.

"Why don't we ride over to see Charles Rogers?" suggested Darrell. When Charles found out he would probably only have to work two weeks out of the year and get paid a hundred dollars, he accepted.

Charles, Darrell, and Sheriff Bass rode over to the Hills' general store so the sheriff could swear in each one and give them a deputy badge. Darrell rode back to Bryans Mill and told Gene McCoy what had happened. He knew it would be all over the countryside if he knew. It was late when Darrell got home, and the next morning, Art told him, "Maybe we can use this deputy thing to help protect us."

"Why do you think I did it?" asked Darrell. The rest of the week, Art and the others poured on the "deputy thing" until Darrell got mad about it. From then on, everyone just called him deputy every once in awhile.

Dr. Lilly was beginning to be in high demand due to a terrible smallpox epidemic breaking out. His advice was to close the few schools for the month of December and for people to stay home, even from church and visiting. "Stay at home!" was his message. Dr. Lilly felt he could try to inoculate the people with cowpox, and that would protect them from smallpox. The problem was getting to everyone to get them protected against the smallpox. It took him all month to get everyone inoculated against this terrible disease. By January, the crisis was over, but it took a lot of care for those smallpox victims that had high fever for several days and were left with scars for several weeks. There were ten deaths in the county, mostly the elderly that already had other medical conditions. Not many families escaped without someone being affected by this crisis.

In addition, people were having trouble making ends meet. Most of the people that were around Art and Darrell seemed to not only be making a living, but building, increasing land, money, cattle, or horse holdings. The boys had developed the reputation of making good decisions and were not afraid to take action on their decisions. They were also known as pretty handy gunmen and would not back down from anyone.

CHAPTER 22

Since Darrell had become deputy, the boys and a posse were going to make a large sweep north of Sulphur River to get rid of all the outlaws living between Sulphur River and Indian Territory. The boys discussed attacking the outlaws before the outlaws attached them. The posse consisted of Art and Darrell, the Anthony boys, Gene McCoy, Charles Rogers, Joe Boyd, Ace Sutton, and Onnie Shaw. They took one extra horse each and two pack mules to feed ten men for ten days. The plan was to buy horse feed in some of the small farms that were around the area.

It was raining when the posse took off early Monday. Charles and Ace were scouting one hour ahead of the rest of the posse. The plan was to zigzag all the way to the Red River. Charles and Ace were to go seven miles northwest from Sulphur River, and then northeast fourteen miles with Onnie trailing three hundred yards behind with the pack mules. They spread out two hundred yards apart, going directly north, and found a camp with five men ten miles north of Sulphur River. They were planning to make an outlaw raid somewhere in the area. When the posse approached the camp and identified themselves, two of the men started firing at the posse. The other three separated themselves, and in about thirty minutes, the posse had the suspects surrounded. Being outnumbered, they finally surrendered. Deputy Darrell questioned them, but they wouldn't talk. When Art and Mark rounded up three rattle snakes and stretched the men out with the snakes twelve inches from them, they confessed. The two suspects had robbed a big farmer near Clarksville and shot a hand that worked for him. They didn't know if they killed the farmer's help or not.

Early the next morning, Chandler Anthony and Onnie Shaw took the two suspects to Clarksville with a note from Deputy Darrell to the sheriff. It was late that afternoon when Chandler and Onnie returned to the posse. Darrell had sent the three other men back to their home in Clarksville. They said they didn't have any money and had been starving trying to farm. Darrell told them if they cut twenty logs and got them to the sawmill, they could earn sixty dollars. They said they didn't have any way to haul, and Darrell volunteered Art's log-hauling wagon. They left, promising to bring forty logs to the sawmill. Art told them to go by Bryans Mill and get ten dollars' worth of groceries. They could kill some game and survive at least a month or two. That night, Darrell said, "We have been on this posse two days, and Art already converted three of the five men we caught. You should have been a preacher going around saving people."

The posse was now ten miles from the Red River and staying at the place the Jensons were living in when Art found them over a year ago. That night, Deputy Darrell posted a guard with the horses, and Art took the last watch at 4 a.m. Within thirty minutes, Art saw at least ten riders at a gallop leaving a clump of pine trees about one hundred yards from Art and the horses. He immediately shot and dropped one rider, woke up his camp, and within minutes everyone was close to Art. He just pointed as he now noticed ten other riders were coming in full force from another direction. The posse concentrated their fire on the nearest riders, cut down four more riders, and one group took cover fifty yards away from the camp. They immediately turned on the other ten and got off twenty rounds within another minute. They stopped and took cover, but they were surrounded by ten outlaws.

Darrell got three men and moved the horses and mules to a rickety old barn. The position the posse was in was not really defendable because they did not anticipate being attacked by outlaws. As far as they knew, there were only ten men fighting them now. Darrell said, "Chandler and I are going out to scout and see if we can find out what we are up against. Art, don't let them shoot until they actually see someone. We don't have a lot of ammunition." Hunter showed them where the attackers were on the east side, and Hunter showed Darrell and Chandler where he thought the ones were on the west side.

Darrell and Chandler took two six guns and one knife each. They took off crawling toward the west side attackers. After twenty-five yards, they could hear three men talking, and it sounded like about ten yards northeast of their location. Darrell pulled a gun and motioned for Chandler to go around the other way and on his signal, try to capture them and find out what they could. If they could capture just one of them, they could get the information they needed. Darrell and Chandler crawled about eight yards and found themselves four yards from the three men. Darrell was the first to tell them, "Don't move or we'll kill you." Two of the men went for their six-shooters. Darrell and Chandler each shot one man, and the other said, "I give up." They took all the IDs, boots, guns, ammunition, and money off the dead men. Most of the same items were taken from the captive. Darrell, Chandler, and the captive crawled back to the small fort. They all ate, and then began to talk to the prisoner. The prisoner said, "The men you're fighting are four gangs that took off when they found out a posse was in the area. They got together and planned to kill or take all your horses. There were nineteen to start with and out of the ten from the west side, that left three." They thought there were more on the east side.

Darrell said, "I have decided we should wait until night time to try and see how many men are on the east side."

As soon as it was dark, Darrell and Chandler left crawling toward the place they thought the outlaws were located. They were shocked because the first attacker was about twenty-five yards away, watching the posse's camp, and they were able to get the drop on him. After gagging him, they tied him up and kept going until they heard talking and could see five men sitting around. Darrell told Chandler, "Go around and see if they have a guard on the horses." When Chandler got to the horses, there was no guard. Chandler then hobbled all eight horses and came back to Darrell. Darrell circled around to the other side of the men and then from a well-protected tree, and said, "Drop your guns." When the men went for their guns, Darrell and Chandler shot four of the five men, and the other dropped his gun and put up his hands. They quickly picked up all the guns and two wounded men. Then they put the two dead men on a horse, making the other two men walk back to the posse's camp.

When they got back to camp, Darrell asked, "Art, will you and Hunter go get the horses, saddles, and anything else of value and bring it back to camp?" He then tied all the dead men of the gang on two horses and sent them toward the east side of the outlaw camp. He then had the three prisoners call out to the men and tell them they were the only ones left and that they were surrounded. The outlaws tried to ride off, but Darrell had positioned all of his deputies around their position and therefore they were easily captured.

Darrell gathered all the dead, wounded, and captured outlaws and started for Naples to turn them over to the sheriff and explain what had happened. The boys decided to also have Charles and Ace scout to see if there were signs of other outlaws close by. They also decided Art should go ahead to Naples to tell the Sheriff what had happened, and that the posse was bringing these people to jail. Art rode hard and got to Naples at midnight and woke up Sheriff Bass. When Art told him what happened and that they were bringing in all the outlaws, he immediately told Art, "I'll go out with you, and when they ride in tomorrow, there won't be a problem." What he really meant was he would come in with the posse so he could get credit for the action. Art said, "I'm tired and I'm going to bed, but if you're going to meet them, it would be helpful to take a wagon." The sheriff assured him he would.

Art got a room and was up and dressed by eight o'clock the next morning. At nine o'clock, he went out to the Union Army camp and told the lieutenant what had happened. The lieutenant asked, "What area did the posse cover?"

"Maybe you could try to cover the area the posse didn't," Art suggested.

The lieutenant wanted to leave before the sheriff rode into town. He left on his patrol by ten o'clock, anxious to go out in the area north of Sulphur River. The army didn't ever want to be outdone by the local law.

Art talked to Mr. Hill about what was happening and said, "What I really wanted was for the sheriff and the army to clear out all the outlaws hiding between the Indian nation and Sulphur River. This would help protect me, my family, and all the law-abiding citizens in that area. Would you tell Deputy Darrell I have returned home?" Art then left for his farm in Bryans Mill. He had been gone for seven days.

When Darrell and the posse arrived in Naples around three o'clock, they caused quite a stir. Of course, Sheriff Bass took the opportunity to let everyone know he had done it all and took the credit. As soon as the other members of the Posse turned everything over to Sheriff Bass, they headed home. By that time, it was around seven o'clock. Everyone was ready to go home, and they felt good about a job well done.

CHAPTER 23

It was now December 10, and the weather turned below freezing for a solid week. Everyone was busy making sure they had plenty of firewood and that the livestock was fed and protected from the cold. The horses and mules got in the barns during the night. The boys had built about eighteen sheds eight feet tall, sixty feet long and twenty feet wide with covering on the north and west sides for protection from the wind. The barns and protection sheds were where they tried to feed the cattle. This was where they also put haystacks. There was going to be a shortage of feed this year. Art, Sharon, and everyone else had a shortage of food for their families because of the draught. Their only salvation was that there were plenty of ducks, rabbits, deer, and fish to eat. Art and Darrell and everyone else were staying close to home. About every other night, Art's family would go over to Darrell's and play dominoes. Darrell's dad really enjoyed the game, and they usually stayed up until ten o'clock.

Darrell and Charles had warned everyone that an outlaw gang led by a man named Rob Lee had been killing, robbing, and rustling; especially if he found out they were black or anyone else who was helping blacks. Lee had stayed around Marshall, Jefferson, and Linden. He had a gang of fifteen to twenty men. The Union Army knew about him but had not been able to capture or kill him. Art and Darrell had discussed Lee and tried to be extra careful. They even had guns hidden in their barns and other safe places on their farms, just in case.

Criminal Rob Lee was beginning to expand his territory and had come up to Hughes Springs. He recruited the three men who had tried to steal Darrell's horses. They not only told Lee about Darrell and the Anthony horses, but about the one thousand plus head of cattle Art had. Lee planned to scout Darrell's, Art's, and the Anthony's farms for about a week while they camped north of Sulphur River. They planned to attack all three farms. Darrell had picked up the tracks on Wednesday. On Friday, their six Indian Choctaw friends, including Hawk, Running Bear, and Straight Arrow, came to the Sulphur. The Indians came up to Art's house, which was unusual, and Art invited them into the house for lunch. Hawk said, "You know there are twenty outlaws five miles on the other side of the river. I'm sure they're going to take all your cattle and horses. What can we do to help?"

Darrell had come to Art's to listen to what the Indians had to say. The boys told them, "If we could see where the outlaws were scouting and exactly how many men there were, that would be a big help."

On Saturday, the Indians said, "The men are scouting Art's, Darrell's, and the Anthony's farms." Darrell rode to Naples and got a promise from the Union Army that they would quietly have a squad there by eleven o'clock. Joe and Jed were sent over to help the Anthonys. Gene McCoy and the townspeople prepared to meet the outlaws. The women and children were all at Art's and Darrell's homes. Darrell had his dad, Mr. Jenson, and his son Paul. Mr. Shaw, Onnie, and Louis were at Art's home. Art, Darrell, Ed, and the six Indians were waiting on Art's home farm. They tried to make it look like everyone was sleeping late and having a late breakfast. Art, Darrell, and the Indians were well-hidden in a strategic location where the outlaws would have to come.

Sunday came, and the first thing Art Jr. and Eric did was get their dogs and put them up in an enclosed place in the barn, where they were kept when necessary. Rob fooled everyone and went to Darrell's farm, taking seventy head of horses and sent them south with two of the outlaws. The other nine went to Art's and began to start herding cows together. At that time, Art, Darrell, Ed, and the six Indian friends opened fire from cover and immediately killed or wounded six outlaws. Art and Darrell then shot the horses of the other outlaws trying to get away. The outlaws quickly surrendered, but Rob Lee was not one of them.

Art asked Deputy Darrell, "Would you go to get the sheriff and army to come and help?" Art had kept the Indians hidden and told them, "Go back to the fishing camp. I'll join you later when it's safe." In the meantime, eleven other gang members had attacked the Anthony horse ranch. Mark, Chandler, Hunter, Joe, and Jed were well-placed in the woods, surrounding their horse herd. The gang rode in about ten thirty, and the hidden defenders opened fire. In one minute and over fifty shots, they killed and wounded five of the invaders. The remaining outlaws tried to ride off, and the defenders shot their horses. A long, three-hour fight continued. The outlaws were pinned down and were using the dead horses as cover. Chandler and Hunter had taken all the horses the rustlers were going to steal to another enclosed pasture one thousand yards away. The rustlers were in an open pasture, unprotected from the elements. It was a cold day of fifty degrees, and then it began to rain about one o'clock. The defenders had protected positions which allowed them to have a clear seventy yard shot at the rustlers. The rustlers tried twice to break out, and two more of them were wounded. They were now just hoping for night time so they could slip away. At about two thirty, Art, Darrell, and Sheriff Bass showed up, and the rustlers quickly surrendered.

The sheriff said, "I'll need some help to take the wounded prisoners back to Naples." He had disarmed all of them, and Mark was going to provide a wagon to transport the rustlers. Joe and

Jed were going to accompany Sheriff Bass back to the Naples jail. Darrell did not yet know about the seventy horses being stolen. The two gang members who had stolen them from Darrell went through Marrietta.

Several farmers were suspicious and went to Deputy Charles. Charles got Ace and three other friends to ride out with him. They overtook the rustlers in Hughes Springs. The two men did not have a bill of sale, and Charles recognized Darrell's brand on all the horses. Charles and his crew took the two men and drove the horses to Darrell's farm, where Darrell confirmed they were his horses and that these men had stolen them. Charles sent his helpers back to Marietta, and he took the two rustlers to the Naples jail. He filed a report with the sheriff. By this time, it was midnight so Charles spent the night at the jail because he was dog tired and slept until eight o'clock the next morning. Sheriff Bass took him to breakfast, and then Charles went to his parents' home in Marietta. He told them of the happenings both at Hughes Springs and Bryans Mill. His mother immediately wanted to go check on Sharon and her family. Charles assured his parents that his sister and family was okay. He then had to go home and take care of his farm.

As far as anyone knew, after all the action the past couple of days, they still had not wounded, killed, or captured the leader of the outlaw gang, Rob Lee. This really was a worry to all who knew the facts. This had been the largest attack in this part of the country since the Indians attacked Bryans Mill and the surrounding area. Everyone was worried and wondering when he would be back.

Now that it was safe, Art went to the Sulphur River to meet and thank Indian friends for their help. He also planned to fish for a couple of days. The fishing was not good, and they left after two days. Art had killed a steer and cooked it. This was their food for the two days. Art also asked about making a cattle drive this next year. Hawk asked Art, "How much would the cattle bring if taken to Abilene?"

Art replied, "I hope twenty dollars a head. I'll try to start about May first and meet you about six days later. I'll come up and confirm this before starting the drive. Speak to your people to see if they are interested."

CHAPTER 24

It was almost Christmas and everyone was getting anxious to celebrate, especially the children. Everyone took a day off to go out and cut their Christmas trees. The kids and women had a great time decorating. Art and Darrell went to sawmilling and brick-making. They had orders for nine barns and two houses. Art figured they had enough trees to get all this cut in twenty working days. Joe, Jed, Darrell, and the Anthony boys were still on alert and were out checking for signs once a week for rustlers around all the farms. So far they had not found anything.

After a week of sawmilling, they shut the mill down at one o'clock and went home. They all went to Naples to shop, eat, and go to the seven o'clock dance. Everyone left the dance around eleven o'clock and drove home arriving at one thirty. The next morning, they went to Bryans Mill church and social. Art's and Darrell's crews left at three o'clock, arriving home at four thirty. They had to feed and check on all the stock.

The next morning an ice storm hit the area, and the focus was to try to take care and feed the stock. Ed, Louis, Joe, Jed, Darrell, and Art went out with a wagonload of corn with a horse tied on behind. They put most of the feed in the animal shelters, finishing at noon. Everyone was busy at home for the next week. On Friday, the ice storm was over, and Saturday they went back to sawmilling and would continue Monday and Tuesday. Wednesday was Christmas, so the sawmilling stopped until Saturday.

Art and Art Jr. went to check the herd on Thursday and saw the tracks of five horsemen going to and from Sulphur River. At noon, Art and his son had finished checking and feeding all the cows on his farm and also the cows on the old Shaw farm. Art drove over to Darrell's and told him about the tracks. Darrell had also picked up tracks on his farm. Art took Art Jr. home, Darrell saddled his horse, and the boys went to look at the tracks on Darrell's farm then went to look at the tracks on Art's farm. They thought the tracks were the same, so they checked out the old Shaw, Parkinson, and Lassiter farms. They didn't find anything there. It was four thirty and getting dark, so the boys decided they would start tracking early in the morning.

Sharon told Art, "I'm going to my parents until Sunday afternoon."

Darrell's dad said, "I'll ride part of the way with Art's family."

The boys took off on Friday morning at seven o'clock and had no trouble picking up the tracks. They followed them all day until they came to a small abandoned barn and house where they spotted seven horses. Art and Darrell thought it looked like the outlaw Rob Lee. They overheard the conversation, and the outlaws were waiting for two men driving a wagon with supplies of food, ammunition, and horse feed. There was a small pasture close by, and Art found seven steers with his brand. Darrell also found eight horses with his brand. It was obvious the cows and horses had been here for at least two weeks. Art could see they had previously butchered three of his steers. Art said, "Darrell you go get the sheriff and a posse. I'll keep a watch on this bunch." It was almost morning, and they had a well-concealed cold camp where they were dry and warm.

Darrell took off at 4 a.m. and went to get Onnie. He also took the outlaws' stolen horses out in the pasture. He got to Onnie's around six o'clock and sent him to get the sheriff and the Union

Army squad stationed at Naples. Darrell put the eight horses in Onnie's corral. Darrell then went on and got Joe and Jed, and they rejoined Art at eight o'clock.

Darrell did send word to his wife about what was happening.

The army posse finally got to Art's camp about 1:00 p.m. that afternoon. It had taken longer because it had started to snow. Art said, "The two men with a wagon arrived with supplies around six o'clock that morning. I think the nine men have mostly been drinking since then." He told Darrell, "I don't believe they even know you took the horses from the pasture."

The army lieutenant wanted to just go charging in. Darrell said, "There's no reason to get any of us hurt. We're going to get as close as we can by crawling." The lieutenant finally agreed. He said, "Two of your men watch all our horses, and the two of you stay on saddled horses in case any outlaws get to their horses and try to escape after the shooting starts."

Art told Joe and Jed, "Try and stay behind us when the shooting starts. After the shooting stops, I want you to put bridles on the outlaws' horses and lead them to another clump of trees.

Art and the sheriff were sneaking up on the south side and got to the barn before anyone got to the house. Just as the boys were getting ready to go in the front and back doors, two of the outlaws came out. They were able to club them over the head and knock them out. The rest of the army posse then charged into the front and back doors. The posse was able to capture and disarm the outlaws before any shots were fired. Sure enough, one of the men was Rob Lee. Art and Darrell showed the branded cattle and horses, proving they belonged to them. Art also gave the sheriff three hides from the butchered steers. That morning, the army put all nine men in the wagon, and the boys took ten horses and seven steers toward home. It was cold and Art said, "Darrell I think I deserve two of the outlaws horses."

Darrell replied, "Take three."

It was cold and snowing off and on. The boys met Mr. Shaw, Onnie, Louis, and Ed about ten miles from the river, and they said they would take the stock on to the pastures. Art and Darrell took off for home. Art had come home to a cold house, and it took him a couple of hours to get the fires started and get himself warmed up. Velma sent her son Eric over with a supper consisting of beans, potatoes, and deer steak. After he finished eating, which was about eight o'clock, Art went to bed, making sure he had plenty of wood to keep the fire going for three or four days.

It was now the fifth of January, and Art decided he wasn't going to do much the rest of the week. He would go over to Marietta and get his family when it was warmer. About eight o'clock the next morning, Darrell came by and said, "I put three horses in the barn and fed them. I'd leave them close so you can feed them back to health." Darrell continued. "What do you plan to do today?"

"Nothing," Art said. "I'm going to feed and check all the stock. Then tomorrow I'm going to Marietta to pick up Sharon and the kids." It took Art until six o'clock to look after all the cattle, horses and check his other farms and, of course, visit with Ed, Louis, and Mr. Shaw. He even rode over to see how Joe and Jed were doing with their farm. He ate some ham and cornbread Sharon had left, built up the fire and went to bed.

CHAPTER 25

The next morning, Art was up by seven o'clock, went out and collected a lot of eggs, fixed bacon and four eggs, and was ready to ride at eight o'clock. It was some warmer. He made a quick two-hour ride to the Roger's house in Marietta and his family. He received a great welcome, especially from Sharon, Art Jr., and Patricia. Charles came by and had lunch.

After listening to Art's story of the happenings over the last ten days, Charles said, "Art, you and Darrell should get the reward, and I'll try to collect it when I'm in Naples today." He also said, "The governor under the direction of General Sheridan is forming a state police force which would have almost unlimited powers. I'll come by and see you with whatever news I have." He continued, "But I'll certainly have the reward money." Charles took off at two o'clock as he wanted to get to Naples by six o'clock. He caught the sheriff at home having supper. Charles told Sheriff Bass, "I really needed to talk to you." After the sheriff finished supper, Charles asked, "Where is the reward money Art and Darrell are due for capturing the Rob Lee Gang? It should have been around five thousand dollars."

Sheriff Bass said, "No, it was six thousand dollars, and all the boys did was locate the outlaws. The army and I did all the shooting and actually captured them."

Charles said, "You know that's a lie. Art and Darrell are better fighters than any of the others that were there, and you know it. I won't let you screw them out of that money."

The sheriff said, "I can't pay Darrell because he's a deputy, but I'll give you a three thousand dollar check for Art."

Charles said, "If you say a deputy can't take money, how can a sheriff? Where does the other three thousand dollars go?" asked Charles.

The sheriff never answered. Sheriff Bass said, "We have bigger problems. I understand the new state police will take over the first day of February and the head of the northeast area in Texas is going to be Jess Lassiter."

"The boys will have a fit!" exclaimed Charles, "Are you still going to have a job and will you still need deputies?" he asked.

Sheriff Bass told Charles, "I'll still be sheriff, and I'll still have deputies, but the new state police will have almost complete power." Sheriff Bass wrote out a check for three thousand dollars for Art and gave it to Charles. "Is this good enough?" he asked.

Charles replied, "You know it isn't." He rode over to Mr. Hill's house and asked him to put the check in the bank for Art the next day.

He got to Art's house about nine o'clock and woke Art up. He told him about the three thousand dollar check and what Sheriff Bass had said. That made Art mad, but when he told him about Lassiter going to be appointed over the state police in the area, he couldn't believe it. He walked over to Darrell's and woke him up to tell him.

Darrell said, "We're just going to have to kill him. We'll do something in the morning." Charles was spending the night in Art's home and already had gone to bed when Art returned home.

On February first, the state police did take over most of the civilian responsibilities and the outlaw Rob Lee and the other members of the gang escaped from them in Naples. This happened when a special state police detachment had come from headquarters to transport them for trial in Austin.

CHAPTER 26

After Darrell finished feeding his horses and Art had fed his cattle, the boys rode to see the judge, Tom Downing, who had helped stop Lassiter from the county judgeship. They were in luck as the judge was at the courthouse in Naples. He told Art and Darrell, "You need to get signatures on a petition to stop the appointment. Then you need to go see the governor. I'll get you an appointment." He had his secretary change the previous petition the boys had used to stop Lassiter's to the judgeship and sent a telegram to the governor stating Lassiter should not be appointed as leader of the new state police in northeast Texas and gave him the reasons. He sent the telegram from Mount Pleasant in the afternoon. The governor asked the judge to send the petition, and he would consider not appointing Lassiter.

Art and Darrell were out and about collecting names the next week. They also had to come up with someone that the governor could appoint. The judge had found out what the real problem was: George Murphy, the man that was the present head of the new state police. Art thought Colonel Nance would be a good choice, but the judge came up with the name of Amos Wright, a Texarkana sheriff that was defeated in the last county election. He was not a Confederate soldier and was considered a fair man. Art and Darrell thought they could live with him. Art told Darrell,

"If Amos Wright is appointed, maybe we could get ex-ranger Todd Berry to be in charge of this area which might be a help to us." The judge Tom Downing sent the petition with 1,500 names to the governor, along with the recommendation of ex-sheriff Amos Wright.

The boys waited two weeks, and then the judge sent for them. When they saw the judge, he said, "The governor stopped Lassiter's appointment, but it was going to cost three thousand dollars."

Darrell told him, "We will have the money in two days."

When they were away from the judge, Art said, "I'm not going to pay this. It's time other folks helped get rid of Lassiter."

"Who else is going to do it?" asked Darrell.

Art said, "I don't know, but I'm going to ask some people."

They headed to Mr. Hill's store. "I'll give four hundred dollars if Lewis Rogers will also give that much," Art told him. "I'll be back in a couple of days." The boys then went to the Simmons brothers and got four hundred dollars. They asked everyone they talked to and also asked if they knew anyone else that would help. They then headed for the Rogers' home, and Lewis said, "I'll give you six hundred dollars, but Hill has to match it." The boys went home for the night.

The next morning, Art and Darrell went to Bryans Mill and talked to Gene McCoy. He said he would help and gave the boys six hundred dollars because he knew about Lassiter's previous tactics. Then the boys went to the Anthony's horse ranch, and Mark gave them six hundred dollars. They now had $2,800.00. Art told Darrell, "That's all we are going to give the judge. If he wants, he can throw in the other two hundred dollars. Not a bad two days work, huh, Darrell?" The next day when the boys delivered the $2,800.00 to Judge Downing, he decided to furnish the other $200.00, making the total $3,000.00 going to the new governor. Art and Darrell were real pleased because all it had cost them was three days' work.

The next Monday, the boys rode to Texarkana to see the ex-sheriff Amos Wright. He was glad to talk to the boys, and they told him all their background. "When you become head of the new Texas state police, who are you going to appoint as chief for Northeast Texas?" asked the boys.

Amos said, "First I have to get the appointment."

Art asked, "Would you consider appointing Todd Berry?"

He said, "Sure, but I don't think he would come to work for the state police."

"If we get Todd to say yes, would you hire him?" asked the boys.

"You know I would." replied Amos.

Mr. Berry owned a one-thousand-acre cow and calf operation just outside New Boston. The boys took off to talk to him. After two hours telling Mr. Berry how bad things would be if he didn't take the job, Mr. Berry promised the boys he would. Art and Darrell then went home. The next day, Art went to see Sheriff Wright and told him, "Todd Berry told us he'll work for you in the Naples area."

Sheriff Wright assured Art, "I'll definitely hire Todd if I get the appointment." Art then returned to his home with a good feeling about the situation.

Art and Darrell discussed the fact they had taken over two weeks to try and stop Lassiter. Darrell said, "It's almost worse than fighting him."

Art said, "But when we fight Lassiter, we have to kill people. If we stop him from this appointment, Lassiter will surely come after us." On February twentieth, ex-sheriff Wright was appointed head of northeast Texas's new state police force. Wright rode out and confirmed that ex-Texas ranger, Todd Berry, would work with him. After a week, Berry moved an office to the courthouse in Naples. The boys were to meet him in Naples as he needed to appoint a black deputy. The boys recommended their good black friends, either Robert or Sherman.

Todd rode out to the black community that had grown to forty homes and about two hundred people. Robert and Sherman wanted to split the job since it paid $240.00 a year for a part-time police officer. Berry told them, "Come to my office next week for two days of training."

They replied, "We'll be there next Thursday at eight o'clock in the morning."

Berry explained to Robert and Sherman, "You'll get paid at the end of each month and you will start March first ." Robert and Sherman were glad to have the money as it was somewhat steady and farming was seasonal, plus the fact that it was a prestige thing being in the state police. They were also afraid of the whites that would want to harm them, or their families. Art, Darrell, and Todd all had lunch with the two black families. The boys pledged their support. Todd told the boys, "I plan to use the local sheriff Bass and his deputies to help control the area."

He also warned the boys, "You'll need to be careful and watchful for Lassiter."

CHAPTER 27

It was now the first of March and time for everyone to start thinking about planting, but it was still wet and colder than usual. Darrell had not been able to harvest his oats, and that was a serious problem. The crop wasn't going to be great, but all of Art's farms needed this to feed their horses and mules, which numbered about 65 head. Of course, Darrell had the largest problem because he had 125 head with his horses and mules. On March fifteenth, Art, Darrell, Mr. Shaw, Onnie, Mr. Jenson, and sons Paul and John all helped Darrell harvest the oat crop. After six days of long hours, they had finished harvesting the oats, and Darrell got Joe and Jed to begin hauling four wagonloads to all of Art's farms. Darrell said, "We have about sixteen loads of oats left, and I'll need that to take care of my horse herd."

It was planting time, and everyone was in the fields plowing, harrowing, and getting ready to plant corn. The only exception was Darrell who was on guard duty and worried about Lassiter. Several days later, Art, Mr. Jenson and son Paul, Mr. Shaw, and Onnie had 130 acres ready to plant corn. Planting of corn was finished by March twenty-fifth. Mr. Shaw and Onnie then began to plant 30 acres each of cotton. Onnie, Mr. Shaw, and Paul Jenson had made a separate deal with Art to plant 30 acres of cotton on his farm they lived on. Everyone had their cotton planted by April fifteenth, and by then it was time to harrow the weeds and grass out of the corn. The corn was all weeded by April twenty-fifth, and it was then time to start weeding the cotton.

It appeared Mr. Shaw was going to marry the widow Lucas and move to her farm. Onnie wanted, in the worst way, to buy the old Shaw place, but Art didn't want to sell it to him. He said, "I have a spot of six hundred acres on the north side of the Sulphur River I'll sell you."

Onnie said, "The only way I would buy it is to have a barge that could cross the Sulphur."

Everyone pitched in and built a barge that could hold a wagon and team or ten head of stock and was easily pulled back and forth on the river. Art estimated this barge might last three years, but it satisfied Onnie. When his cotton was sold, he was going to buy the 600 acres and a special barn the boys sold from their sawmill, for twelve hundred dollars. When he wasn't working on Art's, Mr. Shaw's, or his own crops, he was across the river, clearing land and making corrals and pens for working stock. He had also fenced 30 acres for pastures. The boys were impressed with how well he had worked.

Art knew he needed to begin planning a cattle drive for next year, but he and Darrell knew they could lose everything. Lassiter would have all of their land, stock, and equipment if one of them was not guarding. Darrell said, "I have seen big herds of two thousand-plus head this past spring going north, probably going to Kansas."

Mr. Shaw and Onnie had been living in the old Loggings' farmhouse since the Indians had burned the old Shaw place. Art and Darrell were aware things would change in the fall. Mr. Shaw was going to marry the widow Lucas and buy six hundred acres beside her twelve hundred acres, which would mean they had eighteen hundred acres to farm. Mr. Shaw would only be available to work at the sawmill part time. It was a good thing Mr. Jenson and his son Paul had taken over his duties with the boys. Onnie was buying six hundred acres on the north side of Art's land on the Sulphur River and building a barn that was also going to be his house. He was seventeen and would be on his own. Joe and Jed were going to marry Ashley and Sara Lucas. They had their own twelve hundred acres with a new barn where both couples were going to live. Charles Rogers was going to marry Katelyn Yeiser.

He had been courting her since February. They were going to live on Charles's twelve hundred acres outside of Marietta.

Art was going to build a rock house and a good barn on the old Shaw farm and let the Jenson family live there and sharecrop on this land. These poor people had been living in the office at the sawmill for over eighteen months. During the summer, the house and barn were finished on the Shaw place, and the Jensons moved in the last of August. Mr. Jenson was planning on a corn and cotton crop next year. He was also going to run about twenty sows or gilts. He knew he could get in the hog business cheaper than other livestock, and there was a lot of demand for hogs in the area.

CHAPTER 28

Art and Darrell had been left alone by all the rustlers, diseases, and other hardships. The crops were good due to the right amount of rain at the right time. The boys and their families and friends had gone to three summer dances and church picnics every other weekend. Sharon, Velma, Mrs. Jenson and daughter Sue, Mrs. Lucas, Ashley, Sara, Mrs. McCoy and daughter, Katelyn Yeiser, Haylee, Louis's wife and daughter, and Sharon's parents had all taken a steamboat trip from Bryans Mill to Texarkana for a two-day shopping spree there. Art and Darrell had paid the two hundred dollar cost of the trip. Everyone had living arrangements on the boat. Art made arrangement of everyone to have breakfast every morning on the paddle wheeler. There was even a play being held at a tavern that everyone attended and very much enjoyed.

The shopping was intense, and Art had to loan money to some of the women. Velma and several others wanted to buy a chest of drawers and other furniture. Art stopped them because they could buy those items locally made by people in their home area.

The local people needed the work and money. In fact, Art changed the minds of several people buying furniture, beds, chairs, and tables. Many of those merchants got mad at Art for telling the people not to buy. The women still bought about two thousand dollars' worth of products. Art had reluctantly agreed to go because the boys thought that many good-looking women together could cause quite a stir. The only trouble Art had was at the tavern when a man grabbed Sharon and another grabbed Katelyn and pulled them onto their laps trying to kiss them. Art moved quickly, clubbing both men with his gun and disarmed them. Everyone in that group quickly moved out.

Before leaving Texarkana, the two men Art had clubbed at the tavern called Art out while they were shopping. Everyone told him not to go, but Art sent Velma to get the sheriff and then told Sharon and her mother to take shotguns and make sure some of these toughs' buddies weren't going to shoot him in the back. Art gave them five minutes to get into position and in about ten minutes, he proceeded to go outside to face the two men. The men began to mouth Art about what they were going to do to him.

Art said, "I'm tired of your mouth, go ahead and draw so I can kill you." He continued, "You're just a bunch of yellow cowards and afraid to draw."

Meanwhile, Sharon had seen a man behind Art, with a rifle aimed at him. She let go with both barrels of the shotgun. She didn't kill him, but several of the shotgun pellets went into his back, and it really scared him. Art went over to where the man laid and said, "You were going to shoot me in the back."

He nodded yes and asked Art, "Am I going to die?"

"No," answered Art, "but you should!"

About that time, the sheriff came running up with Velma. She had told him the whole story, and he promptly arrested the two men who had called Art out and the hurt man who was going to shoot Art in the back. Art told the men, "If I ever see you again, I'll kill you."

This was to be the last night they were in Texarkana, but the sheriff said, "Can you stay tomorrow because court is in session and I want a quick trial? I'll need all of you that were here to testify tomorrow."

Art got rooms for himself, Velma, Sharon, and Katelyn so they could stay over and testify. Art said, "We'll take the stage to Bryans Mill Marietta cut off. Tell Darrell to pick us up there at four o'clock." The next day, the paddle wheel took off, with the others of the party, for Bryans Mill. It took four hours to arrive at Bryans Mill at four o'clock in the afternoon. When Darrell found out the trial would be the next morning, he hooked up the two-seated buggy and his horse on the back and was on his way to Texarkana. He arrived at four o'clock in the morning and he was ready to shoot somebody. The sheriff and prosecuting attorney went for breakfast the morning of the trial, and everyone went over and rehearsed their story for the prosecuting attorney. He said, "If they want to prosecute Sharon for shooting the man, then I'll prosecute him for attempted murder."

The trial began, and the three men were complaining about the injustice of it all. After the prosecutor had everyone else's testimony, the three men that were charged got up and lied about everything. They were trying to change the whole story. They denied grabbing Sharon and Katelyn. The judge said, "I was there and saw what happened. You men started it, and Sharon's husband handled it the correct way. You three did exactly what these others witnesses said you did."

The jury took twenty minutes to find all three guilty and recommend they all be sentenced to six months in jail and fined one hundred dollars each. If they couldn't pay the fine, they would have to stay in jail for nine months. The prisoners were mouthing the group, and Art told them, "Remember if I see you anywhere, I'm going to kill you." None of the prisoners had the money to pay their fine, so all three were sentenced to nine months in jail. The sheriff was really upset because he was going to have to put up with those three characters for nine months, and he wasn't sure he could do that. All of Art's crew thanked the attorney and the sheriff for all their help. After the trial, Art's group had lunch, and then departed from Texarkana in the buggy with Art driving and the other ladies also in the two-seated buggy. Darrell was riding along on his horse. They all vowed to never return to Texarkana.

They arrived at their homes in the Bryans Mill area by seven o'clock, and everyone was glad to see them. Darrell told Trixie and Mae, "I'll take you home in the morning." They were okay with that.

The next day, Darrell took Trixie and Mae home, which was north of Naples. Darrell had lunch with Robert, Sherman, Trixie, and Mae. Robert and Sherman told Darrell, "We need some oats to feed our horses and mules." They hitched up their wagon and drove behind Darrell when he returned to his home. It was about four o'clock in the afternoon. Robert and Sherman loaded their wagon with oats and started on the trip home. They arrived home at about 8 p.m.

CHAPTER 29

That evening, Darrell and Art had time to talk. The next day was Saturday. Art had time to look over his stock and the crops. On Sunday, he visited Mr. Jenson, Ed, and Louis. They wanted to talk about planting cotton next year on the shares. They could see the sharecroppers were making extra money which would allow them some day to get their own farms. Art promised Louis, Mr. Jenson, and Ed, "You can plant thirty acres each next year if it looks like cotton will sell at a good price." He told them, "We need to cut fifty logs each before we start harvesting. Ed, will you find out if Joe or Jed have any logs?" As it turned out, they had twenty logs on the ground.

The next Sunday, everyone went to church and the social dinner afterward.

Art and Darrell rested on Monday, and Art went over to see the furniture maker named Bohannon. Bohannon was a pleasant man, hard worker but strictly a business man and not a mean bone in his body. Art said. "I think if you would come over to the Bryans Mill area and bring samples, you could sell a lot of furniture."

Bohannon said, "I'll bring samples over in the next two weeks and see if any of the wives want to buy anything like I make."

When Bohannon came over to visit the farmers and ranchers in the Bryans Mill-Marietta area, he brought a sample of a table, a couple of chairs, one chest of drawers, one kitchen chest, one bench, and two beds. He sold all that and got orders for three more tables, eight chairs, two chests of drawers, two kitchen chests, and four bed frames. The ten families that ordered from him were really pleased with the quality of the furniture that he built and the price. Bohannon was also very pleased with the sales he had made. The people who tried to shop in Texarkana for furniture figured altogether saved about five thousand dollars buying from Bohannon in place of the furniture shops in Texarkana. Their husbands were also well pleased about the money savings.

On the week before the harvest started, there were four weddings that took place in the Bryans Mill Church. Joe and Jed married the Lucas sisters, Ashley and Sarah respectively. Mr. Shaw married Ms. Lucas and Charles Rogers, Sharon's brother, married Katelyn Yeiser, the daughter of the local school teacher that was killed during the Indian raid. Also next week, Onnie was going to marry Katie, whose father farmed next to Art's farmer friend, Ed Wright, south of Naples.

CHAPTER 30

Harvest was started on the corn crop, which looked good and in four weeks, the corn harvest was complete. Art had two hundred acres, and he figured he had eight thousand bushels. Art, Paul, and Onnie would fill a wagon up with corn as they harvested. As soon as the wagon was full, Art would take a load directly to his other farms or to Darrell's. This saved double-handling of the corn, and they already hauled four wagonloads to his own five farms or to Darrell's farm. The deliveries were made with four mules pulling two wagonloads. On October first, everyone in the area began picking cotton and was finished by October 31. Art had netted about six thousand dollars from his share of the cotton harvest. Mr. Shaw, Onnie, and Paul made two thoushand dollars each for their portion of the sharecroppers' cotton.

Onnie immediately paid for the land north of the Sulphur River that he had bought from Art, and also paid for the barn he had purchased at the sawmill. Three days later, the community got together and had a barn raising for Onnie. This would give him and his new wife a place to live while he was building up his farm. Art and Paul began delivering six loads of corn to Gene McCoy's store. This took six days. Art told Mr. McCoy, "I won't deliver any more corn until January." That seemed okay with him. Art still had promised him five more loads of corn. Two of those loads would go to Mr. McCoy's farm. He also had to deliver five more loads to each of his own farms.

Before Art could complete all his deliveries, it was Christmas time. All the people that Art and Darrell worked with came to Art's home for a big Christmas party. All the children received great gifts because the crops had been good. Art and Sharon gave Art Jr. a horse and a new tack to go with it. He immediately wanted to ride out by himself and check all the cattle and stock. That activity was stopped because of their guests. Forty-five people attended the party, and most of them arrived at 10 a.m. and left at 4 p.m. It was almost dark at that time. The group enjoyed several games such as competitive shooting, checkers, dominos, sack races, some singing groups, and of course, a great meal.

Between Christmas and New Years Day, they had a cold ice storm, and no one in the area was prepared. Everyone was doing the best they could to get the stock to protected areas so that they could feed them ear corn. Art had put most of his hay by the protective sheds. You could not even ride horses because it was so icy.

They had to ride mules, but of course they were able to pull the wagons. It was a terrible week to get around the farms and get the stock fed. Art now had over one thousand head of cattle that were over one year old.

Art and Darrell discussed another trail drive north to get top dollar for their cattle with the guests at the party. Joe and Jed had 100 head, the Anthonys one hundred, the Simmons brothers 400, Mr. Shaw and his new wife 200, Mr. Rogers and Charles had 200, Ace had 100, and Robert and Sherman together 140 heads. Art was planning to take 1000 head of his own. It was going to be hard to get enough cowboys to take approximately 2,300 head of cattle to Kansas and the railroad head. Art told Charles and Darrell, "Not only will we have trouble getting enough cowboys for the drive, one of us will need to stay here and protect our property from attack." They realized they would have to leave May first, and the trip would take about seventy days.

Darrell said, "Art, you know if you could get Robert, Sherman, Mae, and Trixie to go, their wives could do the cooking, and of course, Robert and Sherman are good hands."

Art said, "It would be a big help if I could have Charles and a scout along, except through Indian Territory, but I don't think Charles wants to leave this new wife, Katelyn."

"I can't say I blame him," said Darrell. "She's a beauty. Art, you know Sharon is going to throw a fit."

Art said, "Well you know, Darrell, so is Velma." Whoever stayed behind was going to have to protect the farms and work the crops for everyone that went on the drive. Art could only think of himself, Robert, Sherman, Ace, Onnie, Paul Jenson, Mae, and Trixie.

Darrell said, "We would have a lot of help until we got you across the red, and then if you had ten Indians along with the other six or seven people going through Indian Territory, you would have enough to do the drive. I could stay here," he continued, "and in forty days, I could take a stagecoach up to the Indian Territory-Kansas line and help with the final leg of the drive."

Art said, "We'd better start preparing, and I'll go over to talk to Robert and Sherman tomorrow."

The next day, Art went over and talked to Robert, Sherman, Mae, and Trixie about the cattle drive. They were all anxious to go and assured Art that the ladies could handle the cooking, and Robert and Sherman would be good cowboys. They wanted to see that part of the country and also had seventy heads of cattle each to take on the drive. The boys decided anyone who was not going on the drive but sending cattle would have to pay them three dollars a head for selling their cattle for them. Art knew he had to make a trip up into Indian Territory to recruit ten Choctaw Indians to help with the cattle drive. The Indians would join them at the Red River. Art figured it would take at least three horses per cowboy for this drive, horses which he didn't have. He would have to convince the Indians to bring enough horses for them, and then pay them for the use of their horses on the drive. Everyone could help get the livestock across the Red River, and then those not going could return home. That would take at least six days.

The next Sunday, all the folks went to Sunday school, church and the afternoon feed, and social. Art was surprised to see Onnie and his wife with Onnie's sister, Ion, and her two-year-old son with Mr. Shaw and his new wife, Ms. Lucas. As they were all eating in their different areas, Art went over to see all the Shaw clan. Ion asked Art, "Does Sharon know about me?"

Art said, "Yes I told her everything."

Ion said, "I'm coming over to meet her when you return back to your group."

Art and Darrell had told very few people about the pending cattle drive because they didn't want anyone to know, especially Lassiter. As soon as Art returned to his family, Ion came over to meet Sharon. She told Sharon, "Art was my first boyfriend."

Sharon replied, "Oh yes, he told me all about you."

Ion, now Mrs. Lassiter, did not like the tone of her comment. Ion continued, "I don't know how y'all stand it living out in this godforsaken country, which is so desolate and with no friends. We enjoy almost two parties a week, one in our home and another at one of our prominent friend's home. Our house has sixteen rooms, is colonial style with four pillars. I have a housekeeper, cook, and yard man." She asked Art, "How are your mom, dad, and sister?"

Art explained, "My dad died six weeks after you left the area, and my mother remarried the following March. They live on Mr. Martin's plantation in Red Oak, Louisiana. Your dad and brother were great support for my mother and sister when my dad died. They've been great neighbors, and I think they've done well, especially after the war." Ion was really getting mad, and this was exactly what Art wanted. He couldn't wait until she left.

As Ion began to walk away she said, "You thought things were great when you were trying to get over to my house every chance you got to see me."

Art replied, "Ion, you were always ready." He continued, "You've been living in Naples well over two years. Why haven't you come to see your dad and brother before now?"

She did not answer and went back over to the Shaw group's picnic area. The preacher came over and asked, "Art, what was that all about?"

"Oh" Art answered, "Ion was just trying to cause trouble for me."

Mr. Shaw and Onnie came over and told Art, "We think you've always treated us fairly and consider you more of a friend than our daughter and sister."

Art assured them, "Nothing has changed. Don't worry about it." Art did worry though as Ion and her husband just could cause a lot of problems, especially if they knew Art was going to be gone a long time on a cattle drive. Again, Art warned Mr. Shaw and Onnie, "Do not tell Ion anything about the cattle drive because her husband will find out and know when to attack our farms."

CHAPTER 31

The boys found out Lassiter's next move as he began building a new and more modern sawmill in Naples with the intent of running Art's and Darrell's sawmill out of business. During the next six weeks, the boys were busy cutting enough lumber and brick for six houses and six barns. They had no longer finished their sawmilling business when they found out Lassiter was opening his sawmill April first. There wasn't anything the boys could do to stop Lassiter from opening his sawmill.

All of the farmers, including Art and Darrell, were plowing, harrowing, and planting corn. The boys had one half of the corn crop planted, and it was now March 30. Late that night, around eleven thirty, three riders had come to the boy's sawmill. They tried to damage the sawmill equipment and start fires, burning the wood parts of the sawmill, but the boys were lucky as Darrell was about one half mile away out in the pasture with a sick horse. He thought he heard horses and other noises over at the sawmill and went to investigate. He found the three men had already set fire to the office building and stored lumber. They were also using large sledge hammers, trying to damage the machinery. Darrell shot twice, hitting two men and when the third tried to ride off, Darrell shot his horse.

Darrell shot and shot until Sharon woke Art up and said, "I hear something that sounds like shots coming from the sawmill." Art headed for the sawmill and arrived about fifteen minutes after the shooting was all over.

Art told Darrell, "I'll go get the state police." Art knew that was Todd Berry, the ex-Texas ranger, and he would get Dr. Lilly to come out for the wounded men. When state policeman Captain Berry arrived, he questioned the three men for a couple of hours and could not get them to talk. Art said, "Captain Berry, why don't you go over and look at the damage at the office while Darrell and I question these arsonists?"

Art and Darrell staked out the three thugs on the ground. Art had captured two live rattlesnakes several days before. He showed the men the cage and the snakes, and he told them, "I'm going to release the snakes if you don't talk." They still would not talk, so Art opened the cage. When the snakes began crawling out of the cage near the men, they all began screaming that they would tell them what they wanted to know. Art successfully put the snakes back in the cage.

Darrell said, "You're going to fool around with those snakes and get bitten and die." One of the snakes had come within two feet of one of the wounded toughs, and he was really scared!

When Captain Berry came back and started questioning the three men, he found out they had each been paid one hundred dollars from one of Lassiter's foremen named Jelly. Captain Berry then took the three toughs to jail and put them in cells away from all the other jail cells. Not even the sheriff or other deputies knew the toughs were in jail. Berry then went to Lassiter's farm and arrested his foreman, Jelly, putting him in jail with the other three toughs. No one really knew where these men were. He quietly got all the paperwork ready for the charges that would be filed against these four men, knowing the court would be in session through next week. Captain Berry wanted these men tried before court went into recess for two months. Foreman Jelly of course denied everything.

Berry was even the one getting food for those prisoners at times when no one would see him or them. He got away with it because there was an old jail behind the new jail, and no other police went in or out of there. He then sent for his two black deputies, Robert and Sherman, and swore them to secrecy while hiding them in the old jail. Art and Darrell as usual took all the money, horses, and tack for those horses from the three toughs that had tried to burn their sawmill.

The following Friday morning, the judge had the four in court and set their bail at twenty-five hundred dollars each. Lassiter was going to have to post bond and bail to get them out of jail. Their trial was called for two o'clock that afternoon. Lassiter had not even had time to get the foreman and the three toughs out of jail on bond. They were escorted to the courtroom, and all toughs identified the foreman Jelly as the man who had paid them and told them to destroy Art and Darrell's sawmill. After all of the testimony, the case was given to the jury, and they found the men guilty as charged. The three toughs were sentenced to three years, only because they named Foreman Jelly, who got ten years in prison and ordered to pay five thousand dollars in fines, or jail time would double. Lassiter was going to have to have enough money to put up five thousand dollars for Jelly, plus pay him a lot of money to keep his mouth shut. At the time Lassiter, could not get his hands on that kind of money. Lassiter bribed the sheriff to keep the prisoners in the Naples jail for at least six months so that he could try to get the money together. At six o'clock that night, Foreman Jelly asked to see the judge and state policeman Berry. He said, "I'll make a statement in front of a jury that Lassiter had asked me to hire somebody to destroy the boys' sawmill."

The judge said, "If you'll testify against Lassiter, I'll reduce your sentence to three years in jail, but you will still have to pay five thousand dollars in fines." Mr. Jelly made a statement, and Captain Berry arrested Lassiter that night, and the judge would be able to set bail the next Tuesday. The Court would not be in session again until May first.

Lassiter's bond was set at ten thousand dollars. That meant he was going to have to now come up with twenty thousand dollars. He did have over one hundred highly bred horses and called for Mark Anthony to come see him. When Mr. Anthony arrived, Lassiter sold him one hundred horses for ten thousand dollars cash. Ion got the horses together and got the money from the Anthony boys. On their way home, the Anthonys sold fifty of the horses to Art, Darrell, Joe, Jed, Gene McCoy, Charles, and Lewis Rogers. The Anthony boys then took the other fifty good horses home and hid them. Lassiter was of course out of jail on bond and was in a hurry to leave the state so he didn't have to stand trial. Lassiter gave the new sawmill to Ion and began selling his cattle and farms. Art bought one hundred head of great cows for only nine dollars each. The Simmons brothers bought five thousand acres from Lassiter for ten thousand dollars. He then told Ion, "You're going to have to run the rest of the twenty-thousand-acre ranch." He then left for Arizona. When the trial was called in May, he was not there; however, they tried him anyway. He was sentenced to ten years in jail, and the court put out a wanted poster with two thousand dollars reward for him, dead or alive.

Art and Darrell knew this would mean guard duty since they were beginning to gather the heard for the drive north to Abilene. Onnie had come to see Darrell and said, "Ion wants you to take fifteen hundred head of Lassiter's cattle on the drive."

Darrell told Onnie, "Tell Ion no."

Mr. Shaw and Onnie went to Art, and he said, "I'll do it if she'll send ten cowboys and pay me and Darrell three dollars a head. Also, Onnie, you'll have to be the one in charge of her cattle and the money received when the cattle are sold. The money is to be turned over to you, not me or Darrell." Art even had the judge draw up papers and have Ion and Onnie sign them.

She said, "Well, I could drive them myself for a lot less than three dollars a head and ten cowboys." Art and Darrell told her, "Go ahead and do it." She decided to stick with the deal. Darrell said, "Art, no wonder she's so mean to you."

CHAPTER 32

After the crops had been planted, Art took a trip up to see his Choctaw friends in Indian Territory. After telling the chief all about the cattle drive, the chief said, "I will be glad to help by sending ten braves including Hawk, Straight Arrow, and Running Bear." The chief also promised, "I will sell you enough oats to feed the mules and horses for four weeks on this cattle drive."

Art asked, "Hawk, will you scout the area going north that will give us the least trouble with the other Indian tribes and settlers? And also find out what you can about the herds going up to Abilene."

Hawk told Art, "We have probably 250 head we want to take to Abilene."

Art readily agreed to take their cattle also. Art said, "Hawk, you had better have ten Indians ready to work hard on this drive."

Hawk also asked, "Do they need to provide their own horses? I think we can provide thirty horses for our people driving the herd."

Art was worried about the drive in Kansas that would go to Abilene because many of the farmers had given trail herds a lot of trouble. The boys certainly didn't want that.

Hawk assured Art, "I will try to talk to some of the cowboys coming back from Abilene and find out what I can."

Art spent the night with Hawk and his family. All the Indians now had their own farms and seemed to be doing okay. Hawk told Art, "There are still many people bitter about the Civil War and the Trail of Tears. That could cause us trouble."

He answered, "Meet us at the usual Red River crossing on May twentieth. I'll have plenty of help crossing the Red, then nine of the cowboys helping to cross the Red River will be returning to their homes."

Hawk assured Art, "I understand what the cattle drive needs and the route information I must collect."

Art then departed for the Red River and his ranch on the Sulphur River.

About a week before the cattle drive was to start, Ion told Art, "My cowboys and I are going to drive Lassiter's cattle to Abilene by ourselves."

"Okay," he said. "That will probably be better." After the boys crossed the Sulphur River driving the herd toward the Red River, they discovered Ion and her herd was about two miles behind them. Ion did everything she could to hire Onnie and the blacks to help her. Art finally told her, "If you or your men come to my camp anymore, they will be shot."

Darrell and Ace were scouting ahead the four days it took to reach the Red. It took a day to cross the Red with 2,240 head. Ion's herd tried to cross in another place and lost about twenty-five cows in the quicksand. It also took her two days to cross the Red. Art told Hawk, "Get your people their wagons and take those dead cows to your friends. They will be good food for them." It was obvious Ion's reason for trying to cross the Red downstream was to get ahead of Art's herd. Ion's herd and herders rested a day after crossing the river. That put Art's herd about twelve miles ahead of them.

After seven days, his herd arrived at the Indian town, and he told the chief about the Ion-herd problem. The chief, "I'll take twenty-five men out and make them pay fifty cents a head for crossing Choctaw land." Twenty-five Indians in war paint and heavily armed surrounded Ion's herd. All of her cowboys were afraid, and Ion paid the Chief $750.00.

She only had about $1,000.00 left. Ion told the chief, "Art has a large herd also crossing your land."

The chief said, "He is our friend and is always helping us." This made her madder and more determined to drive her herd to Kansas.

After five more days, the herd was out of Choctaw territory and crossing Creek and Seminole land without permission, which took three more days. Of course, the Creek Indians found out. Art and Hawk went to talk to the Creek Chief. After listening to their story, the chief asked Art, "Will you take fifty head of cattle for us to Abilene?"

"Okay" he said, "if you will send a couple of Indians to help with the drive." The two Indians turned out to be pretty good cowboys. The chief made it very clear his boys were to take orders from Art. Art asked the chief, "Do you have some horse and mule feed you could sell us?"

"I can sell you enough to last a week," the chief said. Art promptly paid the chief $100.00 and loaded the feed.

The herd was now in Cherokee territory, and they were met by some other people who told them where to drive the cattle to avoid trouble. It would take Art's herd ten days in Cherokee territory. The Indian scouts told Art. "Ion's herd is four days behind, and she had to give the Creek Indians fifty head of cattle for crossing their territory."

Ion had sent word she was giving up and wanted to join herds and honor the original agreement. She now had only 1,400 cattle left. Art found this extremely amusing. The hands found a three-hundred-acre meadow close to the Kansas border, and Art said, "We will wait two days here for Ion's herd to join us." Her herd was able to merge with them in three days.

Ion told Art, "I'm going to a stage station in Oklahoma and go back to Naples." Art sent Onnie and Paul to go with her and make sure she got to the stage okay. She really didn't like Art sending someone to help her. Before she left her cowboys, she informed them, "You're all to take orders from Art and help him all you can."

Right after Art and the herd crossed the Kansas state line, Ace, who had been doing their scouting, met up with them and said, "We're okay for at least the next forty miles." He drew a map for Art to follow.

Darrell had taken the stage from Naples to Oklahoma and bought a horse at the Oklahoma stage stop area to ride out and meet with Art and the herd. The second day in Kansas, Onnie and Ace had gone up past the forty miles to explore the best route to take to avoid trouble. Art told Darrell, "Let's wait until Onnie and Ace get back, and you can take a turn with Ace on this route scouting." One of Ion's riders was a lot of help, and a great cowboy on the drive. His name was Arch, and he wasn't even a foreman.

Ace returned when the herd was ten miles from Wichita. Art sent Arch, Ace, Trixie, and Mae to Wichita to buy supplies they needed for the rest of the trip. They each rode horses and took two mules to put the supplies on. Onnie drove the chuck wagon while Mae and Trixie were gone. The four were gone for nine hours when they caught up with the herd. Arch and Ace said, "We had a little trouble with a couple of the local boys, and we probably better double the guard tonight."

Darrell asked, "Any killing, shooting, or fighting?"

"No," said Ace, "but they sure called us a lot of bad names and threatened the whole herd." Darrell set up the guards and then set up extra guards further out, trying to locate them on higher ground. Sure enough, fifteen men rode out to the herd. Before anybody could do anything, Darrell was in front of these men and five yards behind him were Art, Ace, and Arch. On the left-hand side, there were three other cowboys.

The spokesman for the Wichita group said, "We don't like you Texas-rebel cowboys coming up here and taking over and crossing over our territory. So we're going to shoot you and several of those steers."

Darrell said, "Now, we can shoot it out right here and at least several of your men will die, or get wounded. But I got a better idea, loudmouth. You and I will shoot it out, and we won't have near as many casualties. I'll remind you there are ten repeater rifles aimed at your group right now."

"No" said the Wichita group. "Let Neely fight. He's faster."

"Okay," said Darrell. "If loudmouth liar here doesn't have the guts to fight me, then have Neely do his fighting."

Neely came up to Darrell and said, "May I talk to you in private?" When they stepped away from earshot of everybody, he said, "I saw you delivering horses and cattle to the Union at Fort Gibson one month before the end of the Civil War, you saved our bacon. I don't want to fight you, but these men from Wichita want a fight."

Darrell said, "Why don't we shake hands where everyone can see us, and you go back to your group and tell that those two Johnny Rebs could have killed you during the war and didn't?"

Neely said to his cowboy posse, "I recognized Art and Darrell right off and suggest we let them go on with their herd and forget about this fight. They not only saved my life but others at Fort Gibson."

All of them said okay except for the loudmouth. The other fourteen began turning around, leaving him alone to face the boys and their helpers.

Darrell said, "I suggest you go join your posse." Loudmouth then turned his horse around and galloped after his posse.

It was now ten o'clock at night. Art said, "We need to get this herd to the river nine miles away and get across it by ten o'clock in the morning." They pushed those cattle hard and were ready to start crossing the herd at 5 a.m. In five hours, the entire herd of cattle, along with the horses, was across the river. Art posted lookouts, sending a man two miles south and also two miles north of the river they had just crossed. Trixie prepared a big steer with potatoes and tomatoes which was eaten by all. Darrell posted guards, and the boys and herders relaxed all afternoon.

About seven o'clock, Neely came riding into the camp and told the boys the route they should take to Abilene. Art said, "How much would it take for you to show us the way? Would you do it for one hundred Union dollars?"

Neely said, "Yes, but I need to return and tell my parents that I'll be gone fifteen days as I live with them." He was back, reaching the herd about noon the next day and began scouting ahead. He returned about eight o'clock that evening and showed the boys the route they should take the next twenty miles. The herd was actually on the Chisholm Trail Westside. The route to take on the Chisholm was dependant on the terrain and farmer's attitude on which side you trailed. The boys followed Neely's directions for the next two days, and the herd moved twenty-three more miles during that time. Everyone's spirits was lifted. Neely returned that evening and said, "There is one more river and one more stream to cross in the next fifty miles." After four days, when they were a half mile from the Abilene stockyard, the boys posted guards and prayed nothing would happen that night, and nothing did.

Art figured he had lost 30 head of cattle. Other owners in the herd had also lost cattle. Ion had started with 1,500 head and only had 1,335 left. Art accepted a bid of twenty dollars per head after rejecting two other bids of nineteen dollars and nineteen fifty. The next morning, everyone began moving cattle into the stockyards and actually loaded twenty-five stock cars where the train engine was ready to take them to Chicago for slaughter. When all the cattle were in the cattle cars or the stockyard, Art, Darrell, Ace, Onnie, Hawk, and Buffalo, one of the Creek Indians with the drive, went to the buyer's headquarters in Abilene to collect the money for their stock. Everyone was in high spirits.

Darrell had rented a home in Abilene for two days that had five rooms and a kitchen. They all looked the town over until six, then met at a tavern that had good food. Everyone ate plenty! Darrell, Ace, Ed, Onnie, and Neely went out on the town, leaving their money with Art. The boys posted four Indian guards from eight to twelve, and four other Indian guards from twelve to five. The ones that had gone out on the town got home at two o'clock in the morning. Art had given the Creek Indians two Sharps carbines that were loaded, and you would have thought he had given them a million dollars. The next morning at eight o'clock, Art had sold the chuck wagon but not the mules. His plan was to have the mules take their supplies on the trip home. That way, they would be able to return to Sulphur River more quickly. When Art returned to the house, he told Darrell, "I want to get started today. If you don't want to go today, then you can follow tomorrow with the ones that want to stay and have a good time in Abilene." After talking with everyone, it was decided they would try to leave by ten o'clock that morning. Everyone including Darrell was ready. They got needed supplies and packed as best they could.

Before leaving, Art wanted to give the money for each group's cattle to that representative, and he also wanted to pay each man the promised wages. He presently had $74,360.00 on him from the sale of that trail herd. He paid Neely $100.00, Ace $200.00, Ed $200.00, Onnie $200.00, Paul $200.00, Robert, Sherman, Mae, and Trixie $900.00, Hawk and nine other Choctaw herders $3,000.00, they received more because they furnished their own horses and finally the two Creek Indian herders $50.00 each. That was a total of $4,900.00 in wages. Since Art had charged $3.00 a head for Ion's herd and $3.00 a head for the Simmons brothers' herd that was a total of $5,175.00, which more than took care of paying the helpers.

Art immediately gave all of Ion's cattle money to her brother Onnie and made him sign a paper that he had received the money and was responsible for it. Art would pay the others when they returned home. This was more money than any of these good old boys had ever seen!

Everyone on the trip knew they would have to go home military-style in order to fight off even a large number of robbers who by now knew this group had a lot of money and it would be worthwhile to see if they could rob them. They rode two abreast, five yards apart and ten yards in between each double rider. The first two days, Neely scouted ahead approximately one half mile in front of the group. The fourth day, Hawk became the point man and would continue until they got out of Indian Territory. When they left Kansas Territory, Neely left them, shook hands with everyone and said, "Come back when you can."

Art said, "You're also welcome to come to Texas anytime."

The fourth day of the trip, they covered seventy-five miles and made camp about eight o'clock. When they crossed into Oklahoma Territory and Creek, Seminole area, the Creek chief came out to meet the group and his Indians that had helped on the drive. He was glad to get the $980.00 for the forty-nine head of cattle that had been driven to Abilene, but was really pleased when Art gave him a loaded Henry rifle. He tried desperately to get the group to stay there for the evening, but Art said, "We're all anxious to get home to our families."

That day, they covered ten more miles after they left the Creek town. Unknown to the group, the Creek chief had sent two braves to help them if they needed it. The Indians had stayed well behind and out of sight but came into the camp to sleep and eat that evening. They told Darrell, "We will ride with you for one half the day tomorrow and then return to our homes." When the group started, they had one extra horse per man, plus the six mules. They could ride on a mule in a pinch if needed. On the tenth day of their trip home, they entered the Choctaw village of Hawk and his fellow Indians. There was a great party that night, celebrating the trail drive success. The next morning, Darrell, Ed, Ace, Onnie, Paul, Robert, Sherman, Trixie, Mae, Ion's cowboys, and Art again started on the trip home. This time, they were also in military formation with each group ten yards away from the other riders.

Hawk and Running Bear were accompanying them to the Red River. When they were about twenty-five miles from the Red, ten shots rang out in less than a minute. Everyone took cover in a gully where they could protect themselves, their horses, and their mules.

Robert and Sherman quickly shot two rattlesnakes that were also in the gully threatening them. It was midday and very hot, but they had plenty of water and ammunition. In the field of fire from the gully, it was clear on all four sides except for five pine trees in each direction. They built several shelters to protect the group from the hot sun. When nightfall came, Hawk and Running Bear rode out to assess the situation but found no one. The attackers had obviously gone on, and no one felt safe staying there overnight thinking that these attackers might come back with help. They got the group together and left, getting to the Red River at eight o'clock the next morning. Hawk and Running Bear left to return to their people. Art and Darrell were extremely grateful for all their help. During the six years of knowing these Indians, they had always enthusiastically helped the boys.

CHAPTER 33

Art and Darrell wanted to push on for at least ten more miles and stop to rest at that time and continue on the next morning. That would give the animals time to rest, so that is exactly what they did. The next morning, Robert, Sherman, Trixie and Mae, along with Ion's cowboys, left the group to go to their homes just north of Naples. Everyone else continued their trip and about ten miles from Sulphur River, they were attacked by a number of gunmen that seemed well organized and pretty good shots. At that time, there was only Onnie, Ed, Ace, Paul, Darrell, and Art. They were backed up to a small hill, and it was going to be tough to protect that position. Onnie and Paul had already been wounded by the attackers, and after attending to their arm wounds, Darrell decided to make a run for an area about a mile away that could be easily defended and would protect not only them but the horses and mules. When they decided to go to the new position, it caught the attackers off guard, but they still wounded two of the mules. They beat the attackers to a small spring, which was easily defended because there was no cover for the attackers within one hundred yards on any side. Darrell asked, "Art, will you ride on to the Sulphur and get help? Probably Joe and Jed's place is the closest." The boy's group had five men left, and they did their best to slow down any of the attackers trying to catch Art, which proved to be successful. Art crossed the Sulphur close to Onnie's ferry. He didn't use the ferry since the Sulphur River was down and made it easy to cross. Art prayed he wouldn't get in any quicksand. He was glad Onnie's wife had stayed with her dad while he was on the trail cattle drive.

Art knew there was still one man following him about a half mile back. He went to Joe and Jed's place and luckily they were both at home. Joe and Jed put their wives in a buggy and sent them to Louis's family which was about two miles away. Joe and Jed said, "Tell Louis to ride to Bryans Mill and get as many men as they can to help." When Art, Joe, and Jed left the boy's house, they went by and picked up Mr. Shaw. All four of them were heavily armed with a lot of ammunition, two Henry rifles, two sharp carbines, and four six-shooters. Joe and Jed's wives barely got to Louis's house before the attacker began to shoot at the girls and everyone in Louis's house. It took Louis about two minutes to find out what was going on and get his guns and return the attacker's fire. Louis certainly could not go for help and leave his family and these other two women. Louis's son John was stuck in the barn where he was doing chores. John was a good shot and hunter, but he had sense enough to hide because he didn't even have his gun with him. He was definitely scared in that barn with the outlaw outside shooting at his family.

After Art, Mr. Shaw, Joe, and Jed crossed the Sulphur, they heard several men talking while hiding out in a clump of trees. As they came close to the trees, Art's foursome knew these were the same men that attacked Art and Darrell's group. They knew they didn't need to go help Darrell and his four other friends, they needed to follow these guys to see where they were going.

They could be going to attack their homes and burn them down. Following about a half mile back of these eight men, it became apparent they were trying to set fire to Onnie's barn. Art's foursome caught them by surprise and wounded three men and shot three of the other's horses. The outlaws had taken refuge in Onnie's barn. Joe and Jed got on either side of the barn and felt they could stop them from getting away. Art wanted to go and get the rest of the crew. Joe, Jed, and Mr. Shaw kept the attackers in the barn. When Art returned with Darrell and the other four men, they tried to get the attackers to surrender.

They refused, so Art and his crew shored up their attack positions and sent Onnie and Paul to Naples to get Dr. Lilly and the state police captain, Todd Berry, and bring them to help. In the meantime, Joe thought he should go and check on the wives at Louis's place. When he arrived, he discovered the one attacker had Louis and everyone in the house pinned down. Joe surprised him and shot him. Louis decided he would take his family along with Joe and Jed's wives to Art's home and warn them of the danger so they could be prepared to defend themselves. Louis then rode to Bryans Mill and got Gene McCoy, his son and the local gunsmith, to go see if they could help the boys on the Sulphur.

By this time, it was getting dark. Louis thought he should go back to Art's house and help protect all of the women and everyone there. When he arrived, Velma and her family had come over, and they were all together in Art's home. Captain Todd Berry arrived at Onnie's barn with five men about the same time that Gene McCoy arrived with three from Bryans Mill. Now they really had these attackers outnumbered and began a ten-minute barrage of shooting into the barn. After the random shots had wounded two more of their men, the attackers all gave up. Dr. Lilly had brought his wagon, not his usual buggy. He treated the five wounded attackers and made them ride in his wagon.

Captain Berry then made all the other attackers ride back in Dr. Lilly's crowded wagon, being guarded by him and the posse.

The boys took all their guns, horses, and money right in front of the state policeman, Berry. Art said, "They owe me for killing my mule." Captain Berry said nothing as the prisoners and posse rode off toward Naples.

It was three o'clock in the morning when everybody got their families and got back to their own homes. Everyone decided no work tomorrow, and they all slept in and did the minimum of work around the house that needed to be done. Art went over to Darrell's and tried to pay him three thousand dollars for helping with the cattle drive. Darrell said, "That's too much money." Art finally convinced him to take it. Art took out one thousand dollars for himself and hid it at home, and put the other fourteen thousand dollars in his money tree.

CHAPTER 34

Mr. Shaw, Louis, and Mr. Jenson had weeded Ed, Onnie's, Mr. Shaw's, and Art's corn and cotton. Those crops looked pretty good. Louis told Art, "We've had four good rains in the sixty-eight days you were gone."

Art said, "If we get a couple more good rains in the next three weeks, we can make a real good crop."

Art needed to go over and pay the Simmons brothers for their cattle. Art asked, "Joe, will you ride behind me about twenty yards over to the Simmons' farm, which is south of Naples?"

Joe said, "Sure, I will." So they proceeded over to the Simmons brothers' farm. The brothers were delighted because they would be able to pay their last payment on the ranch, which was $1,200.00. Now the Simmons brothers thought they could make it!

Art and Joe then went over to his farmer friend Ed and some others to see if anyone had any cows or heifers for sale. Also he wanted to know if anyone wanted to buy any good-blooded English bulls. Art ended up buying 170 cows and heifers, which cost him $1,700.00, and selling two Hereford and three Shorthorn bulls for a total of $250.00. It was late in the evening, so Art and Joe decided to spend the night at Ed's and drive Art's new herd back to the Logging's farm the next morning. They arrived about three o'clock in the afternoon, and the farmers came and picked up the bulls that they had purchased from Art. They headed back for home even though Art tried to get them to spend the night. Sharon had a big meal for everyone before the farmers left. Art Jr. was happy because he helped round up the five bulls the farmers had bought. After they left, Art went to bed and Joe went to his home.

Art had not seen Darrell for two days. The next morning, he decided to go over and see what he thought was going on around all of the farms, and if he had seen any signs of people checking out their land and livestock.

Art, Darrell, his son Erick, Ed, Louis, Louis's son John, Mr. Jenson, and his two sons were working hard to make sure everything needed was ready for the cattle, horses, and mules to survive the winter. They placed as much hay as they could in the vicinity of eighteen protective sheds. Everyone could see that the animals would not have any grass after September, so they would have to start using their supply of hay earlier than they had planned. The livestock would be out of hay by the end of January. An option would be to plant wheat and have the livestock graze during February and March. The boys decided they would plant forty acres of wheat on each of the five farms as soon as they could get the seed. Art told everyone present, "I'll go to Bryans Mill to see if McCoy has the seed. If he doesn't, I'll go to New Boston, Clarksville, or Naples to get the seed."

Darrell said, "My dad's sick, and I'm going after Dr. Lilly in Naples."

Art asked, "Would you have time to pick up the wheat?"

"Sure," Darrell answered. "I'll just take my wagon and pick it up."

Darrell told everyone, "There's a pack of wolves around here. They killed three of Art's calves night before last. I tried to locate and kill them last night, but I couldn't catch up to them by myself. I could hear them," Darrell continued, "but I couldn't catch them. I'll take three men tonight, and we'll stake out a calf about seven o'clock and see if we can kill off the whole pack. I'll meet Art and Paul here at seven o'clock, and the rest of you better tell Mr. Shaw, Joe, Jed, and Onnie. We need to tell everyone around here about these wolves. I'll warn Naples if someone will tell the folks in Bryans Mill, okay?"

Art asked, "Darrell don't you think you would rather stay with your dad tonight?"

"No," replied Darrell. "I'm going to get those wolves, see you at seven o'clock."

That night, Art, Darrell, and Paul roped a calf and tied him to a tree where the wolves had been running. They listened to the calf bawl for six hours while his mother was there trying to get him loose. After the calf and mother retuned to the herd they watched for the wolves until sunup. While they were quietly waiting, Darrell said, "Dr. Lilly told me my dad had yellow fever and was not doing very well. He also said he wanted all of my family to stay in our house and not let anyone else come in or let anyone go anywhere else." Dr. Lilly had quarantined Darrell's family.

"How did you get out tonight?" asked Art.

Darrell answered, "I just walked out and left while Velma was screaming at me." The wolves did not come to Art's farm that night.

The next morning about eleven o'clock, Joe, Jed, and Onnie came to talk to Art. They each had two calves killed on their farms. Art told them, "I lost three calves to the wolves the night before last. We all stayed up last night to try and get the wolf pack, but we didn't. We tied a calf up and let it bawl, trying to get the wolves to come close so we could shoot them," Art explained. "Darrell's dad has yellow fever with a high fever, and his house is quarantined."

They said, "We'll spread the word about the wolves and the yellow fever. We're going to try staying up, staking out a calf and try to get the wolves."

Ed came by and said, "Louis and I didn't lose any stock."

Art told Ed, "Darrell's family is quarantined because his dad has yellow fever and Joe, Jed, and Onnie lost several calves last night." He continued, "We all need to be out at night trying to kill those wolves. The tracks we saw looks like there are nine in the pack."

Darrell came over about seven o'clock and said, "My dad's really sick, and I think he could die. Therefore, I can't help with the wolf patrol tonight."

Art asked, "Is there anything we can do to help?"

Darrell replied, "Just pray."

For four more nights, Art roped a calf as they had done previously. Also Ed, Louis, Onnie, and Mr. Shaw all staked out a calf on their farms just like Art, but again no one saw the wolf pack. Everyone was tired and upset from lack of sleep. Darrell's dad continued to become weaker and weaker from the yellow fever. Darrell was worried sick because Dr. Lilly had said there was nothing anyone could do but try to get the fever down and keep it that way. Dr. Lilly was now more worried about other people getting yellow fever.

Not only was yellow fever a concern in that area, but farmers had lost over twenty calves to the local wolf pack. You could not run wolves out of a territory once they knew there was plenty of food and water. They just had to be killed. On the fifth day, Gene McCoy called a meeting at his store to discuss getting rid of the wolves. Some men were there from Marshall, and they had traps. They claimed they would trap the wolves for $250.00. None of the local farmers were willing to pay. Art suggested to the trappers, "If you'll trap at least five of the wolves, we'll pay you $250.00, and if you trap eight, we will pay you $350.00, but we won't pay anything up front."

"Okay", said the trappers. "It's a deal if we can have food and a place to sleep." All were in agreement.

Art suggested, "Why don't you start at my place, and you could eat supper and breakfast there and sleep in the barn?" The others made arrangement for them coming to their farms for the next seven days. The three men rode out with Art. They had their traps and supplies on their mule. Art showed them where the calves were killed. He then showed them where they had staked out the calves for bait before they arrived. They went to the Sulphur River and found out where the wolves were drinking water. Then they began to set their traps. They also went one hundred yards from the trap and began cutting small trees and built a fence around the traps. They then wanted a calf without a mother. Art roped one and put a rope bridle on it with a rope about ten feet long. They staked him out twelve feet from the traps. They camouflaged and located themselves seventy feet from the traps. After the traps were set, they all went home and Sharon had fixed a big steak dinner which everyone enjoyed.

The trappers sat around talking for a couple of hours, and then rode out alone to their designated hidden trap place on Sulphur River. They didn't catch anything for five days, but ate and spent the day sleeping with other neighbors, never moving the traps but letting the calf go every morning. The sixth night paid off. They trapped five wolves and shot two others, including the alpha male. They claimed only one escaped. The trappers brought the seven dead wolves to Art and wanted their money. Art paid them and had them sign a paper that Art had paid them. Art said, "Thanks for doing a job we couldn't do. Should we worry about the wolf that got away?"

They answered, "He might stay around for a couple of weeks but will probably leave to try and join up with another pack. If you'll watch the river, you can probably shoot the remaining wolf." Art had made up his mind he was not going to spend any night time looking for that lone wolf since Sharon was now sick and running a high fever. Dr. Lilly was to be at his house in about two hours. Art decided he would post a fifty dollar reward for killing the one wolf that was left.

CHAPTER 35

Dr. Lilly had told Art Jr. and Patricia to stay out of Sharon's and Art's bedroom, and sent for Sharon's parents to keep the children. Art was trying to keep Sharon comfortable by putting cloths dipped in cool water on her forehead. Art was kind of disgusted with Sharon because one day while Art was busy she had gone over to take care of Mr. Stroud while Darrell, Velma, and the kids were gone for nine hours, taking care of different things. Art was really concerned she had exposed herself to the disease. He had no way of knowing how much fever she had but knew is was high.

Dr. Lilly finally arrived and confirmed Art's fear that Sharon now had yellow fever. He said, "Quarantine her and try to keep her comfortable and try to get her temperature down." He was very concerned because Sharon's temperature was over 104 degrees. After Dr. Lilly left Sharon, he went over to see Mr. Stroud, who was in bad condition. Mr. Stroud's fever was still 102 degrees, and he was in a much weakened condition. He told Darrell, "I don't see how your dad can live much longer this way. I'm also treating twelve other people with yellow fever." He continued, "I need to go see them also."

Darrell asked, "Why if you can't do anything for them?"

Dr. Lilly replied, "I'll try to do my best to help."

Art continued to nurse and worry about Sharon and his children. Sharon's mom and dad finally came over the next day and had another suggestion. They said, "Why don't we take Sharon home with us?"

Art said, "You don't know anything about yellow fever, so it could be something already in this house. And why should we spread it to your house?"

"We agree you're right," they replied. They gathered everything they needed for the children so they could leave quickly. Sharon's parents spent two hours with Sharon, and her fever was so high Art was not even sure she knew they were there. About four o'clock, Mr. and Mrs. Rogers, Art Jr., and Patricia left and got to their home at seven o'clock. Everyone was crying because they didn't know if they would even see Sharon alive next time. They said, "Art, be sure to get a hold of us if there's any change."

The next day Dr. Lilly said, "Sharon's fever has dropped down to 102 degrees." He continued, "Mr. Stroud is very weak and might not last the week."

Art went to see Mr. Jenson and his family. He explained, "Sharon has yellow fever, and Mr. Stroud is also extremely sick with yellow fever. Be sure to tell everyone not to come to either house. Paul, I need you to work my place until I can get Sharon well. Could you do that?"

"Of course, I'll be glad to help," Paul replied.

Art also told them, "Also, tell everyone the trappers got seven wolves, and I paid them $250.00, and I'm offering a $50.00 reward to anyone that kills the last wolf."

After a lot of instructions from his mother, Paul rode off with Art. Art told Paul, "I need you to work around the barn the rest of today and tomorrow." Art wanted to let Ed, Joe, Jed, Louis, Mr. Shaw, and Onnie about the yellow fever situation and the reward for the wolf and find out when they could start planting wheat. He told Paul, "Tell them Darrell got the wheat, and it's in my barn. The planting equipment is outside my barn. Also, to always come to the edge of my house and holler in the morning and also when leaving in the afternoon."

Art went back to the kitchen and tried to fix something to try and get Sharon to eat because she had not eaten anything.

He had fixed pancakes and, to his surprise, she ate two and then wanted some cold milk. She didn't want anything else to eat all day long and wouldn't drink water. She would drink tea, so he made enough to last a couple of days. At supper time, he insisted she eat a steak. Just as Art was going to prepare it, Mr. Jenson came to his front porch with a pot of vegetable beef soup his wife had made. Art gratefully accepted the soup and said, "Thanks a lot. I appreciate it and don't forget about Darrell's family." Then he poured out one half of the pot of soup and said, "Please take this over to Darrell's and find out what's going on at his house." He also said, "Find out how Darrell is getting along. Tell him about Sharon and that your son is helping me. Ask Darrell if he needs help with anything." Sure enough, Darrell wanted his wife and two kids taken somewhere else. He felt his dad was near death because his temperature had just gone from 102 to 104 degrees. Dr. Lilly was now coming by twice a day, and of course, since they lived so close together he was also checking on Sharon.

Three days later, Sharon's brothers, Charles and Buddy, showed up to see how their sister was doing. Art cautioned them, "It's best you do not touch anything in Sharon's room or anyplace else in the house to keep down the chance of catching yellow fever." They visited for three or four hours, and Sharon was exhausted.

Much of the conversation was about what Art Jr. and Patricia were doing at Sharon's parent's house and how much they missed their mom. The kids not only missed their home, but also playing with Darrell and Velma's two kids. Charles asked, "Is there anything we can do for you?"

"Yes," Art said. "Would you and Buddy check over the cattle, horses, and mules on this farm and tell me if there is anything I need to do? Also, please get me four gallons of rubbing alcohol so I can disinfect the whole house."

Charles and buddy went out and looked over all the cattle, horses, and mules and felt things were okay. They also talked to Paul Jenson, who was taking care of Art's place while he was trying to care for Sharon. They hollered at Art at the porch and when they left said, "Everything looks okay, and we'll bring the alcohol next week."

Paul Jenson told Art, "Everyone's going to start planting wheat on each of your separate farms next Monday."

Ed and Louis came by and talked to Art out in the yard, discussing the business on each farm. Art only had seventy cows and heifers, three English bulls, and ten horses on each of his farms since they had just finished a cattle drive. Ed had planted wheat before, so he would be in charge. Art told them, "Darrell wanted twenty acres planted on his farm."

Ed said, "Just show us where, and we'll get it planted." He had walked over to Darrell's and discussed the wheat-planting and other matters, mostly about the yellow fever. He wanted to know what Darrell was doing to keep his dad comfortable. The preacher came by and talked to Art and Darrell.

Darrell was still concerned about getting Velma and the kids out of the house. The preacher told the boys, "I have been trying to find a place, but people were awfully reluctant to have anyone who has been in contact with yellow fever around them or their farms." The boys both understood that, still they were frustrated because they just couldn't really do anything that helped their loved ones. Really there was not much anyone could do about the yellow fever.

Dr. Lilly was now coming by three times a day to see Mr. Stroud and Sharon. They were very much concerned with their lack of progress.

Friday came and Mr. Stroud died. Dr. Lilly wanted him buried right away. Art told Darrell, "You can bury him next to my dad's grave at the Loggings' homestead." He had been wanting to make that area a family plot. He never dreamed anyone around them would need a place to bury a loved one. The preacher came Saturday, and Darrell buried his dad next to Art's dad's grave. Charles had gotten a casket made in Bryans Mill.

Darrell prepared his dad's body for burial and asked Art, "Will you help get dad's body to the burial site?"

"Of course," Art said. "I am glad to help." Charles had dug the grave, so Charles, Darrell, and Art took Mr. Stroud's body to the grave site on Darrell's wagon. The preacher spoke for twenty minutes.

Darrell, Velma and the kids, Charles, Mr. and Mrs. Rogers, and Art were the only ones at the burial. Folks were just plain scared about the yellow fever and tried not to be around it in any way. Later, Darrell got ten notes from folks around expressing their sympathy about Mr. Stroud's death and explaining they were afraid to come over to Darrell's or Art's home because of the yellow fever. The boys understood.

After the funeral, Art went back to his house to take care of Sharon. Her fever had spiked up to 104 degrees again. Her mom, dad, and Charles came over to Art's house and stayed until Dr. Lilly came and left after one hour. Dr. Lilly was concerned about Sharon. He said, "She can't keep going with this high fever, and there isn't a thing I can do to help her." He told Art, "We might try packing her in ice."

Art said, "You told me that the shock of the ice might kill her."

Dr. Lilly replied, "We need to try it, or we will lose her for sure." Art knew he would have to go to Texarkana to buy the ice and get it back to Bryans Mill before it melted. Art was going to send Mr. Jenson in the buggy to buy two hundred pounds of ice and transport it home in six hours.

Mr. Jenson told Art, "I'll leave at twelve midnight, get there around 6 a.m. and be back by twelve o'clock noon tomorrow." Art got a wooden box and lined it with several quilts and had the shade for the buggy to keep the sun off. He took the back seat off and also had a tarp to keep the ice colder. Dr. Lilly had said he would be over to check on Sharon about twelve o'clock tomorrow.

Art was not sure they could get the ice. He gave Mr. Jenson money to get the ice. Darrell came by, and Art said, "I'm going to try this ice thing and hope it works." He also gave Darrell two gallon of alcohol and said, "You should try to wipe down the room your dad slept in—walls, floor, bed, and everything."

Darrell said, "I'll do it, but I'm not sure it will help." Darrell was very discouraged.

Art said, "You need to get away from here for a week, and we'll look after your place."

Darrell said, "You beat all, you have got more problems than you realize!"

Art said, "Of course I do. I just don't want to think about it."

Mr. Jenson came with the ice, and Dr. Lilly was there. They prepared an ice bed for Sharon. Sharon told Art and Dr. Lilly, "I don't want you to put me in that ice bed." Art said, "It's the only way we know to get your fever down. I am so sorry to have to do this but believe me when I say it is our only hope." They went ahead and put her in the bed which had cloth on top of the ice to protect her skin from direct contact with the ice. After thirty minutes, they put her back in her regular bed. Dr. Lilly took her temperature and it was down to 103 degrees. Thirty minutes later, they again put her in the ice bed for another thirty minutes and continued this treatment six times. At five o'clock, her temperature was only down to 102 degrees and by morning, it was back up to 105 degrees. When Dr. Lilly came, they tried the ice treatment several more times and brought her temperature back down to 102 degrees, but next morning it was 105 degree again. Dr. Lilly said, "We're still fighting, but Sharon is very weak. Stay close. I'll be back this afternoon to check on her."

Sharon's temperature was now above 105 degrees. Art tried to talk to her but she was too delirious and burning up with fever. About three o'clock, she finally passed. Art was so upset he just sat and cried and cried. He was in terrible shape when Dr. Lilly came and said, "Art, go downstairs, take two shots of whiskey. And that's an order!" Art obeyed him and finally started calming down. Art walked over to Darrell's and told them Sharon had passed and asked, "Darrell, will you see that Sharon's parents are notified?"

"Of course I will," he replied. "Don't worry. Just do what you have to do."

Art returned home, and Dr. Lilly said, "I am so sorry I was unable to help. You know she will have to be buried as soon as possible." He continued, "Let's do it tomorrow around noon."

"Yes, sir," said Art. "I'll be okay. Thank you for all you do for us and everyone in the area. You have been a true friend to all of us." Art went up and made sure Sharon was laid out properly and talked to her, even though he knew she was dead. He wanted her buried close to his dad so she would be close to the kids and himself. He decided he could more easily explain everything to the kids later when they could better understand.

Sharon's parents, brothers Charles and Buddy, Art's children, the preacher, Darrell, Velma and their children, and Dr. Lilly were there. Art got no static about burying Sharon close to home. Art had gone out and dug her grave at six o'clock that morning. Dr. Lilly had brought a casket from Naples. The sermon and burying was a terrible event for Art. He felt so bad all he could do was cry. He had about thirty minutes by himself to talk to Art Jr. and Patricia and try to console them. They really didn't fully understand. Art said, "I love you both and need you very much, and we can get through this together."

Everyone knew no one should go back to Art's home until he had time to clean it up. Charles and Katelyn wanted to take Art Jr. and Patricia for a week and then bring them home. Art Jr. wanted to take his horse, and that was okay. Art asked Lewis, "Will you spread the word around Bryans Mill and Marietta?"

He said, "Sure. I'll do it on our way home."

Art told Lewis, "I'm going to burn the bed, her clothes, and anything else in the room." He had already scalded everything in the kitchen. Art then took the bed, bureau, chairs, and clothes to the burning pit and burned them. Then he went upstairs and used the two gallons of alcohol trying to clean and disinfect the whole upstairs. Velma sent Art some black-eyed peas, tomatoes, and cornbread. He was exhausted and after eating, he slept for at least seven hours that night.

CHAPTER 36

It was Saturday, September sixteenth, and Art knew he needed to get started on the corn harvest. The next morning, he talked to Mr. Jenson and Paul about beginning the harvest. They decided to get everything ready today and start tomorrow. The boys then went out and looked at all their cattle, horses, and mules. Art brought up eight cows and two horses that would need watching. There were no tracks to indicate anyone had been looking over the herd on any of the farms. Louis and Ed didn't have any trouble, and both said they would be over tomorrow to help with the corn.

When he got home, he found pork chops and potatoes from Mrs. Jenson and a note from Paul that said everything was ready for the corn harvest tomorrow. Again, Art was super tired and got about seven hours of hard sleep. When he awoke, he was still tired and depressed. He knew he needed to go get three headstones for his dad, Sharon, and Darrell's dad but that would have to wait until after the harvest.

Art, Paul, Mr. Jenson, and Louis's boy Luke, Louis, and Ed started as teams and by 6 p.m. had four wagonloads finished and had picked twelve acres of corn. They had a great start. Art had supper with Darrell and his family and talked to Velma about what to do about getting someone to take care of his kids during the day. Velma said, "I'll take care of them one week, and Mrs. Jenson is coming to take care of them the next. That way, I can clean your house every other week."

Art was going to drive a double load of corn to McCoy's in the morning. He delivered five hundred bushels by nine o'clock. By two o'clock, he had delivered another five hundred bushels. He got home about seven, and there were two more five hundred bushel loads ready to go. They finished the corn harvest in eight days, and it took another day to finish hauling the corn to Art's own farms. Art paid Paul and Luke $25.00 each. He now had $1,700.00 credit at the McCoy's store. So Art asked Darrell, "Will you start buying all your purchases from McCoy's store in my name?"

Darrell and Velma both said, "Yes."

Art went over to Marietta to get Art Jr. and Patricia. They stopped by their grandparents to visit. It was late when they got home. Paul, Mr. Jenson, Ed, and Louis were starting on the cotton crop in the morning. They had planted thirty acres each.

CHAPTER 37

The kids and Art went to see the furniture maker Mr. Bohanan south of Naples. Art needed a bed, mattress, chest, quilts, sheets, pillows, and blankets. He bought six quilts and two sets of sheets and pillows. All together it cost over three hundred dollars. Art told Mrs. Bohanan, "I'll pay you extra if you will wash all the quilts, sheets, and pillow cases."

She replied, "I promise I'll wash them for you, and they'll be delivered when my husband finishes the bed and chest."

When Art was getting ready to go, a neighbor came up and began demanding, "Bohanan, get the wagon ready. You're supposed to take me to Naples to shop and bring money because you're going to pay for it." The neighbor told Art, "You go on home and come back later. Mr. Bohanan needs to take care of me now."

Well, that was enough for Art. He said, "Listen, puss-gut! I don't know who you are, but you are not going to order me or anyone else around." The neighbors name was Ted, and he had threatened Bohanan and his family ever since he had moved there two years ago. He had taken cattle, crops, money, and had beaten not only Bohanan but also his wife and children. This had been going on over two years! Art further told him, "Go strap on your gun because I'm going to kill you." Ted went into a rage, charging at Art. Art ducked aside and then hit him in the kidney and back of the head. Ted went down but was not hurt. Art then began to beat him until Mr. Bohanan pulled him off. Art said, "Are you going to take this?"

Mr. Bohanan replied, "I can't stand up to him."

Art said, "I'll take him home with me and beat the hell out of him daily until he learns to leave you alone."

Mr. Bohanan said, "He does this to two other families around here."

Art told him, "I'll take him to the sheriff in Naples if you will come with me and sign a complaint against him." Art's kids were horrified and Art had to calm them and reassure them things were okay. While Art was talking to his kids, Ted tried to again threaten him and Bohanan. Art went over to Ted and hit him three more times and told him, "If you don't shut up, I'm going to shut you up."

Art finally got him tied up and in the buggy. He was tied up in the back, and Art and the two kids were in the front seat. He had tied Ted's hand and feet, but Ted kept on mouthing off and threatening Art's children so Art gagged him. Bohanan and another family, named Tony Young and his daughter Katie, that Ted had beaten loaded up in wagons and went to the sheriff in Naples. After the two families talked to the sheriff about the beatings they had gotten from Ted, the sheriff arrested and put him in jail. When Art came into Naples, he went to Mrs. Hill's and she was glad to take care of the children for awhile. He spent two hours at the sheriff's office and picked the children up at five thirty. Mrs. Hill had made them a picnic to eat on the way home, and it really hit the spot.

The big conversation on the way home was about the events that took place. The kids asked, "Daddy, why did you get so mad and hurt that man?"

He replied, "I don't like to see people being mean to other people, and I tried to stop it." He continued, "I know you kids don't like to see some people push others around and hurt them."

They both said, "Yes, we know that's not right." It was 7:30 when they got home, and everyone went to separate beds, but all in the kids' room.

Art said, "We'll all sleep in one room and if you get scared, all you have to do is holler, and Daddy will be there in one second." The kids seemed to be okay with that.

CHAPTER 38

The Logging family woke up at six the next morning, and Dad cooked pancakes and bacon. Everyone had eaten and was dressed by seven thirty. Mrs. Jenson came over at eight o'clock. Art said, "I'll see you kids at supper." His assignment for the rest of the week was to take wagonloads of cotton to the cotton gin in Marietta that was five more days. Mrs. Jenson thought the children were getting along real good.

The next morning was church in Bryans Mill and the picnic afterward. Art did not take any food but successfully scrounged enough off other people, and the kids had a good time playing. It was the first time Art had a chance to meet the new school teacher, Phyllis Williams. She was a widow woman from Mount Pleasant. Art couldn't help but notice she was a real looker. She was about five foot four inches tall with a great body. Her hair was light brown with golden highlights and a slight hint of auburn, which complimented expressive green eyes and a quick smile. The best part was she was not aware of her beauty or the fact when she walked by heads would turn. She had baked a delicious cake, and the kids had gone to her table to talk to her. She invited the kids to eat cake with her and when Art came over, she invited them all to eat with her. When they got home at five thirty, the kids wanted to go see their mother's grave. They spent about thirty minutes there remembering, talking about their mother.

Art had decided he would continue with the Bible study for the children every day after supper. Sharon had been telling Bible stories to the kids daily. They seemed to enjoy this and liked to learn and be asked what they had learned. Dad was surprised at Patricia's young age just how much she had learned. Art made up his mind to talk to someone else, to help him determine how he could best teach them more. Maybe the new school teacher he met last Sunday would have some good suggestions. He was just realizing what a hard job he had ahead of him raising his kids without their mother.

After three weeks, Mr. Bohanan delivered Art's bed, chest, mattress, and the other items he had bought. Everyone that saw the furniture thought they had to have a fine bed like that. Darrell and Mr. Jenson each ordered special beds from Bohanan. Art asked Mr. Bohanan, "What about that bully, Ted?"

He replied, "Ted got out of jail a week ago, and no one has seen him. We all figured he was to busy trying to finish harvesting his crops, and I just hope he doesn't bother us anymore."

CHAPTER 39

Art was surprised when his mother, her husband, and sister came riding up to his house in their two seated buggy. His mother said, "Your sister and I were shocked to hear about Sharon dying. We're here to help, and if you'll let us, we'll stay a whole month."

Art replied, "I'll gladly let you help, and it'll make me happy to have you here with us for awhile." He was beginning to feel overwhelmed by his family responsibility.

Abe, Art's mother's husband rested for one day, and then the two men rode out and looked over five thousand acres of land and the sawmill. They didn't ride over to see the five thousand plus acres on the other side of the Sulphur River. Art asked Abe, "Do you have any advice about what I can do to improve my farming operation?"

Abe replied, "The only thing I could suggest is to make more fenced pastures so you can rotate the grazing cattle, especially when it's dry."

Abe left the next day and told his wife and Patricia, "I'll come after you in a month." Mrs. Martin and her daughter, Patricia, coming to his home gave a reprieve to Mrs. Jenson and Darrell's wife, Velma, as they were splitting the job of taking care of Art's children.

It was Thanksgiving, and they had a great holiday. Art's mother and sister asked, "Would it be okay to invite all of your friends to a big Thanksgiving dinner party?"

"Of course," he said. "I think that's a good idea." They invited Darrell and family, Onnie and his wife, and Mr. Shaw and his wife, Mr. Jenson and family, Joe and Jed and their wives, the Anthony clan, the Rogers, Charles and his wife, Buddy, Ace and his family, Ed, Louis and his family. They even invited Ion and her family, and also Gene McCoy and his family. Over fifty people were there, and Art barbequed a steer. They had potato salad and fifteen pies, eight peach and seven pecan. The games played were horseshoes, dominos, shooting contests, and a checkers tournament. The party started at eleven o'clock and ended at five o'clock. Mrs. Martin and Patricia got to see some of their old friends and met a lot of Art's friends. The only invited guest that did not come was Ion and her family. Ion and her son came over a week after the party. Ion was civil to his mother and sister. They stayed and visited most of the day, and it turned out to be a pleasant time, and they had a good time.

Art's mother and sister were pleased with their idea and thought it turned out really good. Most of the women worked hard for at least two or three hours to make sure everyone was fed. That still gave them about three hours to really visit and corral the kids. They were lucky the weather was great, summer like and sixty-five degrees. The two women were so happy, but Art's mood turned sad because he only had memories of Sharon. Mrs. Martin said, "Son, it is all right to have memories. You will always have memories. In fact, you should never forget that part of your life." She continued, "You should also know Sharon would want you to move on with your life, not only for your sake but for the sake of the children. Also, while your sister and I are here, let us help you find someone to live here and take care of the house and children."

"Okay, Mom," he replied.

On December first, the boys looked over all the farms and the livestock. The livestock was fine, and they still did not see any signs of anyone lurking around any of the farms. It looked like they had enough feed to last through January. Everyone was hoping the wheat they planted would provide enough feed for the livestock through February and March.

Art discussed with Velma and Mrs. Jenson if they would still alternate weeks taking care of his children. They would be able to take over as soon as his mother and sister left in two weeks.

His sister, Patricia, had been saying she was going to stay at least three months to help her brother with his children. Sister had not been getting along with Cynthia, the daughter of her mother's husband. This had been an agonizing problem for sister for the last three years. She told Art, "I'll do anything to get away from Red Oak." She would never discuss the real problem, but her mother knew. It was agreed the sister would stay and that again reprieved Velma and Mrs. Jenson of taking care of the children. It appeared one big problem was solved at least for now.

Patricia resembled her brother. She was a rather tall woman, slender and quite attractive. She had been raised with the same principles as Art and they got along very well. He was looking forward to her stay.

CHAPTER 40

The boys had six orders for barns and two orders for houses from Ed and his farmer friends south of Naples. They wanted their lumber and bricks before the end of January. The sawmilling began, but what they really needed was about three hundred logs. Art and Darrell started picking up the logs on the ground on all five farms. They only had one hundred five logs. Art went to see Joe and Jed to see if they had any logs. They said, "We could probably have sixty logs for you by January fifth."

He also went to see Onnie and then Mr. Shaw who said, "I think we could also have about sixty logs by January fifth."

Onnie said, "I already have fifteen trees on the ground and could have them delivered in a week." The boys, Mr. Shaw, Mr. Jenson, and his son worked six straight days and had the lumber cut for three barns. Onnie delivered twenty more logs on Saturday. In the meantime, Mr. Brundet had told Gene McCoy, "I have about fifty logs on the ground but will need the log-hauling wagons for about a week."

Immediately, Art took the two large log-hauling wagons over to Mr. Brundet's farm and said, "Just try to be finished in a week." He went over to his friend Ed's place south of Naples. He talked to the farmers in that area saying, "I'm interested in buying logs for my sawmill." Some of these farmers had trees available to cut, and most farmers could use the extra money, especially since Christmas was only a week away. If they worked hard, they could cut and trim at least ten trees in a week, and it would take one day to deliver the trees.

Six of the farmers came to Art and asked, "Will you front us fifteen dollars each so we can have a good Christmas? We all promise at least ten logs twenty-five feet long and twelve inches in diameter."

"Okay it's a deal," he said. "Here is fifteen dollars for each of you."

Four other farmers said, "We would get some logs for you, but none of us have anything that will haul several logs at one time." He told them, "You can use my two log-hauling wagons, which I will bring to Ed's house two days after Christmas." When Mr. Brundet brought the wagons and logs to the sawmill, Mr. Jenson was sent over to Ed's house with the wagons.

As it turned out, Mr. Brundet delivered sixty logs, and the farmers south of Naples came through with ninety-five. By January second, the sawmill was back in business. They finished cutting the lumber for three more barns and two houses after Onnie delivered fifty more logs.

While all this was happening, Christmas had come to Sulphur River, and Art became pretty sad. His sister was determined to make it great for the children. She insisted Darrell and Art take the kids out to cut a Christmas tree. She and Velma spent a whole day decorating a tree at each house. Both families went to Naples the Saturday before Christmas and got presents for everyone. Patricia, Art's daughter, got a doll with extra clothes, and Art Jr. got a wooden rubber shooting gun which would make it unsafe to play with in the house. Art bought books for everyone in his and Darrell's family, a dress for his sister and also one for Mrs. Jenson and Velma because they had been looking after his children. All the people who worked for him got a ten dollar bonus, which is what they had received for Christmas ever since the first cattle drive several years ago. By the fifteenth of January, all the houses and barns that were ordered had been delivered and paid for.

CHAPTER 41

On January thirtieth while the boys were out checking the cattle on Art's home farm, they found five cows down and dying. They didn't know what it was, but they moved the eighty head that were not sick to a fenced forty-acre pasture. Darrell went to check on the other farms, and Art went to get Dr. Lilly. Dr. Lilly didn't get there until the next day. Darrell reported there were no sick or dying cattle on the other farms.

By the time Dr. Lilly got there, two more cows were sick. Dr. Lilly did not have a name for the disease, but he told Art, "You're going to have to kill all the cattle on this farm and after putting lime on their bodies, bury them. This is the only way to keep this thing from spreading. Everyone working around the animals must wear gloves and masks, then burn their clothing including their shoes. You must then warn all your neighbors not to come on this farm." He sent Paul to warn all the farmers in the area. Then he asked Mr. Jenson, "Will you go to McCoy's General Store and buy one thousand pounds of lime, five barrels of coal oil, two picks, and ten shovels? If they don't have all that, get what you can and bring it back here." He continued, "Then go to Naples to Hill's General Store to get the rest of what is needed." Meanwhile, Dr. Lilly had gone to the other farms to see if there was any more sick livestock, and there wasn't any. This was done at Art's request. He wanted a witness that could definitely verify his other cows were not sick. He asked Darrell, "Will you help me shoot the eighty-seven head on this farm? My plan is to kill them and dig several graves six-feet-deep and eight-feet-wide and twenty-feet-long close to them, then use two mules with tarps to drag them into the graves. I'll need to do that by myself because I don't want anyone else put at risk." He took a shovel and one pick and went out to the forty-acre field closest to the cows grazing and began digging the cow grave. By five o'clock, he had dug part of a six-feet-deep and four-feet-wide hole, but only sixteen-feet-long. It was late, and he was tired, disgusted, and really down in the dumps.

He told his sister, "Everyone will have to stay in the yard and stay away from me until I have all these cattle shot and buried." Art was really sick because he couldn't stand to lose any livestock for any reason. He was going to dig for another three or four hours. How he was going to stand it he didn't know because he was already tired and sore from three hours of digging.

Mr. Jenson had only purchased one hundred pounds of lime, three shovels, two picks, two gallons of rubbing alcohol, and one barrel of coal oil. He hadn't had time to go to Naples but planned to go early in the morning and return by noon.

At eight o'clock the next morning, Darrell, Joe, Jed, Onnie, Mr. Shaw, and the ex-slave friends of the boys, Robert and Sherman, showed up at Art's place. They said, "We're going to help dig the graves for the cattle." In three hours, the crew had dug about one half the graves needed for the herd.

Art took mules, a wagon, and a big piece of tarp, and tied chains in the grommets. He didn't tie the tarp directly behind the mules because he was afraid it would scare them. Everyone wore gloves and bandannas to help protect them. Mr. Jenson returned from Naples with four hundred pounds of lime, three more shovels, four gallons of rubbing alcohol, sixteen pairs of gloves, and four barrels of coal oil. Sixteen head of cattle had died so far, and they moved all of the dead cattle to the grave and shot four others that were dying and put them in the grave. They put a barrel of coal oil on their bodies and Art lit the match. It was four o'clock, and the fire burned until eight o'clock that night. The stink was terrible!

The next day, they got the other three large graves finished. Art put one hundred pounds of lime on the burned bodies, and the crew then covered them with the dirt from digging the graves. That afternoon, the boys shot the remaining seventy head of cattle. Three of those were high-priced European bulls and four of the cross bulls. Art was really upset! All the crew went home for the night. Each day, every one of them took off their clothes and washed their bodies with alcohol and changed into clean clothes. This was done in Art's barn. They wiped their shoes with alcohol because they couldn't afford to replace shoes or boots.

The last day of this horror for Art was putting the remaining dead cattle in the graves and burning their bodies with coal oil. At four o'clock, the bodies finished burning, lime was put on the burnt bodies, and they worked until ten o'clock getting the graves covered. They had also burned the wagon and tarp, gloves, all the clothes worn during burying of the sick cattle, and the chains were also thrown in the grave.

The next day, Art was so despondent he slept until nine o'clock. All the men working around the sick cattle had stayed and slept in only one room of their house where there was no one else around. Dr. Lilly came by at ten o'clock, and they went out to look at the graves. Art described all that was done. Dr. Lilly said, "I think you did more than enough. The crowning blow is that you can't run any livestock or raise any crops on this farm this year." This was almost more than he could take. He had lost eighty-seven heads of cattle worth ten thousand dollars, and no crops could be grown this year on his family farm. His only salvation was he did have four other farms where he still had about three hundred head of cattle.

CHAPTER 42

Art decided he would plant one hundred acres of corn and thirty acres of cotton on the old Parkinson farm. He had never planted on this farm since he bought it four years ago. The Parkinson's place was bought mainly for Art's livestock. He only had two fields of sixty acres each that were fenced. The cow dogs would have to protect the new corn plants from the deer and other wild animals. He would have to build dog facilities on that farm. There was a small farmhouse which needed repair. That would take at least two weeks. They had mainly cut hay off this farm the last four years. He also knew he needed to start building a corral and fence some more pastures.

Darrell came to see how things were going and said, "I heard that two farmers south of Naples also lost their herds to fatal sickness just like your cattle had."

"I wonder," Art said, "if the cows I bought from some farmers south of Naples brought the disease to my herd."

More and more people were shying away from Art, his family, and sawmill for obvious reasons. His family farm was right on the road from Bryans Mill and Naples. In the past, many people would stop and get water or visit, but there wasn't much of that any more.

Darrell told him, "I think this might be a blessing for you and your family because really, you were always nervous with people stopping by, especially with so many dangerous people roaming Texas."

CHAPTER 43

Darrell and Velma had decided to go to the Saturday night dance in Naples and leave their kids with Art's sister. Art said, "No, no, no, Darrell, you have to take my sister to the dance. She hasn't been out of this house for two months so you take her, and I'll stay with the kids." After a lot of objection from Patricia, it was decided the three would leave at noon Saturday. That would leave them some time to shop and eat before the dance. Art asked Darrell, "Will you pay the Hills for the supplies Mr. Jenson bought for me to take care of the sick cattle?" He gave him one hundred dollars to pay for the supplies.

On Saturday, Darrell, Velma, and Patricia left about eleven o'clock and successfully shopped until five o'clock then they ate supper, and at seven o'clock were ready to go to the big dance. It was crowded, and they didn't get a table until 7:15. The parade of men started not only to ask Patricia to dance but also Velma. Darrell and Velma danced every other dance, and that slowed down the men asking Velma. Patricia, on the other hand, had a string of men waiting to ask her to dance. She had finally narrowed it down to two guys she liked. One of them was the Simmons brother Bob, and the other was a saddle maker in Naples.

One drunk cowboy that worked for Ion came over and wanted to dance with Patricia or Velma. When they turned him down, he started cursing and yelling, "These women think they're too good to dance with me." Darrell escorted him outside, hit him four quick punches. When the disrespectful cowboy got up, Darrell took his gun and said, "If you don't leave the dance, I will have to hurt you. Also," he said, "you can pick up your gun at the sheriff's office on your way out of town." Darrell returned to the dance, and there were no other problems the rest of the night.

Patricia told the saddle maker she would meet him at church the next day. As if Darrell didn't have enough problems trying to keep the men away from these two women!

The school teacher from Bryans Mill Phyllis came to the dance and joined their table. When she found out that Patricia was Art's sister, you could sure tell she was interested in Art Logging! She kept talking to them until she finally got Patricia to invite her to come have supper with the family the next Friday night. Patricia had decided she would stay with Art and the kids until April when the crops were planted.

The parade of men continued coming to their table until the dance was over at eleven o'clock. They all walked Phyllis back to the room she had gotten. She came to the dance to meet a friend. This friend had expected Phyllis to be friendlier, and they argued. So after that incident, she went to the dance alone. She joined them for church the next morning and rode home to Art's house. She stayed there, visiting with Art and Patricia for about two hours.

It was getting close to dark, so that meant she would need Art to escort her home to Bryans Mill. He hitched up the two-seated buggy and tied her horse behind. Art Jr. and his sister wanted to go along, and Phyllis convinced him to let them come with them. Art already had his pistol but took his Henry rifle and put it in the back of the buggy, just in case he needed it.

This should be about a two-hour trip.

They were making good progress until about three miles from Bryans Mill. A shot went whizzing through the buggy. No one was hit, but Art saw where the shot came from. He said, "Phyllis, here take the reins." Then he crawled in the back with the kids and told the kids, "Lay down flat and be very quiet." He got the Henry rifle and returned six directional shots where he thought the shooter was located, but he hit nothing.

Two shots rang out, but no one was hit. They continued at a fast pace toward Bryans Mill. His last two shots were closer, which meant the shooter was on horseback. Art told Phyllis, "Slow down and try to move the buggy to either side of the road." One more shot rang out, and Art returned three shots to the area where the shot came from. The shooting stopped, and they continued to Phyllis's home. It had started to rain so he said, "I'll talk to you later. I have to get these kids home." She gave him a quick kiss, and he left.

He got a piece of tarp and had both kids sit up front with him so they could wrap the tarp around their heads. It had taken a total of three hours before they got back home. It took another twenty minutes to unhook the team, dry them off, and rub down the horses. On the way home, Art had to admit to himself it was flattering to have a beautiful woman show an interest in him.

Actually, it felt good.

The weather had turned cold, and a lot of logs were brought to the sawmill Saturday. Art Jr. went to help him when he went to the sawmill. A lot of people just dropped logs off without telling the boys, but they would put their names at the cut on the logs. There were about seventy logs there, which pleased them.

When they returned home, the kids ate bacon and eggs with their dad.

It had been snowing for eight hours, and this was to continue until noon. There was already about six inches of snow. So the kids and their dad went outside for two hours and built a snowman, plus two really good forts. Patricia came out for an hour to join the fun. Darrell and Velma had also been outside with their kids playing in the snow. Even two of the cow dogs seemed to be enjoying the snow. The kids begged, "Please, Daddy, can the dogs come inside to get warm?" He finally relented and let them go inside. He then went out and fed the horses and mules and made sure they all had water as well as a place to get protection from the weather. The next morning, Art hooked up the mules to different sleds. He took the kids and his sister sledding for a couple of hours. When they returned home, he then took the sled over to Darrell's and took his family sledding. This was great fun for everyone! It was cold until Thursday, but the snow had all melted by then.

The boys were discussing the incident of the shooting on Sunday while taking Phyllis home. Darrell said, "Ya know, I think that woman has designs on you, so you better be careful. At the dance with Patricia, Velma and Phyllis there I had to fight off a guy a minute." He went on saying, "Phyllis was so busy talking to Patricia about you we couldn't get a word in edgewise. I'm telling you never again!"

Art said, "Let's go see if we can find out anything about our Sunday night shooter."

They found shells from a Spencer carbine. Darrell looked at the horses' footprints and said, "I could identify this horse."

"I'll bet it was the man Phyllis had the fight with Saturday night," said Art. "I'll have a talk with her to see if she thinks he would shoot at us, who he is and where he lives when she comes to supper Friday."

CHAPTER 44

Darrell went back to work on his horse ranch, and Art started his plans for farming the old Parkinson farm for the first time in several years since he could not run livestock or plant crops on the Logging's homestead. He needed to buy another plow, disc, and planter. He went to Naples and bought a new variety of cotton seed and corn seed from Mr. Hill. Mr. Hill said, "I know where you can buy some good used equipment, but I think you should think about buying new equipment even though it would cost about six hundred dollars. I could get it shipped and here in about two weeks. Let me know if you want to get new."

Art went outside town and looked at the used planting equipment. The man really wanted to sell it and sold it to him for $110.00. Art said, "I will pay you $7.00 to deliver the equipment next week.

The man said, "I'll have it to you next week for sure." Art then went back to Mr. Hill's to pay him for the seed and order a new plow, planter, and disc. With five farms, he felt the used equipment would come in handy, and it was really a good price. The used equipment was going to be put on the farm where Mr. Jenson lived because he would make sure it was ready to begin planting. The new equipment would be used on the old Parkinson's place, and tomorrow the present equipment was going to be taken to his tenant farmers, Louis and Ed.

Art was going to see Gene McCoy and get most of the seed he figured he still needed. All his cows were grazing on the wheat they had planted. The cows were beginning to drop their calves, and he needed to check on all the remaining farms that had cattle on them.

The next day, he went to Bryans Mill to talk to Gene McCoy about corn and cotton seed, and he planned to also ask him about Phyllis's boyfriends. There was still three hundred dollars credit on the books. Mr. McCoy said, "I can't buy any corn from you because it's coming from the land you had the sick cows on."

Art replied, "No, I won't be planting anything or running livestock on that land for a year. All my grain is coming from my other farms, and I haven't had any sick cows on any of the other farms. You can ask Dr. Lilly about that."

"Okay," said Mr. McCoy. "In that case, I'll take two thousand bushels at fifty cents a bushel, and if you raise any wheat, I'll take two thousand bushel for seventy cents a bushel."

Then Art asked, "What can you tell me about the new school teacher? Do you know who she's been going with and would any of them get mad enough to shoot her if she rejected them?" He then told him about the shooting incident and what little he knew about the man she had a fight with Saturday night.

Gene said, "There have been three men really coming around these six months. One is a forty-year-old widower, another a thirty-year-old farmer and a man that lives about five miles east of Bryans Mill. His wife left him about three years ago. I think they were only married a couple of years when she left him." He continued, "I don't think the first two would get that mad, but the other guy is about twenty-five and a horse trader with a small place outside town. His name is Hank Wilson. He's close to six foot maybe one hundred seventy pounds. Good looking and always friendly. I have never seen him mad."

"Okay," Art said. "Will you load the seed and groceries I purchased, and I'll be back shortly."

He walked over to the school house and talked to Phyllis for about fifteen minutes. He asked, "Is Hank Wilson the man you had the argument with Saturday night?"

"Yes," she answered. "He's come to see me twice this week."

"Does he have a Spencer carbine?" was the next question.

Again, she answered, "Yes."

"Well," he said, "I'm going to go out to his place and talk to him about trying to kill us Sunday night."

Phyllis said, "He told me he was going to be gone for a week."

Art said, "If you're coming out to our house, I'll wait and we can ride there together." "That would be great," she replied. "I'll be ready in an hour."

He then went back and picked up his loaded wagon at McCoy's Store and went out to Hank Wilson's house and looked around and confirmed he had Spenser carbine shells. He had made up his mind that if he was the shooter, he was going to kill him. After looking around for a while, he returned to Bryans Mill to pick up Phyllis. She tied her horse to the back of the wagonload of supplies.

As they traveled the one and one half hours home, Art voiced his thoughts about the shooting. He told Phyllis, "If I can confirm Hank Wilson is the one that shot at us Sunday night, I'll kill him.

This really upset her, and she said, "You can't kill whoever was shooting at us. No one was hit."

He replied, "Are you crazy? Anyone that shoots at me, my children, and you as my guest needs shot themselves and I'll not rest until I kill them. If they think they can get away with it, everybody will just shoot and kill all of us and take everything we have. I don't take that from anybody, including your jealous boyfriend."

"Why don't you let the sheriff handle it?" she asked. This question was responded to by about two minutes of laughter. Needless to say, supper and conversation was a little tense.

While Phyllis and Patricia were visiting after supper, Art and Art Jr. walked over to see Darrell. They discussed the events of the day and the conversation with Phyllis. Darrell said, "I leave you alone with your new girlfriend, and the next thing I know, you're going to kill her ex-boyfriend. Tell you what, I'll talk to Robert and Sherman, they're with the state police, and I'm sure they'll get someone to arrest him."

Art's reply was, "They'll have to beat me to him."

The next morning, Phyllis left without even saying good-bye to Art. Patricia said, "We'll see her at church tomorrow. You really upset her. I thought she was interested in you, but I'm not so sure now."

He said, "Anyone that tries to kill or shoot at me, my family, or anyone else is going to pay the price. If she doesn't like that, we wouldn't get along anyway. To make it worse, it was a man she was involved with."

Patricia prepared a great picnic for them for after church service the next day. The weather turned out to be sixty degrees and sunny with a light south breeze. Phyllis did not come over to their table but spent about an hour talking to the preacher. The kids did go over and talk to her for about five minutes as they ate cake she had given them. Toward the end of the picnic, the preacher came over and said, "Art, may I talk to you in private? Phyllis is really upset because you're talking about killing someone that shot at you, your kids, and her last Sunday night."

"Yes," he said. "I'm mad about someone shooting at me and my children and her. What I really don't understand is why she's so mad at me when it was me and my children being shot at."

The preacher replied, "She says you don't have enough proof."

"She's right," he said. "But when I get his confession, that will be all the proof I need."

"I told her I understand your point of view," said the preacher. "And wasn't sure I understood her behavior."

After the talk with the preacher, everyone said their good-byes and left for home. Darrell and Velma's bunch was with them and knew everything that was going on. Darrell said, "Robert and Sherman said they would have someone come out Tuesday when Hank Wilson was to return home, at least that's what Phyllis said."

On Monday, Art was moving all the old planting equipment to Louis's and Ed's. He told them the story, and they both thought she might be trying everything to protect her old boyfriend. They said, "If we were in your place, we would feel the same way you do." Louis and his two sons, Luke and John, were going to plant forty-five acres of cotton and twenty-five acres of corn. Ed was going to plant thirty acres of cotton and thirty acres of corn. Mr. Jenson and his sons, Paul and Pete, were going to plant sixty acres of cotton and thirty acres of corn with the new equipment.

Art had decided he would plant eighty acres of corn and twenty acres of cotton. He asked them all, "How are we going to keep the deer out of the new crops?" They all agreed dogs would be the answer to that problem because they could be easily trained for the task.

Louis, Ed, and Mr. Shaw—all three said, "We have about twenty calves each already on the ground, and we think the wheat grazing will only last until about March tenth."

"I'll try to get more corn," Art said. "But you'll have to haul it." Unfortunately, there was no corn to be found. While visiting with Ed, Louis, and Louis's boys, he asked, "Louis, do you think your wife and daughter would fix up the old house on the old Parkinson's place? I'll pay them fifty dollars each, get some bunk beds, table and chairs, and some bricks from the sawmill to fix the chimney."

Louis said, "I'm sure they will. We saw your nice new bed, and I'd like to have two if you would tell Mr. Bohanan."

Ed said, "I'd also like one bed." He would be sure and let Mr. Bohanan know about them wanting beds.

It took three weeks for Louis's wife and daughter, Ruth, to have that old house quite livable. Art told both Louis and Ed, "I'm going to put new barns on the farms you work for me." The sawmilling business was not real good because no one had any money to spend. When the three large special beds were delivered, Art paid for them, and the tenants would pay him back when the crops were harvested. Art didn't owe anyone any money, but his resources were down to $2,500.00.

On Tuesday, the sheriff came by to question Art. He even talked to Art Jr. for about five minutes. Then he went over to talk to Darrell and asked him, "Will you come with me and show me where you found the Spencer shells and the horse prints at the different locations?" Sheriff Bass said, "Since you're still a deputy, I want you to come with me the rest of the day."

They went to see Phyllis, the school teacher. She told them, "Art and Darrel have some evidence that points in Hank's direction. However, he said he was going to kill him."

"I can understand," said Sheriff Bass, "why someone would want to kill a person shooting at them and their children, because I certainly would feel the same way if it were me and my children."

The next stop was Hank Wilson's place. Sheriff Bass asked Hank, "Did you have a fight with Phyllis and decide to shoot her and the people she was with?"

Hank said, "Yes, we had an argument because I thought she was leading me on, but I wasn't mad enough to try to shoot anyone."

Darrell said, "I was looking at your horse's footprint, and I want the sheriff to have a look."

The sheriff said, "This is definitely the same horse that made the prints we found at the same location we found the Spencer carbine shells. Hank, just what do you have to say about that?"

Hank said, "Yes, it was me, but I was only trying to scare her."

"And what about Art and his kids?" asked Darrell.

He said, "I just kind of lost my head but really didn't hit anybody because I'm a better shot than that."

Both Sheriff Bass and Darrell said, "Well, Art Logging is a whole lot better shot than you."

Hank said, "I know Art could shoot me. He came pretty close at two hundred yards."

"Hank," said the sheriff, "you're under arrest, and you need to get someone to take care of your place while you're gone."

"I can get someone," he said. They then went by the school, which was out at that time.

Hank asked Phyllis, "Will you take care of my place while I'm gone?"

She told the sheriff, "You don't have any real evidence."

The sheriff told her, "We don't need any because Hank has already told us he was the one who did it." All three men left Bryans Mill, and Darrell turned off at his house. Hank and the sheriff continued on to the jail in Naples.

Bob Simmons had been courting Patricia and had been coming to see her every weekend since meeting her at the Naples dance. He went to church with them, took her to the Naples dances. In addition, he came over several Friday nights and spent the night.

Darrell told Art all about what happened and that Phyllis was going to look after Hank's place. Boy, that did it for Art, and he asked Patricia, "Are you sure that woman was interested in me and why?" Hank went in front of a judge and told his story. He was fined $2,000.00 and sentenced to five years in jail, which was suspended to serving six months in the county jail. If he was arrested again during that time, he would go to prison and finish serving his four and a half years. He wrote Phyllis a letter, asking her to sell his horses so he could pay his fine.

She bought the horses herself for $1,500.00, and he put that with $500.00 he already put in to cover the $2,000.00 fine. Phyllis said, "Hank, please from now on just leave me alone. I don't want to see you anymore because I want to get on with my life without you screwing it up."

CHAPTER 45

Art found out two of the ten farmers he had bought cattle from also had to destroy their entire herd because they had the same sickness that was found in his herd. Thank God he had not had any more sickness. He now had one hundred calves on the ground and had not lost any that he knew of.

They saw Phyllis at the church picnic a couple of times and when she tried to start a conversation, Art just got up and walked away, so she tried talked to Patricia. The following Saturday, Phyllis came to the house crying and said, "Art, I really have to talk to you. Just listen to me for ten minutes?" They all sat quietly and let her talk. She said, "I didn't know Hank was the one who shot at us and really didn't think he would do that. Anyway, I was afraid you would kill him without any proof. Then I would be responsible for someone being killed." She continued, "Everyone knows how fast you are with a gun, and anyone who comes up against you is going to be killed. This whole thing has made me sick. I can't live with all that responsibility and your condemnation."

Art said, "Why are you worried? Hank is in jail and has lost his money and horses, so he probably won't stay around here when he gets out of jail. I'm not going to worry until he gets out in six months, and if he is going to do anything, it will be then."

Phyllis said, "I used all my money to buy his horses, and now I don't have any way to sell the darn things."

Art said, "I'll buy the horses and get your money back if you'll stop worrying about all the other stuff. What's done is done, and you can't change it." He continued, "We'll take Darrell and look at the horses this afternoon. I'll pay you the fifteen hundred dollars."

Afterward, Phyllis sat down and had breakfast and coffee with Patricia and the kids. She seemed a lot less stressed by then. Art really didn't know what to think about her, but he needed horses anyway. He would keep the good horses and sell the others.

If he could cut some trees, then he wouldn't have to worry about anything. During the past two weeks, Darrell and the rest of the crew had been harvesting the oats and hauling the grain to the five different farms. Thank goodness the oat crop was a good one.

While the others ate, Art walked over to Darrell's and filled him in on what had just happened and asked, "Will you go with us?"

Darrell said, "Are you sure this woman is okay mentally?"

Art said, "I don't know. I just want to get finished with this situation."

"I'll be ready at one o'clock," said Darrell. "And we will go get this fine herd of horses you just bought. Better bring the dogs."

Back at home, he made out a bill of sale and gave Phyllis $1,500.00. At two thirty, Darrell, Phyllis, and Art began looking over the thirty-one horses. Twenty-three were pretty good mares.

Darrell said, "I'll take any of these you don't want, and pay you seventy dollars each. All the mares are pregnant, and I'll ride these eight geldings and let you know after I have ridden them, but their feet and teeth seem to be sound. In fact, I'll ride one home."

Hank also had a milk cow with a calf. Art asked Phyllis, "What are you going to do the milk cow and her calf." All she did was feed the cow daily. "Do you want to sell the cow and calf?" he asked.

She said, "Yes because I'm out of feed anyway, and they should be worth twenty-five dollars."

"Sold," said Art.

She also asked, "Will you help me get this cabin where it looks like someone is living here so it'll be left alone?" She also said, "I can't plant a crop."

Art said, "I can, but you'll have to plant a garden yourself, and I get the money for the harvest."

She said, "Fine. It's a deal." It looked like there was about thirty acres there. He thought he would plant corn and just take it to Gene McCoy and save all that hauling from his other farms.

Art and Darrell went home with their thirty-one horses and one milk cow and calf. They put the twenty-two mares on a small pasture on the Shaw farm, and took the eight geldings over to Darrell's farm. The dogs really were only helpful with driving the milk cow and calf home. Art Jr. came out and fixed the cow and calf up in the barn as it was beginning to rain.

Art had purchased the Jersey cow and calf because he wanted both his and Darrell's family to have good fresh milk and butter. Art Jr. and Darrell's son, Erick, were excited about the cow and her calf. Art said, "How would you boys like to learn to take care of them? I'll teach you how to milk the cow, and you can take turns." He continued, "One day Art Jr. can milk and keep the milk for his family, and the next day Erick can milk and take the milk home for his family. How does that sound?" The boys agreed and were anxious to get started.

There was no way to keep the milk fresh longer than thirty-six hours without a cold spring to keep it cool, then it could be kept good for four or five days. Luckily there was a cold spring on the Loggings' homestead. They could drink one half of the milk warm and churn butter with the other half. But everyone seemed to enjoy cold milk the best. The women were happy to have fresh milk and butter for cooking.

Art told the boys, "You'll need to leave the calf with her mother from five o'clock in the evening until ten o'clock the next morning so it will get all the food she needs to grow. So milking time will be from four until five in the afternoon." It didn't take long for the youngsters to realize milking was a lot harder than it looked. Since Art had not been raised having a milk cow, he was not very experienced in that area and was glad it would not be one of his daily tasks. It took about a week for the boys to learn the process and get the chores running smoothly. Art said, "If you wash the cow's udder with a clean warm rag, it will help the milk come easier, and movement of the hands and fingers is very important. Also," he said, "You're lucky because she's not a kicker. Lots of times they'll kick the bucket or the one doing the milking." Art later told the boys, "I'm very proud of you for helping your families by taking on this responsibility."

It rained Saturday, Monday, and Wednesday nights. It was now March first. The area got another real good rain of two inches, and they were beginning to have some sixty-five-degree days. The next plan was to start plowing and disking all his fields and prepare for the planting. Working hard for ten days, everyone was ready to plant the crops. Art had used the new equipment on the Parkinson farm, and Paul Jenson helped him that week. Then he went over and put the crops in on the Shaw farm. The second week, Art went to Hanks farm and planted thirty acres of corn. He also plowed and disked a place for Phyllis to plant her garden. She really did want a good garden. Phyllis came out and tried to help, taking him cold water, and she had made him a cake after teaching school all day. While he was planting, she worked around Hank's cabin, trying to make it look like someone lived there. She told Art, "I don't like coming here by myself. When you come over to work with the crops, please let me know so I can come also, then I won't be here alone."

He assured her he would. He really liked her coming there, bringing him water and baking him a cake. He wondered what had changed Phyllis. They seemed closer every time they were together. Phyllis didn't seem to resist Art's advances anymore. In fact, she seemed to encourage them, but in the back of his mind he still didn't fully trust her.

All of Art's crew had finished planting the cotton, and by then the corn was up high enough they began to disc, weeding the grass and weeds out of the corn. This took them until May 1. Then it was time to disc the grass and weeds out of the cotton. It seemed he was busier on his crops than he ever had been. Now he needed to get ready for haying the harvest of the wheat crop because he really needed the money. On the different farms, he had planted two hundred acres of wheat. It took three weeks to harvest that two hundred acres. It cost four days' delay when the machinery kept breaking down.

The sheriff had come to get Darrell, saying he needed him to help him pick up two men in Hughes Springs. They were also going to pick up Charles in Marietta. The sheriff told Darrell, "Hank got another four months added to his jail time for hitting a deputy."

When Darrell told Art Hank had to serve more time, he said, "You'd think he would learn." He also told Darrell laughingly, "This is perfect! You wouldn't even know you have a corn crop on your land until it is harvested and sold. Oh well, just be careful."

Art took 2,400 bushels of wheat to Gene McCoy and told him, "I need to be paid cash because I already have $1,550.00 in credit and won't need more than that until the corn harvest." He received $1,830 for 2,440 bushels of wheat. Now he had to sell the other 4,000 bushels of wheat somewhere else.

Besides trying to intimidate people that might want to rob or kill them, the boys competed in several shooting competitions in the area. Darrell said, "Well, Art, the New Boston shoot-out and horse races are next Saturday. Think we should do some extra practicing?"

Art replied, "Good idea. Everyone's excited about going. The families enjoy the festivities as much as we enjoy competing. A little extra practice never hurts."

The boys started practicing every day. They had always practiced once a week to keep sharp on their shooting skills.

Most people believed the boys were very good with guns, and everyone in their area knew it. What they worried about were the people that didn't come to the contests or know what good gunmen the boys were.

Saturday morning, they left their farms about six o'clock on the way to New Boston. Art, Darrell, Joe, Jed, Charles, and Ace were all going to enter both the rifle and pistol contests. The Anthony's were also entering the horse racing competition. Again, Bryans Mill was well represented. The women had prepared breakfast to be eaten on the trip. When they arrived at eight thirty, two hundred people had already signed up, and over three hundred were waiting. The rifle and pistol shooting got underway around nine thirty. In the rifle shoot, Art, Darrell, Charles, and Ace all put six shots in the bull's-eye, along with twenty-five others. The target was moved to 125 yards away, and six shots had to be completed in thirty seconds. Art and Darrell only put five shots in the bull's-eye while Charles and Ace had six along with three others. The judge ordered a five-way tie and each received a hundred dollars. The rifle contest was finished by noon. At the same time, the pistol contest was being held. The goal was six shots in the bull's-eye within fifteen seconds at 50 yards. Art, Darrell, and Jed all got four in the bull's-eye with one close along with twenty others. The twenty-three went to the final shoot at 60 yards. The boys were the only ones to put six shots in the bull's-eye and split the five hundred dollar winnings. The most any of the others contestants put in the bull's-eye was five.

The Anthonys won one race and won one hundred dollars. However, they finished second in the championship race. Mr. and Mrs. Jenson won the horseshoe pitching contest and got fifty dollars. All the kids entered the foot race. After the race, they came back to their families full of excitement, telling them, "We all got a piece of hard candy!" After the contest, the boys bought everyone a barbeque pig plate for supper. It only cost sixty dollars for all eighty people.

The eight wagons and three buggies left at four o'clock. They arrived home at seven o'clock, and Art said, "Everything looks okay. Boy, am I glad." He had learned not having anyone there to protect his farms was a good way to lose all their stock. By the time they had taken care of the horses and got everything unloaded and put away, it was eight thirty before they got to bed.

Everyone got busy haying for three weeks. Between all the farms they harvested so far, they had enough hay for one half of what they needed for the winter. Everyone began hoeing the corn and cotton, but they would have to take a two-week break to cut more hay.

Art had gotten to the point where he really looked forward to seeing Phyllis. One afternoon at Hank's cabin, Art and Phyllis were working around the place. It was a beautiful day, and they were enjoying their work as well as each others company. Phyllis had baked a cake as usual, and Art said, "Why don't we take a break and cut into that great cake?" She started to get the cake, and as she brushed the hair out of her eyes, Art reached out and pulled her to him. She willingly settled into the comfort of his arms, and returned his kiss without the slightest bit of hesitation. At that moment, they both knew their relationship had become much deeper and more meaningful. No longer could they be called casual friends.

At the end of the summer she asked, "When are you going to make an honest woman out of me?"

He said, "After the harvest."

Phyllis said, "I think we should get married now."

"Why is that?" he asked.

"Well, you need me to help you through this trying time coming up, and I love you. Besides, I'm pregnant." She added, "I don't need a big wedding."

Art said, "Wow! I love you too. We'll get married next Sunday in church at Bryans Mill. Now come here and quit talking."

Art appreciated his sister Patricia for all she had done to help him and the children. She had stayed eight months now and made life so much easier for them. He immediately sent a short telegram to his mother in Red Oak, Louisiana. Then he went to talk to Mr. and Mrs. Rogers, Charles, and Buddy. He then went by to talk to the preacher and his wife, and he asked the preacher, "Will you marry Phyllis and me after the service Sunday morning?"

"Of course," he said. "But I want to talk to Phyllis before church Sunday."

Sunday came and a large number of people were at the wedding and picnic afterward. The wedding took fifteen minutes.

Patricia was the maid of honor and, of course, Darrell was the best man. Art's sister came to him and said, "I don't want to be in the way, so I'll be moving out."

"Absolutely not!" said Art, "We still need you, and you'll not be in the way. You can have the bedroom upstairs, and someone will have to take care of Art Jr. and Patricia because Phyllis is still planning to teach. Art Jr. will go to school with her at seven o'clock, and they'll return at four."

Art and Phyllis stayed at Hank's place that night, and Patricia took the kids home. They had just gotten there and in the house when four tough-looking men came to Hank's place and said, "We're going to stay here for a few days." Art and Phyllis decided they would go to her place when two of the men said, "You're going to leave the woman here."

Art said, "No. On second thought, you men aren't going to stay here tonight, and if any of you want to do something about, it let's settle it right now." One man tried to draw his gun, and Art shot him in the leg. He screamed and hollered for what seemed like an hour. The other three were thinking about drawing their guns, and Art said, "Go ahead and pull those guns, but I guarantee you I'll kill at least two of you. So if you like the odds, draw." They decided not to draw and left complaining when Art made them take their wounded buddy with them. He walked the group out to the road and told them, "I'll kill any or all of you if you ever come here again." Phyllis was really upset and afraid they would come back. "They don't want anymore to do with me," Art told her. "I'll bet they go to Texarkana."

Phyllis said, "Please, please let's go to my place. I don't want to stay here after all that."

"All right, darlin'," he said. "I don't want you to be upset all night." He was glad she had convinced him because they had a great wedding night.

CHAPTER 46

The next morning, Art borrowed a wagon from the blacksmith so they could move Phyllis's clothes and some other items. It would take another wagon to get everything. They got to the house around one o'clock, unloaded and placed things where she wanted them. Most of her other things would have to go in the big bedroom upstairs. Jokingly he said, "We can put the rest of your stuff in a stall in the barn."

She laughed and said, "Don't try it, buddy, or it'll all go on your side of the bed."

Art just smiled and planted a playful swat on her back side.

Patricia and the kids woke up from their naps about two thirty and came downstairs and started attacking them. Patricia said, "If you'll take care of the kids, I'll fix supper."

Supper was great! Darrell came over later and said, "I think all of us, including the kids, should go to Naples next Saturday morning, go shopping, have a good meal, go to the dance, and then to church Sunday morning. Come back home in the afternoon."

Patricia, Phyllis, and Art together said, "That sounds great!"

Next Monday, they would need to start the corn harvest. That meant the equipment had to be in shape and ready to go. Phyllis, Art, and his family settled right into the new marriage. Phyllis was on a quest to win the children over and didn't think she had made much progress. Art told her, "You're trying too hard. Just relax, be yourself, and do what you can for them. They'll come around."

Saturday morning, they all were off with Art's special buggy for them, and a regular wagon for the rest of the group. When they got there, Art went to the jail to see Hank about the men that he had trouble with at his cabin. He said, "I wounded one in the leg and ran them all off."

Hank was pretty upset and said, "Those are the ones that usually brought me horses they picked up, and I'd pay them ten dollars for each horse."

He said, "You mean stolen horses don't bother you? Those were good horses."

Hank said, "I know. Now how am I ever going to build up my horse herd again?"

"Well," Art said, "I planted a corn crop on your land and your half of that would be about five hundred dollars. I told your buddies that if I saw them again, I'd kill them."

Hank said, "I think they're in town, planning on going to the dance tonight."

Art asked, "When will you get out of jail?"

He replied, "October first if I don't do something else stupid in here and have to serve more time."

Art said, "When you get out, go to Hill's General Store, and he'll have a horse and saddle for you." When he left, he had this bad feeling he would see those friends of Hanks again soon.

They attended the dance, and everyone had a good time for about two hours. Patricia had met Bob Simmons at the dance, and they were at another table with his brother and his lady friend.

At 10:15 the four friends of Hank's came in to the dance. They were drunk and looked like they were looking for trouble. Art saw them first and told Darrell, "Get ready. Here comes trouble!"

He moved twenty feet from the table and had his gun drawn. The drunks headed right for Phyllis. Art moved in behind them and said, "Put your hands up or you're dead men. I told you if I ever saw you again, I'd kill you." He then clubbed the one man and took their guns before they knew what happened. Darrell had done the same. Two men were down, and the two standing didn't have guns.

The men were cursing Phyllis at the top of their voices when they were heading for the table. Of course, this had already stopped the dance just before the action began. Someone had gone to get the sheriff. When he arrived, the toughs said, "These two guys jumped up for no reason. We weren't doing anything." The sheriff talked to Phyllis, and she told him about the incident at the cabin. Velma joined Phyllis in telling him about what had happened at the dance, how they were cursing and making disrespectful remarks.

Art then told his story of the cabin incident and said, "I shot one of these men in the leg. I'll show you exactly where the bullet entered."

The sheriff confirmed the leg wound and told Darrell, "Take their guns and help me put them in jail."

At the jail, Darrell said, "If you men come up with any horses, I might try to buy them." He also said, "Look north of the Sulphur River all the way to the Red River. You'll find at least one hundred head there."

The foursome replied, "We don't even have enough money to buy food for a month in order to feed and trap the horses. We have four horses now that are saddled and tied up in the front of the dance hall, and they haven't been fed any grain in a week."

Darrell said, "I'll take your horses, unsaddle them, and make sure they are grain fed every day." Also he said, "Your supplies will be at Hill's General Store, and the horses will be in his big corral behind the store." Darrell then went to Mr. Hill's house and told him what he planned to do and paid him up front.

The sheriff told Darrell, "I'll turn these four loose next Friday."

It was one thirty when Darrell returned to their rented rooms and told Art about the deal he had made with the four toughs.

"What!" Art said, "I don't believe you did that. I plan to kill that bunch!"

Darrell replied, "I think if these boys can get some money, then they'll get out of our hair and just go home and change their wayward ways."

They went to Naples's church on Sunday morning. Patricia met Bob Simmons there. She said, "I'm going out to the Simmons' place until Tuesday, and Bob will bring me home."

Art said, "Okay, sister. We'll see you then."

Art Jr. asked, "Aunt Patricia, is that your boyfriend?"

Both Bob and Patricia's faces suddenly became flushed with embarrassment. Bob said, "My mother will make sure your sister will be okay."

"I assure you my sister can take care of herself," Art replied. They arrived home at three o'clock. Eighteen people had gone to Naples. They were the ones that worked with the boys and their families.

CHAPTER 47

The next morning, which was Monday, Art and Paul started the corn harvest. They had filled two large wagons by three o'clock. They emptied those two on the Parkinson farm, where they would be working for eight days. After emptying the corn in the corn crib area of the barn, they continued working until six o'clock and had both wagons one third full. They worked really hard for eight days and distributed most of the corn to each of Art's other farms. It took less than two weeks to harvest the 165 acres of corn.

They took two wagonloads to McCoy's mill. It took Paul, Mr. Jenson, Luke, and Art until eight thirty to unload the corn at the mill. They were still harvesting and had the two wagons filled by twelve o'clock, emptied and back at the field by two o'clock. They finished at seven, and Mr. McCoy stayed open so they could unload before going home. It was nine o'clock by the time they got home. Mr. McCoy told Art, "I'll take two thousand more bushels of wheat at eighty cents a bushel, if you still have some."

Art said, "I can have that delivered in the next couple of weeks."

After delivering Mr. McCoy his wheat, Art still had two thousand bushels of wheat left.

Charles had told Art, "The mill in Marietta will buy your wheat. However, they're not known to pay much."

He said, "Try to find out what they are willing to pay, and let me know."

Art kinda liked the winter wheat because he thought the cows liked grazing on it, and it did better than hay and corn. If he could sell the wheat he had, then he would plant wheat again in the fall. Charles got word to Art that the Marietta mill was paying seventy cents a bushel. He thought to himself, *I'll feed it before hauling it twice as far to Marietta and then getting ten cents a bushel less.*

Phyllis, Velma, and Patricia took the kids and went to Bryans Mill one day. Gene McCoy told them, "Tell Art I'll now pay him eighty-five cents a bushel for any wheat he has left." Immediately, he sent two big wagonloads, which was only 480 bushels. They left at seven and got back by one. He loaded them and sent them again. He did the same the next day.

It was now time to start picking cotton. Everyone, and I mean everyone, except Darrell who sent his son, was out in the field picking cotton. Velma watched Art's little girl. Art only had 20 acres of his own cotton but 135 acres of sharecrop cotton. The price of cotton was down. They got $185.00 for a five hundred pound bale. He raised ten bales equaling $1,850.00. Art made up his mind, he was not going to plant cotton next year.

The Shaws harvested 135 acres of cotton, which produced sixty-five bales. They were all pretty upset about the cotton price. Art got $6,000.00 for his share.

Louis's boys and Mr. Jenson thought their share was just fine. They came to Art and said, "We each want to raise twenty-five acres on the shares again next year."

While all this was happening, Darrell's four toughs had spent three weeks in the area between the Sulphur River and the Red River. They had found forty horses, one stallion, and thirty-two head of cattle; but they were afraid to cross the Sulphur River into Art's land. Darrell paid each one two hundred dollars for his horses. Art finally relented and paid eighty dollars to each man for the cattle. None of the horses or cattle had brands. Art kept the thirty-two cows at Darrell's farm for three months, making sure they did not have the sickness. Darrell hired the four men to help him plant one hundred acres of oats. That took a week and when the toughs left, they each had a total of three hundred dollars. A small family could easily survive on that for a year. Darrell hoped they had mended their ways.

CHAPTER 48

It was way past time to be working cattle, but Art had a calf crop of 285 that badly needed branding, and the males castrated. Also, the thirty-two head he bought from the four toughs needed branding. All that took a solid week. There had not been any rain for ten weeks, and everything was very dry.

It was time the wheat needed to be planted on all five farms. Art had decided he would plant forty acres on each farm, including the Loggings' homestead. It took Art, Louis, Mr. Jenson, and his boys another two weeks to plant the wheat. Art was going to start using his homestead again where the sick cows had been. He burned the forty acres where the sick cows had been buried, and made sure no livestock could go on that part of the farm. Then he brought the thirty-two head of cattle he had at Darrell's over to his farm and put a Shorthorn bull in with them.

There had not been any cattle or horse rustling on any of the boys' farms for quite some time. Joe came riding over Friday morning and said, "Onnie's barn was set on fire, and while he was fighting the blaze, several men began rustling all his stock. Onnie came to our place, and he and Jed rode over to get Mr. Shaw, and they'll return to his farm."

Art said, "Go over to Darrell's and tell him to meet me here as soon as he can." He then packed a mule and saddled his horse.

By that time, Darrell and Joe were there. The three rode over to Onnie's, which took about an hour.

Darrell asked, "Why did you bring that pack mule?"

Art replied, "Just in case we have to trail those guys like we've done in the past."

Sure enough, the fire had destroyed Onnie's barn where he also lived. The rustlers had run off with about ninety cows and five horses. Onnie said, "It looked like they headed northeast toward the Red River. I'm going with you because I don't have anything here to protect."

Art said, "Okay. Onnie and I will go with either Joe or Jed and, Darrell, you and Mr. Shaw need to go back to your places in case they decide to attack there." Continuing, he said, "Have Paul Jenson ride between all the farms and tell the people what has happened. Also, tell him to go warn Mr. McCoy and have him send someone to the other farmers around Bryans Mill including the Anthonys'."

Darrell said, "I'm the deputy. Let me track them with Onnie and Jed."

Art said, "Okay, but you'll need to go now, or you'll have a tougher time catching them. Onnie, were your cows and horses branded?"

He replied, "Yes."

Darrell, Onnie, and Jed took off after the rustlers. Art said, "You'll stay spread out so you won't get ambushed, won't you?" He returned home and told Velma and Patricia, "Board up and get ready for those guys to come here and try to burn the houses or barns." Paul Jenson was sent to Naples to tell the sheriff what was happening. Art took off for Bryans Mill and told Gene McCoy what had happened. He said, "Someone needs to warn the farmers east of here." It just so happened one of the Anthony's wives was getting supplies at McCoy's store. What a lucky break! Art said, "This is real important to tell all your family what has happened about eight miles downriver from here." She hurriedly finished her shopping and quickly headed for home to warn everyone.

Gene said, "I owe you for the wheat. Here is thirty-four hundred dollars in cash if you'll sign here that you were paid."

It was Friday, and school was about over. Art rode over and told Phyllis, "Dismiss early, and do not let the kids play around because they need to get to their homes." As soon as he hooked up the horse to the buggy, they were ready to leave.

Art, Phyllis, and Art Jr. got home at four o'clock. Art unhooked the buggy horse, unsaddled his horse, fed them, rubbed them down, and turned them loose in the barn pasture. He then went over to Velma's and asked, "Do you and the children want to come over to our place?"

She said, "No, we'll be fine here. And besides, we need to keep watch."

"Well," he said, "have the kids keep watch so you're free to fix you all some supper."

He looked around Darrell's place then got another horse and rode to Louis's house to warn him about the attack on Onnie's farm. He asked Louis's son, "Will you take my horse and ride over to tell Ed about the problem?" When Louis's son returned, Art went home. They had supper at five thirty and everyone, except Art, was ready for bed by six thirty. Someone had to stand watch all night.

Darrell, Onnie and Jed had tracked the thieves until six o'clock and spotted them trying to cross the Sulphur River twelve miles south of Onnie's farm. That's where the crew caught them.

About one half of the animals were across the river when the sheriff and deputy were coming up on the south side. They caught the rustlers in a cross-fire, and after two of the five were shot, they all surrendered. The sheriff and deputy took all five to jail and was going to get Dr. Lilly to come treat the wounded.

The sheriff said, "The leader is one of the wounded."

Darrell planned to use that as leverage. Darrell asked the sheriff, "Will you not get Dr. Lilly to treat the wounded at this time?

I would like to question them first." The sheriff agreed. Darrell put the leader, Tom, in a separate cell away from the others and began questioning him. About thirty minutes went by, and he had gotten nowhere.

The gang all said, "It was all Tom's idea. He's the leader." Darrell had a nose for this sort of thing and was suspicious that Jess Lassiter might be behind these outlaws. Darrell finally said, "Tom, for the last time I'm asking who are you in cahoots with? If you don't tell me, I'm going to hurt you."

Tom said, "I'm already hurt. You need to get me a doctor."

Darrell replied, "You ain't getting a doctor until you tell me what I want to know." The men sat in silence for ten minutes. So Darrell got up and threw Tom to the floor and stepped on his hurt leg. Tom began screaming and hollering. The other men could hear him and were frightened because they knew Tom was in great pain and couldn't do anything about it.

He passed out from the pain and woke up ten minutes later, with Darrell still applying hurting pressure on his leg. He said, "I can't stand this anymore. Just stop, and I'll tell you what you want to know."

When the deputy and sheriff came in, Darrell asked the jailer, "Why don't you take a long supper break and then bring back some supper for the prisoners?"

Tom finally told Darrell, "We met this guy named Pete in Clarksville, who absolutely hates you and your partner. He gave us five hundred dollars to steal cows and horses from you two and burn your homes and barns then take the cattle and horses to his farm. Actually, they had attacked Onnie's farm by mistake, thinking it was either Art's or Darrell's place."

"So," Darrell said, "Lassiter knows what you're doing, and have you ever talked to him?" Darrell said to himself, *Where would Pete get five hundred dollars?*

The worst thing Tom said was, "We weren't the only people he made this deal with. There were probably twenty or twenty-two people, including us." He continued, "As soon as we got the money, we came to get it over with"

Darrell asked, "You are sure then that there are other people coming to rustle and burn our farms?"

He answered, "Yes."

Darrell called to the sheriff, "Hey, will you please come in here and listen to this?"

Tom also told them, "Pete told the attacker to do it when the families have gone to church."

Sheriff Bass said, "I'm going to Clarksville with two deputies and see if we can find Pete and any of the others before they come to attack your place. You should go home and try to prepare for their attack. I'll be by after a couple full days at Clarksville. I'm going to put these men in jail in the upstairs cells, and I have called Robert and Sherman to come to the jail to make sure there's not a lot of coverage and see to it they don't have any visitors. I don't want anyone talking to them or finding out what happened to these men." Sheriff Bass finally sent for Dr. Lilly to treat the wounded.

Darrell said, "I want to thank you, Sheriff Bass, for all the help." Darrell was really tired but knew he needed to get home so all their people could start preparing for the attack. He went over to Mr. Hill's and borrowed his wagon to take home ten fifty-gallon wooden barrels for water to fight fires. They had always had rain barrels on each farm for collecting rain water, which was helpful for putting out small fires that were frequent during that time. The boys knew they couldn't burn down their houses but could burn down their barns. They were very concerned about the possibility of starting grass and tree fires, especially since everything was so dry due to lack of rain.

Art, Darrell, Ed, Louis, and Mr. Jennings got two fifty-gallon barrels each. Everyone was told to plow at least ten rows around their houses and barns. Darrell slept for twelve hours and when he woke up, they had to set up their defense with lookout points and different signals by the younger shooters, mainly on Art's farm because he was the one they attacked before. Everyone agreed if the attacker set a number of fires, they would probably lose the fight; but they hoped that wouldn't happen, and they had to try to protect themselves.

They were planning to use a number of young boys to send the signals to everyone. Art said, "I don't think they'll attack the Shaw farm, especially if we move the cattle and horses to the back of the farm where they can't be seen from behind the woods."

Mr. Jenson and Paul said, "We'll do that with the cow dogs today."

Art said, "If we don't guard the Shaw farm, we can more easily guard the other five farms." He also said, "Louis, you stay at your place and send your oldest boy six hundred yards from your house on a hill with his horse so he can be seen by Paul, who'll be on the top of my barn. Ed, you stay at your place, and I want Louis's youngest boy on a hill six hundred yards from his brother so he can see you and his brother, and we can see him." He went on to explain, "The red signal means they're coming and to that location. If Paul raises the red flag, that means they're on their way to mine or Darrell's farm, and everyone come here. If Louis's oldest son raises the red flag, that means they're headed to Louis's. If the youngest raises the red flag, that means they're on their way to Ed's farm. Darrell and Velma's son will be on the old Parkinson farm so he can see Ed's house, and he'll have a white and a red flag to raise whichever is necessary." Art went to the river to see if they crossed there, and Darrell was going to watch the road from Bryans Mill.

Knowing they would need more help, Art went to Marietta and asked Charles, "Do you think you can get Ace and any other help? Looks like we can use all the help we can possibly get." On Sunday, the three Marietta boys arrived. Art was at the Sulphur River, Darrell and the Marietta boys were at Art's barn. The families rode in the two seated buggy with two dummies that looked like the boys. Patricia had put Art's clothes and hat on one, and another dummy was in the backseat that she had dressed to look like Darrell. About four miles from Bryans Mill, they saw ten men on horses. After they passed them, the men started down the road toward Art and Darrell's barns. The ladies said, "They bought it!"

When Phyllis, Patricia, Velma, and the children got to church, they told the Anthony boys what was going on. The Anthonys headed toward the Loggings farm, but they would be an hour behind the rustlers. Darrell saw the ten thugs coming and told Paul, "Raise the red flag, then get down and run into the house." Four of the men headed for the river. All of them were carrying torches soaked in coal oil. Art had seen the men coming. He started toward them through the trees. He was within sixty yards of the men when one stopped to light his torch. Art shot and hit him twice. The other three got off their horses, but by that time, he had shot two horses and one more rustler. He had them off their horses and only two were able to return fire, which they immediately did. Art protected his horses behind a clump of trees, and he took cover behind a tree. He fired six more shots at the two rustlers.

In the meantime, Darrell, Charles, and Ace had opened up on the four men that rode up, got off their horses, and started to light their torches. Darrell and his crew promptly fired a total of ten shots, and all the men were hit. The Marietta boys quickly got the rustlers four horses and rode off after the other two that had headed toward Darrell's with their torches lit. The two men had already started a few small fires. Charles and Ace shot the two men twice, then began to fight the fire. Louis, his two sons, and Ed rode up to help fight the fire. Darrell, Charles, and Ace took off to help Art and the Anthony boys joined them. When the rustlers saw six more men riding up, they threw down their guns and surrendered. Deputy Darrell and Ace took care of the three prisoners, and the rest of the crew went back to fighting the fires.

Even with the extra help, it still took thirty minutes to put the fires out.

Darrell had sent Paul Jenson to Naples to get the sheriff and Dr. Lilly. They had accounted for all the men that had been hired by Pete. Art thought there were probably more, but if this incident got in the papers, maybe others would back off. All of Pete's gang was charged with attempted murder and arson. They all received sentences of seven to fifteen years.

After all the fighting, they were ready for Thanksgiving. Phyllis wanted to have a big party, but Art said, "Let's wait until Christmas." There still had not been much rain since September, and this country was becoming nothing but dust.

CHAPTER 49

Two weeks into December, several men came in the night and burned Art's, Darrell's, and Mr. Shaw's barns and over five hundred acres on Art's and Darrell's farms. They tried to burn the boys' houses, but the families were able to put those fires out because the main part of their homes was made of stone and brick. The roofs were tin. They got the animals out of the barns, but the corn stored in the barns was burned. They were lucky to get the fire stopped on the pastures. They plowed and plowed around the fire and finally got it stopped. The fire had also burned about one hundred acres of trees. They had enough logs to cut for the three barns and had a big barn raising. All three barns were completed by January first.

The boys had a lot of help from many people. The Simmons brothers helped for two days, even though Art thought Bob only came over so he could see Patricia. Ed brought his group of farmers for two days, and the Bryans Mill people came for two days. Mr. Hill brought a group from Naples to help for one day. Even Sheriff Bass brought five prisoners for five days. A couple of the prisoners, David Townsend and his cousin Alex, were really good carpenters. Darrell talked the sheriff into letting the prisoners work for him for a month.

Christmas this year was just so-so. Each house had a Christmas tree, and the kids did have fun decorating the trees. No one had time to buy presents but promised the kids to get them presents when they went to town. Art again gave all his people each a ten dollar bonus. The people that worked with Art were really tired. One of the main jobs was getting fences rebuilt on the land where the trees had burned. Everyone really needed about two weeks of working around their own homes.

On January fifth, they got a two-inch rain and again on the tenth, fifteenth, and twentieth. Then they had a week of fifty- and sixty- degree weather, and the boys could really see an improvement in the oat and wheat crops. The crops were not going to be very good, but they needed feed for February and March plus oats for the horses and mules next year. It rained two inches every ten days during February and March, which assured a better oat and wheat crop. On March 15, everyone helped Darrell harvest the oat crop. It only yielded twenty-five bushels to the acre. That was only one half of what they needed for Darrell and all of Art's farms.

With the help of others, Art rounded up all the seed needed to plant this year. The crops were late, which usually meant fewer yields. They started plowing disking and planting corn and cotton. There were 160 acres of corn planted and on April tenth, they began planting 150 acres of cotton. After that, it was time for the branding of the livestock and the castrating of the male cattle.

Phyllis had stopped teaching on the first of March. Patricia had taken her place teaching for the remainder of the year. On April fifteenth, Phyllis gave birth to a healthy baby boy which they named Kenneth. Art was staying closer to home. Art Jr. and his sister really fell in love with their new brother. They always wanted to hold him or do something, anything they could, for him. Mrs. Jenson came over during the day to help Phyllis, and that allowed Art to go ahead with his planting.

Just before they worked the cattle, two of the prisoners David and Alex that stayed and worked for the boys all of January got out of jail and came to them looking for work. They wanted to sharecrop. Art talked it over with Darrell, Phyllis, Patricia, and Velma. They thought that maybe if they took a chance on them, they would stay out of jail. Art said, "I have a cabin over on the Parkinson farm, go to Bryans Mill, and get supplies you need for a month and charge it to me. Also you better pick up some horse feed from Darrell and get your horses in better shape so they can work harder for you." He also told them, "You'll have to build a corral and do some other things around the cabin to get it fixed up and livable."

They responded, "Don't you worry. We'll work hard." They proved to be very hard workers. They helped work the cattle and helped with the planting. By the end of May, they had actually fenced in all of the crops. They also helped Louis and Ed, shot six deer, and gave one each to Ed, Mr. Shaw, Louis, and Onnie. Alex and Dave were beginning to get a reputation as being hardworking men. When they collected their twenty-five dollars' wages for the month, Art gave them a job for the rest of the summer. He wanted them to build barn corn crib storage for all the farms. Art instructed them exactly how they were to build them.

David and Alex came to Art and asked, "May we go get our girlfriends to come live with us in the cabin? They're having a hard time making it where they live in Vernon. It'll take about three days."

Art said, "Okay. Just don't tell anyone since you're not married. Let it be a surprise."

"Could we borrow a wagon and mules for the trip?" they asked.

After the planting was over, Bob Simmons was almost living at Art's house. Art's sister Patricia said, "We're getting married on Sunday, June first. That will give my mother and his mother time to plan a big wedding at the Livingston's ranch south of Naples."

That meant her mother, her husband, and his daughter would be at Art's house on May twentieth until the day after the wedding. Art loved his mother, but she was used to the very best of everything, and Art's way of living was pretty rugged.

Phyllis and the baby had been sleeping downstairs in the only downstairs bedroom. There would be three more people in the house with one inside toilet and one bathroom. It would be a trying ten days for all. Of course, Mrs. Martin wanted to visit with all her grandchildren and especially the new baby.

Art had gone to the furniture maker Bohanan and ordered one of the special large-sized beds for his sister and her husband-to-be as a wedding present. There would be a wedding shower at the Bryans Mill church the day after her mother arrived, and another one three days later at the Simmons' ranch. Phyllis and Art were really pleased that Patricia would be living close by.

This past year had been a rough one for the boys. They both had lost loved ones, Darrell his father and Art his wife. They had barns, trees, and pastures burned and lost a lot of cattle to a strange disease. They had been shot at and attacked again and again. Also, they had lived through a drought. The boys had come through it all wiser and more mature. They certainly were not the same two young men that they were when they first met in the war. They were definitely now men and had gained the respect of their friends and neighbors.

Art still became sad at the loss of Sharon and the fact the kids would grow up with only memories of their real mother. However, he had learned to love again and now had a wonderful wife and another son, which made three children. His family was great. His sister was getting married and would be living close, and the drought was broken.

Darrell said to Art, "It's already started out to be better for us this year. Maybe things have turned around."

Art replied, "I hope so, but as long as we have our friendship and our families, we'll be all right. What more could anyone ask for?"

CPSIA information can be obtained
at www.ICGtesting.com
Printed in the USA
JSHW032008130621
15616JS00002BA/10